Spectacular RASCAL

Spectacular RASCAL

Cover design by Bootstrap Designs.
Editorial services provided by Help Me Edit.
Interior Designed and Formatted by Tianne Samson with

emtippettsbookdesigns.com

The complete Under His Command Series is Available Now:

Controlling Her Pleasure

Commanding Her Trust

Claiming Her Heart

The complete Bought by the Billionaire Series is Available Now:

Dark Domination

Deep Domination

Desperate Domination

Divine Domination

The complete Dirty Twisted Love Series is Available Now:

Dirty Twisted Love

Filthy Wicked Games

Crazy Beautiful Forever

One More Shameless Night

The complete Bedding the Bad Boy Series is Available Now:

The Bad Boy's Temptation

The Bad Boy's Seduction

The Bad Boy's Redemption

Warning: *SPECTACULAR RASCAL* is a stand-alone erotic romance told from the hero's point of view. No cliffhanger. Lots of dirty talk.

Dedicated to NYC, thanks for an amazing summer.

Hey there, princess.

Yes, you. The one with the copy of *Leaning In, Buckling Down, and Having it All!* clutched to your chest.

The one with the tasteful pink lipstick, Spanx squeezing you in half beneath your knee-length pencil skirt, and the "This can't be happening to *me*, not to *me*," look in your eye. You've spent your entire life bending over backwards to be all the things you're supposed to be—intelligent, well-mannered, ladylike, refined; a rule follower who never leaves an "i" un-dotted or a "t" un-crossed—and look where it's gotten you.

In trouble. On the run. Watching your back and wondering how the hell you're going to get through this, because all the cotillion classes and Ivy League degrees in the world can't protect you when you end up on the wrong side of Dr. Perfect's alter ego, Mr. Tall, Dark, and Psycho.

Going to the police isn't good enough, and you know it.

You're not only well educated, you're well informed. You keep up with current events and are aware of the depressing statistics on domestic violence. You know that every nine seconds a woman in the U.S. is beaten by her partner. You know that three or more women are killed by their husbands or boyfriends every day, and that a restraining order isn't going to stop a man who's determined to prove that no one walks away from him.

At least, not without a few scars to remember him by...

I'm not going to sugarcoat it, sweetheart. You were right to be afraid, but you don't have to be. Not anymore. You've come to the right place, to a man who understands how to fight fire with fire.

Together, we're going to convince your dangerous dick of an ex that you've got a new man, a bigger, tougher, meaner man, who fucks you so often and so well that you don't have any energy left to worry about Douchebag's threats. In reality, our relationship will never go further than a kiss, but he won't know that. He'll assume that you've been claimed by an alpha male with a black belt in kicking ex-boyfriend ass and biceps the size of those spiral cut hams his mama buys for Easter dinner, and realize his best bet is to start walking and never look back.

I was signed on to Magnificent Bastard Consulting for cases just like yours, for exes who need more than a hefty injection of jealousy into their lives. For the guy who needs a reminder that there are more savage creatures prowling the jungle, and that terrorizing a woman half his size is a shitty idea.

But this is going to take more than me escorting you around town on my tattooed arm, or kissing you like I own your sweet pussy every night. I can do Big, Bad, and Possessive with the best of them, but you have your part to play, too. A part so important that there's no way I can do this without you.

So go ahead and close your eyes, princess.

That's right. Close them.

Lie back. Relax. Unzip your pencil skirt, slip out of those Spanx, and let your breath come slow and deep while I take you to a place I like to call No Fucks Left To Give-ville.

Now, now, don't tense up. Hear me out.

I know what you're thinking—*But Aidan, I'm all about giving a fuck.*

I give big fucks, all the fucks.

I give so many fucks that sometimes, at the end of the day, I feel like I'm unraveling in all the places where I've cared so much, tried so hard, given all I could give to be the best I could be. To be the change I want to see in the world, to inspire and lead by example, and lift up my fellow man, and all those other platitudes I post on social media during my lunch hour to avoid talking to the jerk in the next cubicle over...

Yeah, I hear you. I get it. *You care.*

But when is the last time all that "caring" got you somewhere? When's the last time the world changed because you were giving so many fucks?

Probably never, I'm guessing. And that's because giving a fuck is different than caring. Caring is something you do without worrying about the end game. Caring makes the world a better place while costing you nothing.

Fuck-giving is a whole other kettle of rotten crabs.

Here's how it goes: you're so afraid of being out of control of your life, or your destiny, or whatever it is that you're stressed about, that you freak out over things that don't matter, spreading your fucks around like chicken feed to be gobbled up and shit out by the empty-headed flightless birds of the world. You fight to control and persuade, but in the end the fight controls you. You give your power away to the people who enrage you or misunderstand you, people that you're never going to change no matter how many fucks you give.

And sooner or later, you'll have given so many effs about so many stupid things that you'll have no energy left for the stuff that really matters.

No energy for the friend who needs you to talk them out of their post breakup depression. No energy left to notice the woman struggling to get her stroller down the subway steps on the day the elevator is broken while the rest of the world streams past her. No passion for the things you really want to do with your life, for art and music and belly laughs and the rest of the really good stuff.

Maybe that's not what you expected to hear from a guy with a beard and full-sleeve tattoos wearing a muscle T-shirt and a chain on his wallet. But I don't care if I'm not your stereotypical New York City tattoo artist.

That's right—I don't give a fuck.

I've been a resident of No Fucks Left to Give-ville for years, and it's made me a happier, more well-adjusted, more successful person than almost anyone I know. It has given me freedom to be who I am, to go after what I want, and to enjoy the things I enjoy because life's too short to let someone else tell me who I should be.

I call the shots. Not society or religion, not my parents' expectations, or pressure from my friends, or all the unwritten rules and unspoken messages shoved down my throat a hundred times a day by people trying to sell me something.

And that's what I'm here to give you, princess, what you need most at a time like this. Power.

I'll show you the way, and little by little, you'll take back the power the world has stolen from you, power you'll need to convince your big bad ex that there's no point in continuing to fuck with a stone cold bitch like you. Yes, it will take time, and yeah, your ex may employ the usual bully tactics—threats, violence, intimidation. But I'll be there to back you up, to prove to him that you're so well-loved and well-fucked and completely satisfied with your "new man" that his fight is pointless.

You are a wild horse he'll never break, a free bird he'll never pin down, and sooner or later he'll drop his fists and walk away. And on that day, you won't just be free of Mr. Wrong; you'll be free to be anything you want to be.

Now, doesn't that sound nice?

To never go to bed worrying about whether you're good enough or smart enough or pretty enough or successful enough by anyone's standards but your own, ever again? I can tell you're enjoying how much easier it is to breathe without those Spanx…

What's that? You're not convinced No-Fucks-Ville is for you?

You need further persuasion?

Then take my hand, beautiful, and let me show you how right it can feel for a good girl to go bad.

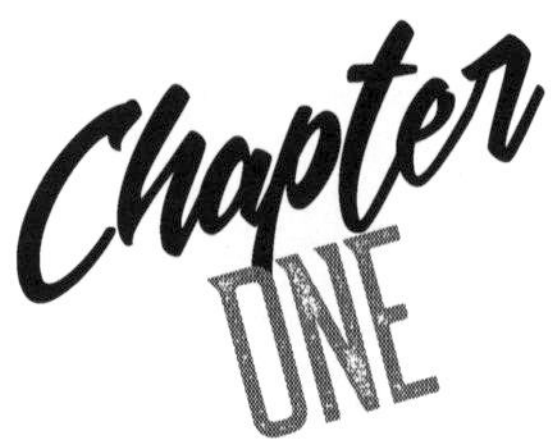

It's a gorgeous summer morning in the city and already hot as balls, a fact I can verify as I'm currently cupping my balls—and my dick—in one hand as I run naked across Prospect Park, pursued by a policeman with an air horn he blares every few seconds, ensuring no one is missing my solo streak around the lake. My balls are hot and sweaty, my not-intended-for-sprinting-boots are digging painfully into my calves, and a group of grandmotherly types walking their dogs just whistled and shouted "nice ass, cowboy, let's see the rest of what you've got!" as I ran by.

Old ladies. They aren't what they used to be, that's for damned sure.

And this sweaty streak is a lot less fun than the last time I went running naked with my Dasher club, when we were all so wasted that streaking across the Brooklyn Bridge sounded like a kick-ass idea. At least then it had been dark, I'd been drunk, and a cool breeze off the East River had kept the ball sweat to a minimum.

But streaking was the only way I could think of to distract the cop who was about to arrest my friends. Better for me to be charged with public indecency than for Bash and Penny to get hauled in for banging in the Prospect Park Lake.

I still can't believe the two of them decided that fucking in public was a good idea. But I guess true love does crazy things to a person's judgment. I wouldn't know, personally. I've never been in that kind of love, but judging from what it's done to my best friend and his usually sweet, levelheaded, keeps-her-panties-on-in-public assistant, it's apparently some intense shit.

As I duck under low-hanging branches near the edge of the lake, aiming myself for the canoe rental station, I decide I'm just fine with remaining a bachelor for the foreseeable future. Scheming to get my best friend and his girl back together so the pair of them would stop moping and crying and killing the summer fun before it could even get started has used up my limited enthusiasm for romance.

Besides, I have a job starting tomorrow. A fake girlfriend who, in exchange for ten thousand dollars, I will pretend to be completely fucking devoted to for the next month. Bash has been too caught up in his full-time pity party to send over the complete file on the woman, but I know her name and occupation: Beth Jones, a lawyer who's having a hard time convincing her creepy ex that their relationship is over for good.

My gut says Bash would be a better man for this job. He's the smooth, successful businessman type who looks like he should be dating a lawyer, but Beth asked for me. She took one look at the pictures in my "Spectacular Rascal" dossier—don't judge me, Bash chose the name; sometimes he's too damned cute for his own good—and insisted I was the guy she needed.

Apparently she wants a man who's "a little bit dangerous."

Of course, in reality, my danger factor is only skin-deep. I'm covered in tattoos, have a full beard that accentuates my "don't fuck with me" face, and am currently risking arrest for a friend, but I'm not dangerous, not even a little bit. I've never hit a man who didn't throw the first punch, never made a risky decision out of anger, and never spanked a woman who hasn't begged me to show her pretty ass who's boss.

I like my sex hot, primal, and as dirty as I can get it, prefer being on top in most situations, and refuse to be fucked with by anyone or anything. But when it comes to the things that really matter, I'm harmless. I literally have "Do no harm," tattooed on my left forearm, right next to the devil dancing in the pale moonlight I had inked at my first pro convention. I don't hurt innocent people, I don't incite conflict, and I don't work my personal shit out in my relationships. I save that for the weight room.

That's where I go to purge my demons and regain my focus. And yes, I'm ripped, and I have to stretch out for a good twenty minutes after I lift to maintain full range of motion. I'm not saying I don't have my issues, just that I deal with them in a sane, healthy, muscle-mass-increasing way.

I'm thankful for that muscle mass as I jump into an empty canoe, setting the captain and his crew free to slap against my thigh as I grab the oar and haul ass toward the center of the lake.

"Dude, you have to pay for that!" the skinny kid in the Parks Department T-shirt manning the rental station shouts after me. But his tone is more bored than outraged. Apparently the fact that I'm naked isn't enough to outweigh the fact that he's stuck working outside without so much as an umbrella to shield his greasy, teenage head from the sun.

"I'll pay when I bring it back, man. I promise," I call, glancing over my shoulder, breathing easier as I see the red-faced cop and his air horn still a good two hundred feet away.

Resisting the urge to shoot the officer a shit-eating grin—no need to rub salt in the wound, or give the man a reason to call for backup if he hasn't already—I duck my chin and pull hard, sending the slim canoe skimming fast across the water. Within minutes, I've made my way back around the curve in the shoreline, into the secluded cove that was the scene of Bash and Penny's crime of passion.

Literally.

Penny's skirt had covered the most pertinent parts of the equation, but there was no doubt what they were up to when Officer Red Face and I appeared on the scene. I suppose some guys would get off on that sort of thing, but I'm not much of a voyeur, especially when it comes to watching my best friend and a sweetheart with a goofy streak a mile wide get it on. Penny's like a little sister to me, and I would pay good money to get the sight of her girl-next-door face twisted in ecstasy out of my head.

As I drag the canoe onto the grassy bank and swiftly pull on the clothes I stashed behind a tree near the water's edge, I allow my thoughts to drift back through my own personal sex-ventures, looking for something to banish Penny mid-orgasm from my memory bank. I've had an excellent start to the summer season of fun, sexy, no-strings-attached hook-ups, and spent time with some very beautiful, very up-for-anything women, who have provided me with ample erotic inspiration.

But for some reason my brain skips over all that sizzling, prime spank-bank fodder I've collected lately and makes a beeline for a night eleven years ago—college graduation. It was my last run with the Pennsylvania University Dashers, the night I handed over the torch as head dasher and came way too close to taking Polka Dot Panties's virginity on a pile of leaves.

I'd never slept with a virgin, not even when I was one myself, and had no intention of getting into deep emotional waters like that with any girl, let alone Panties, one of my best friends and a girl I knew only by her Dasher name.

We all went by nicknames—the raunchier the better—on the trail.

Polka Dot Panties started her freshman year as Mary, as in the Virgin Mary, the way all the newbies to the run hard, drink harder Dasher lifestyle do. Later, after a sprint through the rain that rendered her hot pink running shorts transparent, she became Polka Dot Panties. I was Curved for Her Pleasure, for exactly the reason you might imagine.

She called me Curve. I called her Panties, PDP, or sometimes, just…Red.

Red for that silky red hair that fell all the way to her ass, for the lipstick she wore to Saturday night bonfires after our grueling afternoon runs. Red for the pen she used to write the notes we exchanged, and the color she made me see every time she gave me shit for laying an easy trail or not including enough switchbacks or whatever fault she found with my work as "fox."

The fox (the head dasher) lays the trail, and the hounds (all the other runners) dash after it, following the top-secret markings of our club, fighting to find the true trail and be the first across the finish line. From the day of her first run, Red was a force to be reckoned with. By her sophomore year, she came first in every single race, leaving no question as to who should fill my shoes when I graduated, though the honor of head dasher is usually given to a senior.

That last night I was supposed to hand over the fox binder, the trail marking tools, and the windbreaker with "Polka Dot Panties, Here to Fuck You Up" monogrammed on the back that I'd had made for her as my way of saying "thanks for busting my ass and being one of my best friends." I wasn't supposed to smoke a joint with her, or pull her into my arms to dance in the dark, or kiss her until her sweet, fearless taste was permanently imprinted on my tongue.

And I certainly wasn't supposed to slide my hand down the front of her panties and feel how wet she was for me.

Wet and hot and so ready that she rocks into my hand with this sexy as fuck moan and begs me to be her first. Begs me to take her, right there, on the ground in the leaves or up against a tree, wherever I want so long as I don't stop until I've taken care of her pesky virginity once and for all.

"I don't care if this isn't the way it's supposed to be," she says, fingers tangling in my hair. "I want you. And I trust you. And there's no one else in the world that I want to do this with." Her breath feathers across my lips, making me ache for another taste of her. "Please, Curve. Be with me. Now. Tonight. Before you go away."

"I'm not up for this, Panties. I can't." I groan as she finds the ridge of my erection, rubbing me through the thin fabric of my running shorts.

"You feel up for it." Her fingers wrap around the swollen

head of my cock and squeeze. Her touch is lightning in a bottle, potential energy as dangerous as it is seductive.

This is so fucking wrong. Red is a friend and only a friend.

But damn, I want more than my fingers in her hot little pussy. I want her under me, squirming as I show her just how up for fucking her I am. But she wouldn't lie about being a virgin. Or anything else. Panties is a hardcore truth teller. If she says this is her first time, it is.

Which means if I fuck her, I'm going to hurt her. I'm on the larger size of above average, and I come by my nickname honestly. When I'm hard, my cock curves back to point at my own navel—perfect for hitting the G-spot in a girl who's been around the block, but definitely not a Starter Dick.

Still, it's not the physical pain I would cause that I'm most worried about.

Red holds her cards close to her chest and plays it tough, but she has her share of issues. She's got an insensitive, selfish prick for a father, never knew her mother, and is dealing with a host of other stuff she keeps bottled up and under pressure. She's hardcore, but she's also more vulnerable than she lets on, and not the most emotionally steady person.

Having her first lover be a one-night stand isn't the kind of thing that's going to help her get any steadier. And I don't want to throw her off her game. I like Red.

Maybe even more than like her, I realize, my heart twisting in my chest as she begins to unravel in my arms, succumbing to the slow steady pressure of my fingers gliding over her clit.

"Oh, God," she says, voice catching as she trembles against me. "I've never… Oh God, I can't, I'm going to fall."

"No you're not." I wrap my free arm around her waist and hold on tight. "I've got you. Now come for me. I want to feel you

come, Red. I want you all over my fingers, beautiful."

Her breath rushes out, and a second later she's calling my name as she goes, but it's not my real name. She doesn't know my name is Aidan, and I have no idea what her real-life friends call her.

We're so close, and share a hundred inside jokes, but we're not close enough for this. Not as close as I would want to be if I was going to be the man making love to her for the first time.

And she deserves someone to make love to her, not just fuck her virginity away. She deserves someone she can trust with her heart and her body and her tightly guarded secrets, but I'm on my way out of the country tomorrow. Even if I wanted to, even if I was ready for something as intense as what I suspect I could have with Red, I can't be her someone.

With a pang of regret felt keenly in my heart, my gut, and my furiously aching balls, I realize that I can't let this go any further. No matter how hot Red is tonight, or how desperately I want to give her everything she's asking for.

I emerge from the memory with a shudder…and a hard-on that won't quit.

It seriously won't. Twenty minutes later, after walking the opposite way around the lake to avoid any officers of the law lingering in the area, I'm still fighting a stiffy. As I pay the grouchy kid for the canoe rental and a little extra for fetching it from the cove, I conceal the situation with my T-shirt and then head toward the subway, feeling strangely shitty, considering I've done my good deed for the day.

Bash and Penny are back together, my best friend is out of his despair hole, and no one has been charged with a crime.

At least I don't think they have.

To be sure, I tug my phone free and shoot Bash a text—

All good with you two? No arrests made?

After a moment Bash texts back. *No, we're in the clear and already back at Penny's place. How about you?*

All clear. Though it was touch and go for a while there. I glance over my shoulder to make sure I haven't acquired a tail. But the most menacing thing on the sidewalk behind me is a girl with a Long Island accent talking too loudly on her cell. Hopefully, if any cops show up, they'll arrest her for refusing to text like a decent human being, and leave me the hell alone.

I bet. Bash texts back. *Penny wants me to tell you thank you, by the way. She's says you've got balls.*

Ha. Ha. Very funny.

Not really. Don't ever get naked in front of my girlfriend again.

I smirk. *Why? Worried she might see something she likes?* I watch the bubbles dotting my screen, anticipating a smartass response, but Bash surprises me.

Not even a little bit. Penny is mine. I'm hers. And I'm probably the happiest bastard in New York right now, so... thanks. Seriously. I owe you one. A big one.

Hmm, a big one, huh? I wonder how big... *Does this mean you'll take over with Beth tomorrow? I know she wanted me to handle her intervention, but I don't date lawyers, man. We'll look ridiculous together. She'd be better off with a Magnificent Bastard.*

No way. You can't back out of this, Aidan, Bash shoots back immediately. *Even if I didn't plan on shacking up with Penny and keeping her in bed for the next four days, I can't swing this one. Beth needs someone to scare the shit out of her ex. That's not in my wheelhouse, and you know it. I'm excellent at what I do, but I don't inspire fear at first sight.*

I sigh. It's true. Bash can be a cold, hard, son of a bitch when he needs to be, but at first glance he looks like the kind of guy who's going to shake your hand and ask the location of the nearest whiskey bar, not hunt you down and cut your heart out for fucking with his girl.

Though he would. I know if anyone threatened Penny, Bash would do whatever it took to keep her safe. He proved that when he stole a horse and rode after her like he was channeling John Wayne. But his badass doesn't show on the surface, which means I'm stuck with Beth for the next month, or however long it takes to convince her ex to back off.

I pause near the entrance to the subway and type out a quick—*Got it, I'll take care of Beth. Enjoy your time with Penny*—as another wave of malaise washes through my chest to settle heavily in my stomach.

A part of me wants to blame the lady lawyer and her special intervention needs for the crappy sensation. I don't enjoy taking a week off from my real work for new client orientation. Tattooing is my passion; this gig for Bash is just a way to fast track the funds I need to open a second location of Ink Addicts. But this woman I've never met isn't the problem.

The problem is the look on Bash's face when he saw Penny today. I've never seen that exact expression before, not in almost twenty years of friendship. All the Bash swagger and smartass joking fell away, and there was nothing in his eyes but pure happiness. In that moment, there was no one else in the world but Penny, the woman who is his everything, the friend who knows all of his secrets, the person he needs more than the air he breathes.

Bash has been in love before, and I did my share of hanging out with him and his last steady date, but I've never seen him look at anyone the way he looks at Penny. It's like the answer to every question is right there, in that curvy little body. In those big brown eyes. In the arms of the person who has proven to him that who he truly is, deep down beneath all the bullshit, is enough.

More than enough.

It's been a long time since I've been with anyone who made me want to show my deep-down side. It's been even longer since I let myself start collecting those moments, those memories, those pieces of a person that, little by little, make you wonder if this is it. If this is your shot at something more than a casual connection. If this is the person who is going to prove that love isn't a lie or a fairy tale or something that starts to die the moment it's born. That love is real and that it can last, even though every couple you know is faltering, fading, or broken beyond repair.

Not anymore. There's nothing broken or fading about Bash and Penny.

I grunt as I shove my phone into my back pocket, reminding myself that it's too early in the game to make a call on Bash and Penny. They may have had a perfect working relationship for two years, but love is a completely different animal.

Whenever I hear about a lion tamer torn apart by the cats she trained since birth, or a man savagely murdered by the chimpanzee he saved from poachers, I think about love. Love is a wild, untamed creature. And no matter how beautiful or seductive it is, it can't be trusted not to wake up with a fur ball up its ass and decide to rip your face off.

On the subway ride home, I hold tight to that truth, and by the time I reach my apartment in the West Village the shitty, melancholy, "what if you're missing all the good stuff" feeling has faded, and I'm my old self again.

I stay that way until ten a.m. the next morning, when I walk into Buvette for my first meeting with Beth Jones and see a woman sitting in a corner table, sipping a cappuccino, watching me with cool green eyes that are way too fucking familiar.

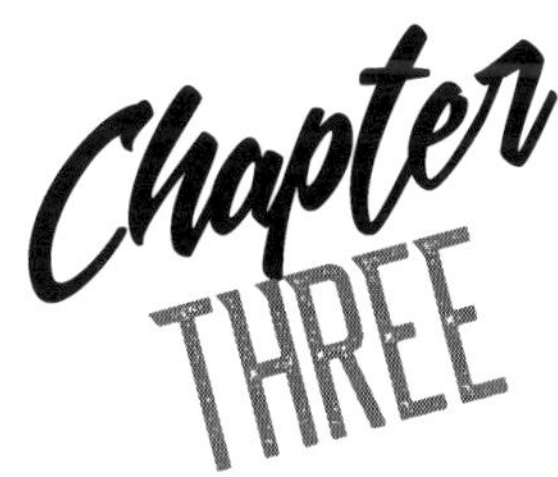

From the collected notes of Curved for her Pleasure and Polka Dot Panties

Dear Curved,
I'm not sure you'll ever read this note—as a lowly freshman, I have no way of knowing if the hole in the butt crack of the union soldier statue is really where the Dashers place top secret messages or if you're just messing with me—but I figured I would give this a try.
If you're hiding in the bushes filming me while I climb the statue and take its butt virginity with this piece of paper, I can only hope that you won't show the footage to anyone outside

the club. I've accepted embarrassment as part of my new lot in life, along with my polka-dot-pantied nickname, but there are people in my world who would NOT be amused by anything involving me and a man's butt.

Even if the man in question is a statue.

Anyway, just thought you might want to know the reason it was so easy for me to find the real trail today. Your dasher trail markers are solid, but every time you lay a false trail, your footprints get deeper and closer together. Anyone who knows the first thing about tracking can take one look at the first few feet of the branch and tell if it's a real trail or a trick that leads to a dead end.

So basically, you're going to have to step up your fox game if you want to fool this hound. ;)

Thanks again for letting me join the group. I can't remember the last time I had this much fun.

Best,

Polka Dot Panties

Dear Panties,

So what you're saying is that you're an Apache scout trapped in a skinny white girl's body. This is good to know, and I'll

do my best to stop making things easy for your polka-dotted ass.
Thanks for the heads-up and don't worry about anything Dasher-related being shared outside the club. As you can probably tell already, we're merciless when it comes to dishing out shit, but we've always got each other's backs.
Your reputation is safe with us.
Welcome to the motley crew,
Curve (C to my friends)
P.S. The soldier lost his butt virginity a long time ago, but it was sweet of you to worry.
Too sweet.
You need to cut that shit out or the rest of the hounds are going to have you for breakfast.

Dear Curve,
Gotcha.
Thanks for the note, the reassurance, and the warning. But don't worry about anyone having me for breakfast. My polka-dotted ass and I are tougher than we look.
See you on the trail.
Try to make me work for it this time?
Sincerely,
Panties

Dear Panties,
I will remind you of your smart-ass note when you're begging me for mercy on Saturday. I'm devising something with seven levels of pain just for you.
Get ready to cry like a freshman,
Curve

Beth Jones is Panties.

Panties is Beth Jones.

My mind makes the connection quickly, realizing that any other explanation for Red sitting at the corner table where I'd arranged to meet my client, wearing the green shift dress my client said she would be wearing, is farfetched.

For years, I've wondered about Panties's real identity. But I resisted the urge to Google my way to a name to go with the memory of the girl who pushed me into becoming the craftiest fox the Penn U Dashers ever had. The girl who was one of my best college friends, and who haunted my dreams for months after that night in the woods when I almost made her mine.

I hadn't wanted a name or any more intimate details. I'd wanted to put her in the past and forget that I almost called off my plans to study with a master tattoo artist to spend the summer buried balls-deep in Red. Forget that it took so long to get her out of my head, or that there are still nights when I find myself alone and nothing the Internet has to offer in the way of erotic stimulation will do.

Nights when I jerk off to the memory of her smell and her taste and the hitch in her voice when she whispered that I was the only one she wanted. Nights when I wonder if it was the fact that we were young and stupid and went out of our way to be fools together that makes me remember her with a tight feeling in my chest, or if it's something more, something I missed out on, something I might never find again if I don't switch up my game.

And now here she is, meeting my gaze across the busy-for-a-Monday-morning French café with a cool, guarded expression that is nothing like the confident, secretly vulnerable Panties I remember, and all I want to do is turn and walk away.

It hurts to see her like this, with her pretty mouth tight around the edges, her eyes shuttered, and a tense curve in her shoulders that is becoming all too familiar. My first two clients had that same curve at the top of their spine, like they were perpetually ready to curl into a ball and hide. That curve assures me that Red hasn't booked a Spectacular Rascal intervention as an excuse to connect with an old college friend. She's here because she is Beth Jones, an attorney well versed in the law, who is still unable to protect herself from an ex-lover who refuses to take no for an answer.

Thanks to Bash's slacking the past couple of weeks, I don't know much about Beth's situation, only that she's being stalked by an ex who wants her back, and that she needs someone "dangerous" on her arm to convince the guy to back off.

No, I don't know much, but I can tell she's in deep. She's

in trouble, and for some reason she thinks I'm the person who can help her out of it. But I'm not. Bash was clear about the rules of engagement from the beginning: never confuse fantasy with reality, never develop a personal relationship with a client, and never let things go further than a kiss.

Panties and I have already gone further than a kiss. Much further. I know the sounds she makes when she comes and the way her fingers feel wrapped around my cock.

Which means this intervention is over before it begins.

"I know this seems strange," she says as I stop in front of her table. Her voice is as husky and confident as I remember, making me hope her situation hasn't reached Dire status. It might take some time to get her booked in with Bash, and I don't want her to be stressed out or in danger while she's waiting for help.

"But I seriously had no idea you worked for this company when I contacted your boss," she continues, fingers curling around her mug. "It's just a crazy coincidence."

"You're kidding." My brow furrows. Red was never a liar, but the chances that someone I know would accidentally become my third client are pretty fucking slim.

She shakes her head. "No, I'm not. Bash helped a friend of mine send her ex to prison for securities fraud last year. She referred me to Magnificent Bastard Consulting, and when Bash heard the details of my situation, he suggested that I take a look at his associate's file. I had no idea it was you until I saw the pictures." Her lips quirk on one side. "Nice portfolio, by the way. I like the shot by the railroad tracks, the one where you're glaring at the camera with your neck veins popping out."

I narrow my eyes. "Are you giving me shit?"

She sees my narrowed eyes and raises me an arched brow.

"Did you have makeup on your stomach in those pictures?"

"The makeup lady ambushed me with eye shadow," I admit with a shrug, smiling as Red's husky laugh fills our corner of the café.

"Then, yes, I'm giving you shit. Just a little bit." Her grin banishes the tension from the corners of her mouth and strips the years from her face, making her look like the Panties I knew, the girl who always had my back, no matter what. "How have you been, Curve?" she asks in a softer voice. "It's been a long time."

"It has. And I've been good. Really good," I say, my smile fading as that sad, shitty feeling from yesterday sweeps in.

I don't enjoy meeting Red again like this.

And I'm going to enjoy telling her that I can't help her even less.

"So are you going to sit down?" Red's gaze shifts pointedly to the empty chair across from her before returning to me. "Or is this Spectacular Rascal thing something you only do standing up?"

"I didn't choose the name," I say, instead of the dozen other things I should be saying. I pull out the chair and settle in, promising myself I'll only stay long enough to catch up a little before I let her down easy. "Bash is in charge of the marketing, the detective work, and all the rest of it. I'm just the muscle."

"I doubt that. But you have committed to the beefcake thing, haven't you?" Her eyes skim down my chest, where I know my tight black T-shirt is displaying my well-earned pecs to their best advantage. "When I first saw the pictures, I wasn't completely sure it was you. The face was the same, but the Curve I knew looked more like a soccer player than a gladiator."

"I took up weightlifting after college." I resist the urge to flex beneath her gaze. I'm not a cheesy, 'roid-chomping meathead, but something primal inside of me wants to give her a reason to keep checking me out.

"You certainly did." Her attention returns to my face, uncertainty flickering in her green eyes. "I'm sorry I sprung this on you out of the blue. I should have told Bash that we knew each other. But I was afraid that if I did, you wouldn't come. And I really do need someone like you."

"Someone who's a little bit dangerous?" The words hit me in a different way now that I know who said them. I cross my arms on top of the wooden table and lean closer. "Surely you know better than that, Beth."

"Cat, please," she says. "My full name is Catherine Elizabeth, but I've always gone by Cat."

Cat. I nod. It fits her so much better than a sweet, old-fashioned name like Beth. It's light, playful, and mischievous, like the girl I used to know, the girl who is still there inside the woman she's become, though she looks every bit the high-powered attorney. From her shining auburn hair without a strand out of place, to her French manicure and designer dress, Cat looks like a million dollars and change.

It's hard to believe this is the same girl I saw covered in mud and sweating buckets on a regular basis. Looking at her now, I wouldn't believe she's ever sweat a drop in her life, let alone had meaningful interactions with dirt.

"So, Cat..." I shift uncomfortably in my chair as I realize we're as mismatched as I expected us to be when Beth Jones was just a name on a file. "I may have put on some muscle, but the scary stuff is all an act. The beef tartare lunch special is more dangerous than I am."

She lifts a perfectly plucked brow. "Is that right?"

I lower my voice so as not to offend the cranky French chef who makes my favorite *Pain Suisse* in the city. "I don't care how careful they are with the cutting and handling, eating raw meat is a bad idea. Put a raw egg on top and you're asking for date with E. coli. But me? I'm harmless. You know that."

She holds my gaze, unblinking. "You really believe that, don't you?"

"I do." I start to smile, but her serious expression cuts my grin off at the pass. "You don't?"

"No, I don't." She mimics my lean across the table, meeting me halfway, until there are only a few inches between our faces, and the familiar lemongrass and ginger smell of her pricks at my nose. "Because I know you, Aidan. I might not have known your name until a few days ago, but I know that you're fearless and boundary-less and give so few shits about what people think of you that you're about two subway stops away from being a sociopath."

The furrow between my brow deepens into a canyon, but she pushes on before I can insist that I'm way more pussycat than psychopath.

"And that's why I need you." She swallows, her pale throat working, making it clear this speech isn't coming easy for her. "I was recently involved with a man who is also fearless and boundary-less. But it turns out he isn't two subway stops away from being dangerous. He's riding the crazy train all the way to the last station, and he wants me in the seat next to him." She blinks faster before continuing in a hushed voice, "And if I'm not where he wants me to be, he would rather I not be anywhere at all. If you get my drift."

I nod, hating the man who put the fear in her eyes, wishing

there was a way to turn back time and keep her from getting involved with a nut job in the first place.

"The only way he's letting me go is if I can convince him that I've hooked up with someone not even he wants to mess with," she continues, holding my gaze. "Someone who has nothing to lose and no reason not to take a fight farther than Nico wants it to go."

I shake my head. "I don't know where you got the idea that I have nothing to lose. I own a business, but even if I didn't I can't—"

"But you're not an attorney working for some of the most affluent sleazebags in New York," she cuts in smoothly. "You're not planning a mayoral campaign, or scheming how fast you can clear a path to the White House. Aside from making sure no one gets an infection from a dirty tattoo gun on your watch, you don't have to worry about your reputation."

The thought makes my hands curl into fists on top of the table. "Don't even mention dirty tattoo guns and my shop in the same sentence. You could perform surgery in my chairs. They're that clean."

Her lips curve again, but only for a moment. "I'm sure they are. But you know what I mean. You don't have to be election-ready careful."

Her hand reaches out to cover mine, sending a shot of heat spreading through my body, making me wonder when the last time such a simple touch made me feel warm all over. "That's why you're perfect for this job. We just have to figure out how to stage our fake relationship so that Nico gets the message as quickly and painlessly as possible. For everyone involved."

I pull my hand away from Cat's and lift it into the air, signaling to the waitress headed our way that we need more time. There's no point in ordering. I won't be around long enough to drink a cup of coffee, let alone to settle in for the lengthy brunch orientation I had planned.

Despite what Red thinks, I'm *not* perfect for this job, and no matter how much I want to help an old friend, getting involved with Panties would break too many rules. I promised Bash I would keep things professional with our clients. And I promised myself I wouldn't get involved with women who are too vulnerable to hold up their end of a grown-up relationship, the kind that ends amicably, with no drama or hard feelings when one party is no longer having a good time.

Ten minutes into this thing with Red and there is already drama. She's insulted my sanity, my profession, and even my abs. But no matter how bothered I am by being called a sociopath, I'm also interested in her in a way I shouldn't be interested in a client.

The past eleven years have been good to her. She's still long and lean with sculpted runner's legs emerging from the short hemline of her dress, but she's also filled out in all the right places. Her features have fleshed out into a softer, prettier version of the face I remember, and from what I can see I'm guessing her ass is even more fucking phenomenal than it used to be.

There were days, back when the Dashers would go on conditioning runs after class, when Panties's round, firm, biteable, spankable, squeezable ass was the only thing that kept me going through miles four and five. Even when we were friends and only friends, I couldn't help indulging in the occasional fantasy about that ass and the girl attached to it.

About what it would be like to dig my fingers into her firm flesh while we kissed, to mold my palms to her incomparable ass as I took her from behind, to turn her over my knee and redden her pretty backside until she couldn't think of a single smartass thing to say. Until her blood was pumping hard and fast, pooling between her thighs, making her squirm and moan and beg for me to slip my fingers between her legs and take care of her.

Take care of her.

I *can't* take care of her. Not in any of the ways I'd like to. It's not my place. It never has been and never will be, and the best thing I can do for Red is to put a swift, painless end to this meeting and direct her to someone who might actually be able to help her.

"Listen, I want to help," I begin, my jaw tight. "I really do, but—"

"No. No buts." She shakes her head, sending her silky red hair sliding over one shoulder. "You can't back out. We have a contract, and I've already paid an insanely large deposit."

"And if Bash isn't available to handle your case, your deposit will be returned in full." I push my chair away from the table, needing physical distance to resist the pleading look in her eyes. "But I'm sure once I explain to him that I have a conflict of interest, he'll be happy to—"

"What conflict of interest?" Her palms flip to face the ceiling, fingers spread wide. "You mean because we almost had sex eleven years ago? When we were both practically children?"

I clear my throat, more flustered by her frank assessment of the situation than I expect to be.

"That's crazy, Aidan," she hurries on. "You turned me down and left the country the next day. Nothing even happened."

My jaw tightens. "That's not the way I remember it."

The way I remember it, she came on my hand and then somehow we ended up on the ground, me on my back in the leaves and her on top, grinding her slickness against the length of my cock, begging me to take her. And if our friend, Empty Tool Box, hadn't shouted for me to come help him put out the bonfire before it burned down the entire forest, I would have.

I would have fucked her bare there in the dirt because I was so out of my mind with wanting her. I was beyond worrying about finding a condom, or the responsibility of taking her virginity, or anything but how desperately I needed to be inside of her. Balls-deep, buried in her sweet, tight body, stroking hard until she made more sexy, coming sounds while her pussy milked my cock dry.

Red, who is thankfully oblivious to the X-rated memories dancing through my head, huffs in irritation. "Well, then your memory is impaired. Nothing happened, and nothing is going to happen, except that we'll work well together, the way we always have."

She threads her fingers together into a double fist, and her tone takes on a vulnerable quality that makes me feel even shittier for getting turned on while I'm turning her down. "We were a good team back in school, Aidan. You have to admit that. We watched out for each other and cared about each other and—"

"We did, but—"

"And this is no different than laying a killer trail or making sure no one gets kicked out of school for fighting on campus," she insists. "We'll get the job done, you'll get paid, I'll get my life back—everyone wins. Right?"

My mental wheels turn, searching for the right words to get out of here without hurting her. But before I can promise to go to bat for her with Bash and do everything I can to convince him to take her case—no matter how little I like the idea of my best friend working his fake love magic on this particular woman—she stands with a hard sniff.

"Fine." She fumbles in her purse, pulling out a few crumpled bills that she tosses on the table. "I get it. I'll call your boss and cancel the contract and…figure something else out. No worries."

"Wait, Cat. Don't you want to at least meet with Bash?" I pull my wallet out and toss another ten on the table by way of apology for causing a scene and stand to face her. "I know he's not exactly what you had in mind, but he's very good at—"

"Don't. Just…don't." She pauses halfway around the table to pin me with a look that makes my breath catch. She's angry, but it isn't her anger that gets me. It's the fear, the terror, lurking behind her pretty eyes that hits me like a fist in the gut.

"I'm sorry," I say softly. "I don't want to—"

"Do you know how hard it was for me to ask you for help?"

My lips part, but she doesn't wait for my answer.

"Insanely hard. I was so ashamed for you to know how messed up my life is, but I came to this meeting anyway. I showed up because I truly believe that you're the only person who can help me." She pulls in a breath, pressing her lips together. "But maybe you're right. Maybe you aren't the man for the job."

She holds my gaze with an intensity that makes me feel like she's looking straight through me, drawing my attention to unpleasant things lurking beneath the surface. It reminds me of the look my stepmom used to shoot me from the door to my bedroom, the one that cleared the teenage head-fog and made me realize that my man cave was two steps away from becoming a toxic waste dump.

"You always did run when things got heavy," she continues. "I don't know why I thought this would be any different."

I reach out to take her arm, to hold her close long enough to get it through her thick skull that comments like that are the reason why I can't be her knight in shining armor—we have baggage, and a past that's clearly weighing on both our minds—but she's as fast as she ever was. Before my fingers can capture her elbow, she's slipped away and fled the restaurant. She bursts out onto the sidewalk, setting the bells above the door to jangling and sending a puff of warm, garbage-scented air oozing in to mingle with the smells of toasting bread and herbed omelets bubbling in cast-iron skillets.

It's starting to smell like summer in New York. By the start of July, the stench will be so bad anyone with someplace better to be will have fled the city to spend weekends with relatives upstate or down at the Jersey shore.

For a moment, I wonder where Cat spends her long summer weekends and how having a psycho ex-boyfriend will affect her plans. And then I think about Kayla, my first client, a dancer who came to Bash for help after her ex-boyfriend ambushed her in her apartment and tied her to a bed for nearly a week.

By the time she escaped, she'd pulled at the ropes binding her to the frame so hard they'd cut into her skin. The burns around her ankles got infected and she had to take time off from her dance company, losing her first soloist role. But it wasn't losing the gig that convinced Kayla that drastic measures had to be taken to get her ex out of the picture; it was his promise to cut off her feet the next time she tried to leave him, ensuring that she would never dance again.

There are men like that. Men who are prepared to destroy the women they claim to care about, all to ensure that they won't be named losers in the game of love. They want control, and they want it bad enough to burn down the world to rule the pile of ash left behind.

And one of those men has decided Cat belongs to him, and he's going to do whatever it takes to get her under his thumb, or die trying.

No, he's not going to die.

But she *might.*

You realize that right, asshole? That this Nico character might do more to her than scare her and bully her? He might hurt her. Maybe even kill her.

And if that happens, you can take a long look in the mirror and see exactly who's to fucking blame.

I curse beneath my breath and start toward the door.

Ignoring the curious stares of the group of yoga-mat-wielding women settling into a booth in the opposite corner and the glare from the older man buying bread at the to-go counter, I hurry across the restaurant and out the door.

I have to do whatever it takes to convince Cat that Bash can help her end this thing with Nico. I'll pin her down and sit on her until she listens to reason if I have to. Her life is too precious to do anything less.

Outside in the early morning heat, I search the sidewalk in both directions, but there's no sign of a woman with silky auburn hair. Cat is gone, vanished into the crush of people bustling around the West Village, and I have no idea where to start looking for her.

I tug my phone from my jeans pocket, intending to call Bash and get her address, but before I can dial, I catch a flash of green out of the corner of my eye. It's Red, hurrying back toward the restaurant, her chin tucked, shoulders hunched, and hair falling around her face.

Her gaze is glued to the sidewalk in front of her, and her fingers are clutching the strap of her purse so hard her knuckles have gone white. She looks like she's trying to avoid attracting attention, but she's easily the most stunning woman on the street. Even if I hadn't been looking for her, she would have drawn my eye.

There's something about Cat that makes you want to take a second look and then a third. There always has been. She's not stereotypically beautiful—her face is a little too narrow, her mouth too wide, and back when she was younger there were times when she was all elbows and knees—but she stands out in a crowd. It's like the light inside of her has been cranked up a notch brighter than everyone else's.

And I'm not the only one who has noticed.

A moment after I catch sight of Red, my gaze is drawn to a dark-haired man behind her. He's about a block and a half away, wearing reflective sunglasses and a gray suit that fits his long, broad frame like nothing off the rack ever could. Walking with a brisk, confident stride, he doesn't appear to be in a rush, but he's steadily closing the distance between him and Red, and there's no doubt she's the reason he jogs to get across the street seconds before a taxi roars around the corner, nearly mowing him down.

I can't see his eyes behind his glasses, but I can tell he's looking at her. It's like there are laser beams shooting out of his forehead to dance between her shoulder blades. He's got a bead on her, and she's hauling ass away from him as fast as she can without breaking into a run.

Which means that this fuck in the thousand-dollar suit must be Nico, the man who won't take for no for an answer, the man who insists that he and Red are in it to win it, and who experiences temporary hearing loss every time she tells him the thrill is gone. The man who has scared the shit out of a woman I know for a fact doesn't scare easily.

I was there at the Death Valley marathon when Red kicked a rattlesnake out of the trail and then, when the thing had the poor judgment to slither back for round two, took it out with a rock to the head. I was there when a section of our usual trail gave way after a week of hard rain, and Red and another freshman went sliding down into a ravine. By the time we got a crew down to drag them out of the mud, the other newbie was hyperventilating and had to be carried back to his dorm room.

Not Red. She was pale and filthy, but after a drink of water and a minute to squeeze the mud out of her hair, she ran the trail and stayed up until midnight drinking beer with the rest of us. If she hadn't already been dubbed Polka Dot Panties, on that day she would have earned a much more badass trail name.

She's a tough cookie, but this arrogant, entitled, stalking sociopath has her on the run. He's the one responsible for the fear in her eyes, and he's so fucking crazy he's tailed her to a brunch meeting she insisted she would do her best to keep top secret.

The second I make the connection, everything changes. Now that I've laid eyes on Nico, there's no way I can turn Cat's case over to Bash.

Even from a block away, I can tell this guy is more than Bash can handle. My best friend thinks he's a stone cold bad ass, but deep down he believes that most of the people in the world are on the better side of okay. He expects a certain baseline of common decency and would be unprepared for a man like Nico. A man who thinks it's acceptable to treat an independent, intelligent, accomplished woman like an animal he bought at a pet store.

Or worse. I've known men like Nico before. They'll backhand their wives without a second thought, but most of them wouldn't dream of laying a hand on one of their dogs.

The thought of this douchebag laying a hand on Red

makes me see the same color. Before I've had time to think it through, I move into her path, stopping her with an arm around her waist and pulling her against me.

Her lips part, and her palms press against my chest, but when she sees my face she stops fighting.

"Look at me, nowhere else," I say, driving a hand into her silky hair. "Let's give that sack of amputated goat anuses a show he won't forget."

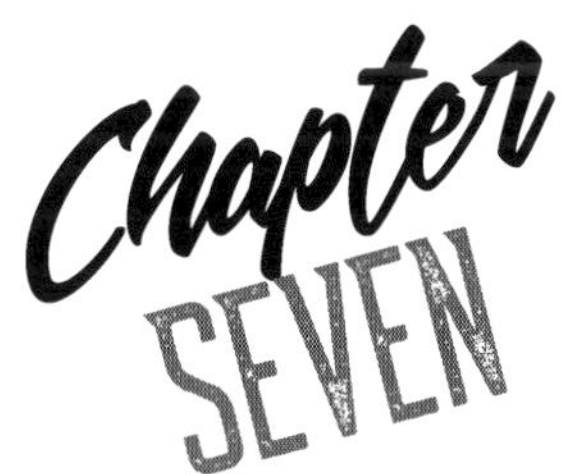

Chapter Seven

Bracing my free hand against the side of a long, black car parked by the curb, I lean Cat back against the sun-warmed metal and bend my face closer to hers.

"That's right," I whisper inches from her lips as I leverage one leg between hers, forcing her skirt higher on her thighs. I run a hand from her hip to mold around her ribs, just beneath her breast, feeling the heavy beat of her heart beneath my fingers. "Look at me. Focus on the sound of my voice while I tell you a story about all the things I'm going to do you as soon as we're alone."

"What kinds of things?" she asks, chest rising and falling faster.

I'm pretty sure it's fear of the approaching psycho that's making her breathless, but it doesn't matter. Arousal makes your breath come faster, too, and I'm going to do my best to ensure Nico buys that we're hot for each other—hook, line, and sinker.

"First, I'm going to kiss your lips. Slowly, thoroughly, thoughtfully, to prove how much I love taking my time with you." My thumb drifts back and forth, lightly caressing the under curve of her breast through her dress, watching her eyes darken as I hold her gaze. "And then I'm going to kiss you hard and deep. Give you a taste of what I'm going to do to you when we get home."

"What are you going to do?" Her tongue slips out to dampen her lips. "Tell me. I want to hear you say it."

"I'm going to own your pussy." The hair at the back of my neck lifts, some instinctive part of me warning that a predator is getting close even as my cock thickens inside my jeans. "I'm going to fuck you until you know who you belong to, and then I'll fuck you again just for the pure joy of watching you fall apart when you come."

I lean in, pressing my hips to hers, pinning her against the car. Despite the awareness of our audience, I'm rock hard, and I know there's no way Cat is going to miss it. Still, the moment her breath catches and her pelvis rocks against mine sends a bolt of lust surging through me. It's intense, mind-blowing, and powerful enough to make my knees weak.

I'm grateful for the support of the car as I bring my mouth to hers and murmur against her lips. "I'll fuck you until you can't stand and I have to carry you up to the roof for round three. And then I'll have you up there, while the stars come out, and make you call my name so loud people three blocks over will hear you screaming when you go again."

"I want that." Her palms skim down my back to cup my ass, making my cock swell even thicker. "I want *you*. I want you so much I wish you could take me right here. Right now.

Just turn me around, lift up my—"

I silence her with a kiss, and not the soft, sensual one I promised. This kiss goes from zero-to-sixty in three seconds flat. One moment we're two people standing close, the next my tongue is in her mouth, and her leg is hooked around my calf and the hand I've been careful to keep beneath her breast lifts high enough to brush her nipple through the thin fabric of her dress.

She moans into my mouth and arches into my hand while her fingers smooth across my body, exploring with a feverish appreciation that makes me even harder. By the time soft laughter sounds behind us, I've almost forgotten that this is all for the benefit of someone else.

But that laughter—low, deep, and seemingly sincerely amused—is like a bucket of ice water poured down my back. Or something worse. A bucket of week-old squid, maybe. Or a bucket of circus peanuts with razorblades hidden inside.

It's a laugh that says we're not fooling anyone with our hot kiss, and I can tell Cat hears it by the way she stiffens beneath my touch, but I'm not about to give up that easily. I keep kissing her, stroking my tongue against hers, waiting until the bastard standing behind us has the balls to do something other than laugh.

I don't have to wait long. A few seconds later Douchebag speaks up in a rich, lightly accented voice that it pains me to admit is nice to listen to.

"Imagine seeing you here, Catherine," he says. "What an unexpected surprise."

I turn to face Nico, who has removed his glasses—the better to glance condescendingly from Cat to me and back again—and curse silently. I'm not one of those men who pretends he can't tell when another guy is attractive, and this turd burglar is a damned good-looking guy. And a damned dangerous looking one.

I twine my fingers more tightly through Cat's, silently offering my support.

It's best if she takes point right now. I don't know enough about the situation to make a judgment call on whether Nico will take the message that she's finished with him more seriously if it's coming from her or from me. But judging from the way his dark eyes are fixed on her face, I'm betting her voice is the one that matters most.

"What are you doing here, Nico?" Cat's tone is cool, but not cold, which is odd considering I know she has no interest in communicating with this man.

But then she's probably making an effort not to offend him, which is a good idea, though I hate that she's being forced to pander to a big, scary, fuck stick. And damn, but the creep is even bigger and scarier up close.

Nearly as tall as my six-five, Nico is every bit as broad through the shoulders and chest, though more slender everywhere else. Still, there's no doubt in my mind that he would be a bad man to meet in a dark alley. He holds himself with the grace and ease of the prizefighters I've known. I'm bigger, but he would be faster and meaner. No fucking doubt about the meaner part.

Looking into his dark brown eyes is enough to give me frost burn. He's smiling, but there is nothing amused in his expression, and there's nothing at all in his eyes. He's empty, soulless, all the way down to the core, one of those people born without any conscience to go with their consciousness.

Red was right. This dude is riding the crazy train all the

way to the last stop. Thank God she had the sense to get off, and to seek help from someone who will make sure she doesn't get yanked down onto the tracks.

"A better question is why you're kissing another man against my car," Nico asks, his smile never faltering.

Cat glances over her shoulder before turning back to her ex with saucer-round eyes. "Oh my God. I'm sorry. I didn't realize. I never meant—"

"It's all right." He angles his body closer to hers, making it clear he doesn't consider me a part of this equation. "I know you, Catherine. I know who you are, and the way you behave when you're being true to yourself. I'm not worried."

Cat pales, swallowing hard. "Please, Nico. I just want to move on. Aidan and I have been friends for a long time and now it's, um…it's turned to something more." She leans into me until her ribs jab into my side, as if to prove that we're literally inseparable. "I'm sorry if that hurts you. I never intended to rub your nose in our relationship. I honestly didn't realize this was your car until you—"

"There is no relationship." Nico still refuses to look at me, even when I wrap my arm tight around Cat's waist and glare down at him. "You can fuck every man in this city, but in your heart, your soul, you belong to me, and you always will. Nothing you say or do will ever change that."

"Her heart and soul belong to her," I snap, deciding Cat needs backup. Stat. "And no means no, friend. She has no interest in you. It's time to move on and leave her the hell alone."

"We'll talk more later." Nico ignores me, but the muscle in his jaw tightens, proving he heard every word I said. "When you're alone and not covered in another man's sweat."

"You won't be talking to her later and especially not alone." I drop the pretense of civility, allowing the threat of violence to creep into my tone. "You will lose her number and forget her name."

"Please shower as soon as you get home," he continues, "I don't want to catch the smell of him on your skin." Nico's eyes narrow, and I can feel how hard it is for him to keep from shifting his glare my way. "The stink is incredible."

I laugh; I can't help it. "Did you really just insult me by saying I smell? What is this, the third grade?"

"Take care, love," he says in a clipped voice. "I'd hate it if anything happened to you while you were keeping bad company."

"I can take a shower," I continue mildly. "A bad smell washes off. Crazy is a lot harder to get rid of, I hear."

Cat pinches my side in a silent warning, but I don't look down at her. I keep my eyes on Nico, ready to meet his Psycho with my Badass Motherfucker when he finally achieves eye contact, but he glances over his shoulder, instead. "Let's head uptown, Petey. I need to be at the office no later than noon. Take care, Catherine. We'll talk soon," he tosses over his shoulder as he circles around Cat and steps off the curb.

I turn, Cat still held close, to see a beefy guy who tops out at about five six, wearing a dark suit and standing on the other side of the car, which I now realize is a limo. That explains the short guy's chauffer cap, but not the look of hatred on his face. The man shoots me a glare that makes it clear he'd like to pull my guts out through my nose and then shifts his attention to Cat, who he clearly has no love for, either.

If anything, his rage level seems to increase when his gaze lands on her face, and by the time he shuts Nico's door behind him and opens his own, his cheeks are red and his beady brown eyes look like they're about to pop out of his face.

"Nico's cousin Petey," Cat whispers through clenched teeth. "I'm pretty sure he's in charge of disappearing people who piss Nico off."

"Small, but feisty, then."

"Small, but deadly," she corrects.

I nod slowly, knowing further discussion of Petey's "disappearing" skills have to wait until we're alone, but inside I'm putting together the pieces of this puzzle to make an ugly picture. Cat hasn't just gotten on the wrong side of one very bad man. She's gotten on the wrong side of one very bad man, his very bad friends, and maybe even a very bad branch of very organized fucking crime.

Though, I suppose I shouldn't be surprised.

Cat never did do things halfway. Why should her psycho-ex-lover situation be any different?

From the collected notes of Curved for her Pleasure and Polka Dot Panties

Dear Curve,
I hesitated, to write this because I know you're not into the touchy feely stuff, but then I had another beer and decided what the hell? You only live once!
So I'm writing to thank you for shutting down that whiny little shit Marty this afternoon. As you know, I take great pride in winning races fair and square, with a combination of superior skill and keen intellect.
To be accused of kissing you where you pee in order to get the specs

of the trails ahead of time was insulting, not only to me, but to my entire gender. That freshman dick's assumption that the only way a girl can win as often as I do is if she's getting preferential treatment from the man in charge is a huge steaming pile of bullshit.

If you hadn't set him straight, I would have had to kick his ass, and that would have sucked because I'm committed to nonviolent conflict resolution since that time I almost killed a man in Kathmandu.

So basically, you're awesome, and I respect the shit out of you for making a club that could have become a big, fat, unwelcoming-to-girls-and-other-decent-people testosterone fest an enjoyable place to be for folks of all sexes, races, and sexual orientations.

Rock on with your bad self,

PDP

Dear PDP,

The phrase "kiss you where you pee" is probably the cutest thing I've ever read. I debated the wisdom of telling you that you're cute because I know you're probably a super-soldier sleeper spy who's going to lose your shit in a flashback someday and take out anyone who ever reminded you that you're also an adorable redhead, but I couldn't help myself.

I've had a few beers, too.

Related: drunk-note-writing is a lot more work than drunk-dialing.

Maybe we should exchange numbers so I can text you when you're being cute? Let me know. I would like to experience in real time your irritated responses to things I write.

Will keep rocking on with my bad self,

Curve

P.S. No worries about shutting down that dirt-surfing snot goblin. No one fucks with you on my watch, kid.

Dear Curve,

Several things:

One: I am not a kid. I am two years younger than you and I'm going to be able to buy my own beer in less than a year so you should respect my near full adultness.

Two: I am not a super–solider sleeper spy. (Or maybe that's just what I have to say to preserve my cover. Boom. Just blew your mind.)

Three: I'm not sure it's kosher to exchange numbers. Aren't we supposed to respect the sanctity of the hole? It's right there in the rulebook: all Dasher communications outside of running hours shall be conducted via notes stuffed in the Union Soldier statue's secret hole. Respect the hole.

Four: I am not cute or adorable, but it's cute and adorable that you think I am. But don't worry, I won't tell anyone that beneath your tough, take-no-prisoners façade you're basically composed of raindrops on roses, whiskers on kittens, and old lady face lotion.

Respecting the hole and not giving you my digits—but if you want to give me yours, I might make use of them.

Someday.

If you're lucky.

Adorably yours,

Panties

Dear Panties,

Why old lady face lotion? I have to know...

C, aka Raindrops on Roses and Whiskers on Kittens

555-3476

Text from Panties to Curve: My number is blocked so hard you'll never figure out my digits so don't even try, but this is Panties.

Curve: So are you really a spy? Or in the witness

protection program?
Or a former drug lord posing as an innocent co-ed while you hidc out from a rival cartel and plot their downfall?
That would explain a lot of things about you, Panties.

Panties: Lol! Like what? I don't do drugs. If I did, my dad would kill me and then resurrect me through dark magic just to kill me all over again. I don't even drink anything harder than light beer.

Curve: Yes, but for a skinny person, you can drink an insane amount of light beer without getting fucked up.
But you're right. You're not the drug lord type.
I'm sticking with spy. When the feds come sniffing around and suddenly you're nowhere to be found, I won't be surprised.

Panties: Don't be silly. If I'm spying for anyone, it's Uncle Sam. I'm a patriot. I bleed red, white, and blue.
Now, do you want to know why you're made of old lady face lotion, or not?

Curve: Yes. Desperately. Do tell.
Raindrops and roses and whiskers on kittens felt right, but I didn't know what I did to deserve to be composed of one-third stank-ass face cream.

Panties: I didn't mean the stinky kind. I meant the nice kind that smells like cucumbers and sea salt. Like my gram used to wear.
I lived with her when I was little. She was very cool and fun and let me have cookies every day after school. So, to me, the smell of old lady face lotion is the smell of a safe, fun place where there are cookies.
So…there you go…

Curve: Wow…
That's sweet, Panties. Thank you.
I'm glad that the club is a safe, cookie kind of place for you.

Panties: Yeah, well. Whatever.
Don't take any of that too seriously.
I've had four beers and my roommate is watching Sense and Sensibility and Colonel Brandon just confessed his soldier love to Marianne. The combo is making me uncharacteristically sentimental.

Curve: Sometimes I wonder if you drink too much, Red. And if it's our fault for supplying you with beer when you were a freshman.

Panties: Nah. I drank before I came to college.
It's the way I deal with the flashbacks after Kathmandu.

Curve: Sometimes I'm not sure when you're

kidding.

Panties: And that's the way I like it. ;)
Sweet dreams, C.

Curve: Sleep tight, Panties. Don't let the crazy bugs bite.

Panties: Too late.

Curve: For you and me both, kid.

I want to slam my fist into the hood of Nico the Psycho's car and shout after him that it will be a cold day in hell when he lays a hand on Red again. Instead, I stand on the sidewalk with my arm around her waist, doing my best to look bored until the limo is out of sight.

Dicks like Nico love rapping the glass until the animals start freaking out and hurling themselves against the bars, but I refuse to give him the satisfaction.

So I turn to smell the shampoo and sunshine smell of Cat's hair and think smug thoughts about how clearly turned-on she was while I was kissing her and how satisfying it is that Nutjob Nico heard at least part of our hot-as-fuck conversation. But the second the sleek, black Mercedes turns the corner, I release Cat with a growl and jab a finger toward the subway entrance.

"Subway. Now, *Catherine*."

She wrinkles her nose so hard the bridge turns white. "It's

Cat. Red or Panties if you're on my good side. Ms. Legend if you're nasty."

"Thanks, Janet," I say, rolling my eyes. "I thought your last name was Jones."

Her gaze shifts to the right as she picks nervously at a loose thread on her purse strap. "Well, it's not. I gave Bash a false last name. For me, and for Nico."

"And why's that?" I drive a clawed hand through my hair. "Just to fuck this up before we even get started? Or is lying something you do to entertain yourself when being stalked by a psycho starts to get boring?"

"None of this is entertaining," she snaps, her cheeks flushing pink before she lets out an unexpected stutter of laughter. "Okay, so maybe the part where you called Nico a sack of amputated goat anuses was a little bit fun. But that's it."

"Bash and I have a running contest to see who can come up with the best insults for our clients' exes." I concentrate on keeping my scowl firmly in place, refusing to let her husky laugh throw me off course. "So why the fake name, *Cat*?"

It really does fit her, and not just because of the green eyes and the mischief factor. It fits her because she's sneaky as shit and diabolically unpredictable, just like a fucking feline.

"I did it for your own good," she says. "To protect you. And Bash." She glances over my shoulder before turning to peer over her own, back toward the café where a line has formed as the tables fill up for lunch. Finally, when she's sure the coast is clear, she adds in a soft voice, "I didn't want to put anything in writing, just in case he's still reading my email."

"Nico?"

She nods, tugging harder on the purse string. "I change my email password every day, but I'm not sure that's enough to stop him, and I don't—" She cuts off, wincing as the string snaps off in her hand. She shakes it onto the ground with a rush of breath. "We shouldn't talk about this here, and we shouldn't fight in public, either. There's a chance we're being watched. Just because Nico drove away doesn't mean he didn't leave someone behind to keep tabs on me."

I stand up straighter, fighting the urge to turn and scan the crowd beginning to clog the street as the office buildings set their cubicle jockeys free for the lunch hour. "You're sure you're not being paranoid?" I ask, though my gut says she's not. Nico is clearly crazy and also clearly has the funds to pay someone to follow his ex around and scare her shitless.

"I'm sure," Cat says, teeth worrying her bottom lip. "He sent photos to my office last week. He said his associate was following me to keep me safe until he could protect me himself, but the real message came through loud and clear."

My jaw tightens. "That you're being watched."

She shakes her head. "No, that Nico can get to me anywhere. There were shots of me inside a closed courtroom where I was representing a client and at a friend's restaurant where you need a secret code to get through the door." She crosses her arms, her shoulders hunching as if against the cold, though it's at least eighty-five degrees outside. "There was even a shot from inside the dressing room at my gym. I was coming out of the shower. Judging by the angle, I'm guessing the guy was hiding under the lockers. But I had no idea I wasn't alone until I saw the images. If he'd wanted to do more than take a picture I would have been dead before I had any clue I needed to run."

My gut clenches. "Fuck me."

"I didn't think that was allowed," she says, a hint of the old smartass in her tone as she hitches her purse higher on her shoulder. "The contract I signed said that things between us will never go further than a kiss."

"They won't." I ignore the ache in my balls that gives testimony to how ready I was to do more than kiss Red a few minutes ago.

She clucks her tongue as she shakes her head. "I don't know. I think we might have already violated that proviso. I'm pretty sure you stole second base, and that level of dirty talk has to count as at least third. Maybe third and a half."

"Third and a half," I echo, feigning boredom, not surprised she called me on stealing second.

Of course she did. She might look like a sophisticated princess, but she's still Red, a fact that makes me happier than it probably should. Red was trouble, and Red all polished, poised, and grown-up is flat-out dangerous.

"Not that I'm complaining." She holds up her hands in what would be a placating gesture if a shit-eating grin weren't creeping across her face. "I mean, you clearly made an impression Nico won't forget, but I don't want to incur supplemental charges without being aware of it up front. Do you charge extra for the dirty talk and second-base stealing? Is it like per word or per sentence or—"

"Come on, smartass." I reach for her, fingers closing around her upper arm as I set off down the street.

"Where are we going?" she asks, allowing me to lead her toward the subway.

"To a place where we can talk and I know for damned certain none of Nico's spies will be able to follow us."

"Good." The tension seeps from her arm as her muscles relax. "I was beginning to think there weren't any more places like that." She shifts closer, tapping her knuckles lightly against my chest. "So this means you're helping me. Right, Curve?"

"Aidan," I correct, deciding the sooner we get back on purely professional ground the better. "Mr. Knight if you're nasty."

"Aidan," she says softly, the sound of my given name on her lips making this feel *more* intimate instead of less, proving my instincts are shit when it comes to this woman. "So you're helping me? We're taking care of this together?"

"Yes, we're taking care of this. Together." I pause near a halal food stand and turn to face her, hoping the umbrellas shading the area will provide cover from any prying eyes. "But that means no more lies. You tell me the whole truth and nothing but the truth. I need to be prepared for whatever Nico might dish out, and I can't do that if you're not honest with me."

She nods seriously. "The whole truth. I promise. Even though it's embarrassing. I'll spill everything as soon as we're somewhere safe."

"Good." I let my fingers trail down her arm to take her hand and give it a squeeze. "And don't waste time being embarrassed. We've all done things we're not proud of."

"Really?" Her head cants to one side. "Even you? Mr. All Honorable, All The Time?"

"You need to make up your mind," I say, voice low. "Am I honorable? Or am I a sociopath?"

Her lashes sweep down, drawing my attention to her lips, reminding me how fucking good they felt pressed against mine. "I never said you were a sociopath. I said you were two subway stops *away* from being a sociopath. There's a difference."

"Give me a break, Cat."

"Hey, a lot can happen in two subway stops! And even

sociopaths can have honor codes," she insists stubbornly, because she majored in stubborn and minored in being a pain in my ass. "It's just that their codes don't necessarily comp to the honor codes of people who are hardwired in a more traditional way." She rolls her eyes as she waves her free hand breezily through the air. "And who wants to be traditional anyway? Traditional people are boring and predictable and hardly ever have interesting jobs like being a professional spectacular rascal."

"Seriously, Red. Just take back the shit about me being a sociopath and we can continue about our business."

"Speaking of business," she says with a bright smile. "Do you have business cards that say Spectacular Rascal on them? If so, I would love to get one to add to my 'That Time I was Stalked and Had to Hire a Professional Rascal' scrapbook I'm working on for my—"

"I'm serious, Catherine." I squeeze her hand tight enough to let her know I'm not fucking around. "Look at me. Right now."

She rolls her eyes again before bringing her gaze back to meet mine. "Okay, fine. You're not a sociopath."

"Thank you. Now was that so hard?"

"No." Her lips press into a thoughtful line. "I don't know why I said that in the first place. It just came out and then I felt like I had to defend it to the death. I've always been that way, and it's only gotten worse after having a job where I basically argue for a living, so…" Her breath rushes out. "So, I'm sorry. You're not a sociopath. You're one of the most honorable people I've ever met, and I'm incredibly grateful you're going to take my case."

"Thank you. Apology accepted." I study her flushed face,

seeing more of the girl I used to know now that she's relaxed her guard. "And to answer your question, yes, I've done things I'm not proud of. Lots of things, and I almost added another one to the list when I said I couldn't help you."

"Apology accepted. Thank you." Her lips curve in a real smile, a warm, sincere, light-up-the-world smile that makes me wish we'd stayed in touch. No one can be more irritating than Red, but no one smiles like her, either.

"Yeah, well," I say gruffly. "Hopefully you'll still be thanking me when you get the bill for the extra dirty talk."

She shrugs. "Whatever. As long as the talk is good, I don't care if it's cheap."

I'm tempted to tell her that this intervention is on the house, but think better of it. This is Bash's show. Only he can make the call about whether a case should be pro bono, and it's probably best if we keep money involved. Money will remind me that, for the time being, I am Cat's employee, not her friend, and certainly not anything more.

But as we hold hands on the steps down into the subway, it doesn't feel like I'm on the job. It feels like I'm walking back into a wonderful old memory and reconnecting with a girl I never should have left behind.

Cave Fitness is just a few blocks from my shop and open twenty-four hours a day, seven days a week, making it perfect for lunch hour lifting or a quick late night workout after I close up.

But even if it were on the far side of Manhattan, the cave would be worth the trip. Its back to basics mentality, combined with a firm commitment to bulking up without chemicals or sketchy supplements, is one that's hard to find. Add to that a bohemian vibe that welcomes lifters from every walk of life, regardless of sex, gender, color, or creed, and you have a recipe guaranteed to take me to my happy place.

And don't tell the rest of the hardcore power lifters, but the fact that my gym is right next door to Sweet Vengeance, a bakery specializing in fucked-up sounding cupcakes that are insanely delicious, isn't something I'm going to complain about—not like the rest of the babies bitching about sugar going to their guts and concealing their cuts. Cuts are all well and good, and I like my gut on the flatter side, but if a post-workout cupcake is wrong, I don't want to be right.

As Cat and I emerge from the subway, headed for the cave and its spy-unfriendly smoothie lounge, where I'm sure we won't be disturbed—Cavers welcome all, but no one without a membership, or a member to vouch for them, is getting by Reba at the front desk—I'm tempted to duck into Sweet Vengeance for some sugar therapy first. But thanks to Bash's slacking behind the scenes and Cat's less than truthful application, we're already five steps behind. And with a guy like Nico, I prefer to be ten steps ahead, waiting with something heavy I can use as a weapon if the need arises.

Therefore, I heroically ignore the seductive smells of butter-soaked croissants crisping in the oven, and sugar and flour coming together in mouth-orgasm-inducing combinations, and escort Cat into the cave.

"Heading to the smoothie bar," I tell Reba, flashing my membership card. "Knight and guest."

Reba, who resembles a ripped Betty Davis, right down to the smoky eyes and seriously un-fucking-amused pout, gives me a thumbs up, while shooting Red an appraising look. I've never brought a woman into the cave before. It's my refuge from the outside world. I don't consider dating a stress-inducing activity, but I prefer not to risk running into lovers—current or former—when all I want to do is sweat and unwind.

But Red isn't my lover, and I doubt she'll take one look at the cave and want to apply for membership. I appreciate the prison weight room vibe offered by the cinder block walls, concrete floors, and tiny rectangular windows near the ceiling, but most people are looking for something a little more luxurious in a gym.

"I see why you chose this place," Cat says, raising her voice to be heard over the clattering of weights and the grunts and groans issuing from the bench press section. Her gaze skims the crowd of mostly male lifters, an assessing look in her eyes. "Most of these guys look way scarier than Nico's thugs."

"Looks are deceiving in this case. Most of the Cavers are harmless." I lift a hand to a few familiar faces as we make our way through the weight room to the smoothie and juice bar. "I rarely meet a guy in here who isn't made of raindrops on roses and whiskers on kittens."

She laughs. "And old lady face lotion. Can't forget that."

"Of course not. That's the best part." I wink as I open the door for her, letting her precede me into the Smoothie Dungeon.

Inside, whoever decorated the cave even more fully embraced the prison-chic vibe, complete with bars surrounding the blending professional on duty, painfully bright fluorescent lights, and metal tables bolted to the floor. Red and I place our orders—an extra large Green Monster for me, and a Walnut and Whey Protein Blast for her—and settle in at a table by the wall with a clear view of the door.

Except for the guy manning the blender and two women I've seen at the cave before, we're alone. The blender dude is busy and the women are huddled over their Strawberry Explosions, gossiping in hushed tones about someone from their apartment building. They're ignoring Red and I completely, and we'll be the first to see anyone who comes into the bar. We're in a secure, controlled environment, and there's no time to waste fucking around. The enemy has been engaged, and we haven't even started to craft a battle plan. I should dive right in to the gory details.

Instead, I hesitate, a part of me wanting to put off hearing about this man Red used to love before it all went to shit.

Bash may have been sucking at his job since he and Penny split last month—thank God she's back and things at Magnificent Bastard Consulting will soon return to their anal-retentive state of organization—but his intake form on Cat did contain a few useful pieces of information. Evidently, the feelings between her and Nico weren't always one-sided. She copped to caring about him and to being "swept up by the intensity" of their relationship.

I remember that was the exact phrase she used, but it's hard to imagine Cat being swept up by anything.

She isn't that kind of person. She's levelheaded and logical, passionate, but a woman who reserves her fire for issues of societal injustice, not interpersonal relationships. In fact, aside from that one night when she seemed as carried away by the chemistry between us as I was, I've never seen Red lose control. Get angry, get loud, get feisty—yes. But never lose control.

Even that night in the woods, the lapse in her restraint had been physical, not emotional. She wasn't in love with me; she'd just wanted to get rid of her virginity with a friend she could trust.

So what happened?

What opened up a practical woman like Cat to the ravages of a dysfunctional kind of love?

"This is kind of weird, isn't it?" She swirls her straw through her thick shake.

"How so?" I take a deep pull on my drink, approving of the lime to cucumber and kale ratio.

She shrugs, an uncertainty in the gesture that isn't like

the Cat I remember, either. "I mean in some ways we're old friends, but in other ways we're strangers. I know what will make you laugh, but until today I didn't even know your name, let alone anything about your past or what you've been up to for the last eleven years."

"It is kind of strange, I guess. But that's what makes Dasher clubs so great. You get all the fun of a close group of friends with none of the real life drama."

"You're right," she says, with a wistful smile. "We did have a lot of fun. Maybe I'll get back into the lifestyle when all of this is over."

"I run with the Lower Manhattan Dashers. We have a good time."

She nods, casting her gaze down at her drink. "That's a little far for me, but I hear the Brooklyn club is good."

"If you like hipsters in fake retro T-shirts with your alcohol poisoning."

"And who doesn't," she deadpans. "Though I prefer gladiator types in overpriced organic tee shirts."

I grin. "How could you tell my T-shirt was organic?"

"I'm an Apache scout, remember?" She points two fingers toward her eyes before swiveling them in my direction. "Nothing's getting past me." Her smile curdles at the edges. "Except all the things that got past me for the past six months. Like my ex being up to his elbows in dirty money and having mob connections going back five generations."

I sigh, not enjoying having my organized crime suspicions confirmed. "The mob. No shit? What tipped you off, the creepy goons who work for him or the thousand-dollar suit?"

"Touché," she says wryly. "But in my defense, Nico was good at hiding things he didn't want me to see. At least in the beginning." She runs a hand through her hair with a long sigh. "Which is where I should probably start. Or maybe even a little before."

"Go for it." I sit back in my chair and get as comfortable as I can on the unpadded metal seat. "I'll cut in if I need clarification, but otherwise, talk until you're talked out, and then we can go back and fill in any holes."

She nods and gives her shake another stir. "It started when my dad died. It was right after that crazy March snow storm last year, the one that knocked the power out for almost a week."

"I remember. And I'm sorry," I say automatically, though her voice is steady, and she actually looks less upset than she did a few minutes ago.

"Don't be," she says, before adding with a shake of her head, "I mean, you can be. That's fine. I'm sorry, too, but not for the obvious reasons. I respected my father, and I'll always be grateful to him for many things, but our relationship was never what you'd call easy."

She sighs again. "I spent the first fifteen years of my life trying to be just like him and the next fifteen wavering between being too scared to show him who I really was, and trying my best to piss him off. And..." She rolls her eyes as her lips twist unhappily. "Anyway, I'll save that shit for my therapist, but the point is that he died before we could find our way to anything resembling a healthy relationship. Or achieve closure. Or any of that good stuff."

"Dads can be hard." I cross my arms, thinking of my own father. We get along better than we used to, but I'll always be a disappointment to dear old dad. I chose passion over hundreds of years of family tradition, and he's never forgiven me for it, no matter how proud he is of me for building a successful business from the ground up.

Red nods. "Yeah, they can be. And my dad was. Right until the end."

I wince. "No good good-bye?"

"No good good-bye, which I thought I was okay with. But if that was true, I wouldn't have gotten involved with Nico. I knew from the second I met him that he was trouble. Though, I never imagined he was involved with anything illegal." She laughs breathily. "We met at a bar conference, for God's sake. As far as I knew he was just another predictably cutthroat chief legal officer for the Fortune 500."

"So he's a lawyer, too?" I think back on Nico's eloquent condescension and showy suit, and nod. "I can see it."

"He is, but he's not just a CEO's evil legal lapdog." She leans in lowering her voice. "He's also a consigliere, legal advisor to one of New York's last thriving mob families, and third in line to be the big, bad mob boss of the next generation. Which, considering the turnover in that line of work, makes his ascension to the ranks of Al Capone types fairly likely."

"Well, shit, Red." *Fuck.* This is even worse than I thought. Nico's not just a cog in a dangerous machine; he's one of the people calling the shots.

And scheduling the hits.

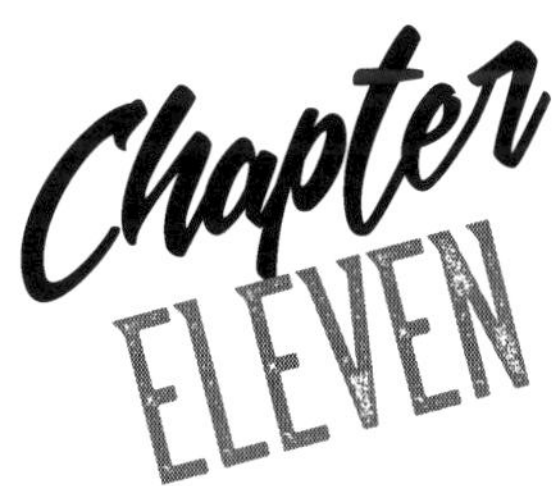

My breath whistles through my teeth. "You don't mess around when it comes to making enemies, do you?"

Cat winces. "I know. But I honestly don't think he wants to grow up to be a crime lord. Like I said, he has political aspirations, even White House fantasies. He's been trying to distance himself from that world."

I snort. "It doesn't matter. A guy with mob ties, even distant ones, is never going to be president."

Her lips twist. "I don't know. When Trump cinched the GOP nomination all my preconceived notions about what the American people will put up with as far as crass, crazy, and weirdly orange are concerned went out the window."

I nod, conceding the point.

"And Nico really does hide what he is very well. When I first met him, I had no clue he was part of organized crime," she says, wadding her straw wrapper into a tiny little ball. "I only knew that he was an arrogant ass my father would have hated with the passion of a thousand white-hot waffle makers. That alone was enough to make me say yes to a first date."

I arch a brow. "And the second date?"

"Well, he was charming in his way," she says, tossing her straw-wrapper ball to the center of the table. "And the sex was pretty fucking phenomenal."

I watch the wrapper roll across the metal surface, ignoring the growly feelings inspired by imagining Nico and Cat in bed together and the voice in my head that insists she only thinks she's had "phenomenal" because I haven't had my chance with her yet. These are inappropriate thoughts and feelings to have for a client, and I should be concentrating on her story, not my own reaction to it.

"But I don't have a fucking clue why I let things go as far as I did." She snatches her drink from the table and sucks vigorously at the straw, draining it several inches. "Maybe I have a brain tumor or something." She pops her straw back in her mouth and takes down another giant mouthful of ice-cold shake.

"Hopefully not, but you're going to give yourself a brain freeze if you're not careful."

"I don't get brain freeze." She sets the drink back on the table. "I'm a super-solider, remember?"

"I do, which is why I don't understand this," I say, shaking my head. "My 'dude's not right' detector started going off the second I laid eyes on that guy. The lights are on, but no one's home. At least, not anyone I want to meet."

"He used to hide it better, I swear he did," she says, that haunted look creeping in to tighten her features. "It's only since I told him I was calling off the engagement that his mask started to slip. I never saw the Nico you saw today before that. He faked having a soul very well."

"You were engaged?" I fight to keep the surprise from my tone. I had no idea it had gotten that serious, that she'd actually agree to marry that scum dumpster before changing her mind.

"Only for a couple of weeks." She glances down at her folded hands, not meeting my eyes. "As soon as I said yes, our entire relationship changed. He started getting bossy with me outside the bedroom and assuming that he was going to have a level of control over my life that was never going to be okay. He wanted me to quit my job and text him every time I left his building. He even talked about putting a tracking device on my car…" She shakes her head. "All kinds of crazy stuff. But he kept insisting it was for my own safety, which made me ask questions I should have asked in the beginning."

She takes another survey of the room. We're now the only occupied table—the two women finished their shakes and left a while ago—but she still leans in to whisper her next words, "That's when I found out that he's been helping launder money for the Mancuso family for years, and that his grandfather pretty much owned Brooklyn in the fifties."

I sit back hard enough to send the front legs of my chair lifting off the floor.

Mancuso.

This keeps getting better and better.

I'm far from up on current events—I prefer to get my news from the Onion and the pissed off political activists who swing into the shop to get inked—but even I know about the Mancusos. They're New York's most untouchable crime family, a group of highly intelligent, highly dangerous criminals who have managed to avoid prosecution for decades, all while ruling an empire built on blood and fear. Federal prosecutors have tried to bring several higher ups in the organization to trial twice, but each time key witnesses vanished before they could take the stand, and the mob bosses went free.

People who have dirt on the Mancusos have a way of disappearing on an alarmingly regular basis.

Disappearing…

The phrase is no longer the least bit funny, and the fact that Petey, the "disappearing" specialist, was glaring at Red less than an hour ago makes me determined not to let her out of my sight. No one is disappearing on my watch. Even if I have to break every one of Bash's rules, I'm keeping Red alive until we can find a way out of this hot mess we've landed in.

From the texts of Aidan Knight and Sebastian "Bash" Prince, with cell phone appropriation by Penny Pickett.

From Bash: End it, Aidan. Right now.
She lied on the application, which renders our contract null and void.
Go home, lock your door, and then give me a call back. We'll figure out together what to do next. You've got a friend at the NYPD, right?

Aidan: Yeah, Lipman made Detective last year. But—

Bash: No buts. Get home and call Lipman. See if he can hook you up with someone who can help Catherine. And if that's a bust, Penny knows a guy who's former FBI.

Aidan: I'll give Lipman a call as soon as I can, but I can't bail on this assignment. Cat's ex already saw us together this morning.

Bash: So what? Did you give him a name?

Aidan: Not my full name, no, but Cat mentioned my first name, and I hear mob guys are pretty good at getting information when they want it. And he's going to want it. Cat says he takes jealousy to the insane place.

Bash: What's to be jealous of? As far as he knows you and Catherine had brunch.

Aidan: Had brunch and then made out on his car.

Bash: Fuck!
No, don't fuck.
So what? Brunch and making out. That's not enough to get a price on your head. I know you like being the hero, but this isn't what you signed up for. We take down average, run of the mill assholes. MBC isn't equipped to take on the mob.

Aidan: I know, but I—

Bash: Get. Out. Of. There.
Now. Ten minutes ago if possible. You're going to

end up in the witness protection program, man.

Aidan: You're not listening.

Bash: Or dead. Mobsters kill people, Aidan!
This is Penny, btw. I took Bash's phone because I text faster than he does, but I speak for both of us when I say that this is crazy pants. We feel for this woman, we really do, but we LOVE you, and we do not want to see you hurt or killed for any reason.
But especially because of MBC.
This isn't even your passion work. This is something you're doing for extra cash, and extra cash is not worth endangering a single hair on your precious, furry, lumberjack face. So come over to Bash's right now, and we'll call my friend who used to be with the FBI and get some advice on how to put this fire out ASAP.
Bash wants his phone back because he thinks I'm going overboard with calling in the FBI guy right away, but I'm not going overboard.
Trust me, I know all about psychos.
My mom dated lots of psychos, including a guy who was with the Croatian mob. And Ivan was scary as shit, and no one has ever even heard of the Croatian mob. Ivan was a My Little Pony mobster compared to this Nico guy. This guy is a wild, angry, baby-eating, Italian-stallion mobster psycho who is fully capable of hiring people to fit you with concrete shoes and make sure your body

is never found.

So get your butt over here right now.

Aidan?

Aidan are you still there?

Aidan if you don't text back in the next minute, Bash and I are going to track you down and kidnap you. I'm serious!

Aidan, this is Bash again. Please don't make me put clothes on and come have a serious talk with you. Just get out of there, go home, lock your door, and call me.

We can sort this out without losing our cool or anyone having to put on pants.

Aidan: I'm staying with Catherine at her place.

She isn't thrilled about it, either, but I can't leave her alone. We were followed when we left my gym today, I'd bet money on it. My skin crawled all the way back to the shop.

I tried to get Cat to stay with me at my place, but she wouldn't. She thinks an overnight might piss Nico off to the point of doing something dangerous. But I say bring it on. The sooner he does something crazy enough to get arrested, the sooner he's confined to a cell where he can't get his hands on his ex-girlfriend.

Bash: *He* might not be able to get to her, but mobsters have people to do this kind of shit for them.

He'll probably send one of them to stab you in your

sleep and then you'll be dead because you are not a cop, or an ex-Navy SEAL, or even in possession of CPR certification—a lapse in excellence and preparedness I want you to remedy as soon as you have a free weekend to take the course down at the Y.

I can't believe I sent you out without being certified.

Penny has threatened to sue me herself just to teach me a lesson about not being responsible for perfectly preventable deaths.

Aidan: I'm glad Penny's back to whip your ass into shape.

Which brings me to another important point: if I'd had a picture of our client beforehand, the way I was supposed to, this never would have happened. I would have been able to see that she was someone I have a history with, and could have turned the job down before we got started.

But now it's too late so we'll just have to get through this the best we can.

Bash: What?! What kind of history? Who is this woman?

Aidan: It doesn't matter. What matters is that this is your fault, Bash, which means the ball is in my court.

If you make the mess, you don't get to tell me how

to clean it up.

Bash: Now hold on a fucking second

Aidan: Don't bother texting again. I'm turning off my phone. I'll touch base when Catherine and I have a game plan in place.

Red puts up a good fight, stalling by riding the 1 train all the way into the Bronx and back again, and then trying to ditch me in Times Square as we move between trains. But I remain stubbornly glued to her side, ignoring her protests that me spending the night at her place is the dumbest idea ever conceived by man.

Finally, around seven o'clock, she gives up, disembarks at the 14th Street Station, and leads me out into the muted evening light aboveground.

We emerge at the edges of a quiet Chelsea neighborhood and turn left along a tree-lined street, moving away from the hum of traffic on the Avenue and the hot dog and gyro vendors selling a quick evening meal to people headed home from work.

"You want a hot dog?" I jab a thumb over my shoulder. "I can run back and get a few. I'm not expecting you to feed me."

"I'd rather fish something out of the garbage," she says, her voice rough after hours of raising it to be heard over the roar of the trains underground.

"Delivery it is." I smile, pulling in a deep breath of the cooling air. "I see you lied about the Lower Manhattan Dashers being too far for you to travel. I'm starting to think I can't trust a word out of your mouth."

"Again, I was lying to protect you," she says wearily. "I didn't want you to feel obligated to invite me into your club and then have it be weird. I was trying to keep your safe place safe, jackass."

"Well, that was a nice reason for a lie, at least," I say, enjoying the way the late evening light warms the stones of the red brick homes lining the street. "Nice neighborhood. You lived here long?"

"Three years." She sighs heavily, clearly determined not to make small talk easy for me.

"I've been in my place five. It's crazy that we haven't run into each other before. I jog through here all the time after I finish running the High Line."

"Speaking of crazy…" She stops beside a planter overflowing with petunias on a stoop filled with so many flowerpots there's barely room to climb the steps. "One last time, I have to repeat that I think this is a bad idea. Can we please, please, please meet up tomorrow morning instead? We can spend the night brainstorming and start fresh with coffee and bagels. My treat."

I stuff my hands in my pockets and tilt my head back, admiring the antique molding around the windows, answering her pleas the way I have the past sixteen times she's asked me to go home—by changing the subject. "What floor are you?"

My gaze tracks back and forth from the sixth floor to the first. "I'm going to guess first or…third."

"Why's that?" Her shoulders slump in defeat as she fishes her keys out of her purse.

"You seem like the white, gauzy curtains type." I follow her up the steps. "Though I guess I could see you with blue flowers, or that who-cares-what-my-windows-look-like shade of beige. But not the superheroes, unless there's something else you're not telling me."

"The superheroes belong to Milo, who is seven and adorable. And you, my friend, are wrong, wrong, and wrong." A smirk curves her lips as she fits her key into the lock. "I'm the second floor."

My brows lift. "No curtains."

"No curtains." She cocks her head, looking up at me through half-closed lids. "I like to walk around naked after my shower and give the firefighters who live across the street a free show. I feel it's the least I can do to show my appreciation for Ladder Twelve."

I swallow, trying not to imagine Cat naked and fresh from the shower, and failing miserably. Spending the past few hours riding the subway and waging a battle of wills with the most stubborn woman in the universe, I'd managed to push the attraction I feel for her to the back of my mind. Now, it comes rushing back again, hitting me hard enough to make my blood rush and my head feel light for reasons that have nothing to do with missing my afternoon snack.

"Not smart," I say, gruffly, covering the flash of awareness with irritation. "Considering you're being stalked by a creep with a camera, curtains would probably be a good idea."

"Relax, I'm kidding." She rolls her eyes as she opens the

door. “I have blinds. I put them down at night or when I’m home and want privacy, but I leave everything open during the day. Fang likes to jump up on the couch and keep an eye on what’s happening on the street.”

“Fang?” I follow her through a tidy entryway where a folded stroller leans against one wall, making me think Milo isn’t the only kid in the building.

“My guard dog,” she says as we climb the narrow stairwell. “He’s pretty vicious. In fact, you’d better let me go in first and get him calmed down before you make an entrance.”

“And give you the chance to lock me out?” I shift around her to lean against her door. “No, thanks. I’ll take my chances with Fang.”

Her mouth puckers. “You think you’re pretty smart, don’t you?”

“Nah,” I say, with a shrug. “Just smart enough, I guess.”

“Well, if your smart ass gets bitten, don’t come crying to me. I’ve been training Fang to attack on command.” Her eyes narrow dangerously. “Sometimes he waits for the command; sometimes he doesn’t.”

I nod. “Got it. No crying to you. But I’m good with dogs. I’m sure Fang and I will get along just fine.”

She mumbles something unintelligible beneath her breath, and then, with one final sigh of resignation, she unlocks the door and swings it wide. “Fang! I’m home!” she shouts as she reaches over to push a code into the security system panel on the wall.

Her words are answered by high-pitched yapping and the light scrabble of claws on hardwood. A second later, a honey brown Chihuahua skids around the corner into the entry hall with a big smile on its face, its pencil-thin legs churning as it struggles to change directions on the slick floor.

A moment later, the terrifying guard dog collides with his mistress's feet and begins full-body wagging hard enough to lift his paws off the floor.

The dog probably weighs about eight pounds soaking wet and, aside from a quick sniff of my shoes and a lick at the hem of my jeans, seems to have zero interest in protecting his mama from the stranger who just breezed into his house.

"Fang, I presume," I say dryly, closing the door behind me.

"Fearsome Fang, actually." Cat drops to her knees to scoop the blissed-out pup into her arms. "Fifi for short."

"He's terrifying."

"He's a she," she says. "There's a way to tell boys from girls, Aidan. We can talk about it later, after the puppy's gone to bed, if you want. I'm waiting to talk to her about the birds and the bees until after she's been fixed."

"Thanks, I appreciate that. Do you need to walk Killer?" I meet her smartass with more bone dry, motioning toward the leash and tiny red leather harness hanging on the coatrack inside the door. "And, FYI, if I'd known you had an animal waiting at home that needed to go out, I would have insisted you get over your stubborn streak sooner."

"Fang is fine." She glares at me as she scratches Fifi's scruff until the dog's tongue lolls out in pleasure. "I have friends who walk her at noon and five during the week while I'm at work. I would *never* let my dog suffer because some big idiot is insisting he knows how to handle my life better than I do."

My jaw clenches, her words getting under my skin in a way they haven't all day. But then even the patron saint of patience probably had a breaking point.

"You came to me for help," I say, voice so low it vibrates through my ribs. "I assume that meant you had some faith in my judgment."

"How can you judge anything when you won't even listen to what I'm saying?" she asks, brows drawing together. "You used to listen."

"I did listen." I step closer, summoning a soft growl from Fang that's about as scary as a box full of cupcakes. "And I evaluated your apprehensions against my own concern for your welfare, and I made a judgment call."

Her lips part, but I cut her off before she can start arguing with me again.

"And that's the way it's going to be for the rest of our working relationship. I will listen to and respect your opinion, but in the end I'm going to choose the course of action that's most likely to result in you remaining in one piece. That's the job you hired me to do, and I'm going to do it."

Her eyes flash, anger and something more intimate flickering in their green depths. "You just can't stand to let anyone else take the lead, can you?"

I fight the urge to roll my eyes. "Give me a break, Red."

"I would love to," she snaps. "Go home. Take a break. Come back tomorrow. I'll be in a better mood after not riding the subway for four hours."

"That's on you, Catherine." I force a smile even though my jaw is so tight it feels like it's about to snap in two. "If you hadn't kept beating a dead horse, we could have been couching it with a beer hours ago and maybe making some real progress on solving your mobster problem."

She makes a choked sound. "Was that a Godfather joke? Are you *joking* about this?"

"No, I'm not joking," I snap. "I'm here to keep you alive, sweetheart, not to entertain you."

Fang growls again, but this time I have a feeling it has more to do with Cat's fingers digging into the dog's tiny chest than me being too close for comfort.

I shoot her hand a pointed glance before lifting a brow. "You okay?"

"I'm fucking fantastic." She leans down to set Fifi on the floor before stepping in close enough that the sharp toes of her sandals jab into the front of my shoes. "But don't you dare call me sweetheart. *Ever.* I know all about your history with that word, and I want no part of it."

"Are you sure?" I can't resist the urge to rattle her cage, even though I know it's not smart. I should be pacifying her and behaving professionally and getting us back on track to solving the Nico problem.

But damn it, she gets under my skin the way she always did. Like no other woman ever has. And she started us down this unprofessional road when she lied on her application and then gave me hours of shit for the sin of doing my damnedest to protect her. Now it's my turn to be a pain in her ass.

I lift an arm, bracing my hand on the wall behind her, bringing my face closer to hers. "I'm not sure I believe you, Cat. You seemed pretty into it this morning, when I had you up against that limo and you couldn't keep your hands off of me."

"That was an act," she says through gritted teeth. "Sadly, for you, that ship sailed eleven years ago."

"Did it?" I lean even closer, continuing in a soft, husky voice. "So if I'd run my hand up your thigh this morning your panties wouldn't have been wet? Not even a little bit?"

Her eyes narrow, but she doesn't respond. At least not verbally. But her breath comes faster, and her pupils dilate, giving me enough encouragement to continue in a whisper, "You weren't wet, Red? For me? Because even though you should have been worried about the man following you, all you could think about was my hands on you and my mouth on you and how much you wanted more of all of the above?"

Her skin flushes a pink so deep it's almost fuchsia, a color I've only ever seen on a redhead and only when he or she was deeply mortified.

But I know this particular redhead well enough to know this blush isn't her embarrassed blush. It's her "I'm about to take you down" blush. And damn it, a part of me hopes she goes for my throat. Right now, there are few things I would enjoy more than wrestling Red until we're both hot and bothered.

Until I have her hands trapped over her head and her body pinned beneath mine and her legs wrapped around my waist squeezing so tight I can feel her pussy throbbing between her thighs. Feel her pulsing against my cock, letting me know she's as turned on as I am.

And she *will* be turned on. She's already turned on.

She can glare and huff and spit insults at me all she wants, but her nipples are tight beneath that sexy little dress, and her lips are parted, and every warm puff of her breath against my mouth is a challenge I'm dying to accept. I'm about to kiss her—willing to risk a fist in my face for another taste of her sweet mouth—when she holds up a hand between us and says, "I invoke Religious Advice," and I have no choice but to stand down.

Once a Dasher, always a Dasher, and when a fellow member calls for Religious Advice, aka, a Top Secret, No Bullshit, Honest to a Fault meeting of the minds (usually involving at least a case of beer), there's only one thing to do: get a drink in your hand and prepare to hear something your friend has never told someone else. Something so secret and scary she's had to invoke sacred space to get it off of her chest.

As I stare down into Cat's wide, troubled eyes I have a feeling I'm not going to like what she has to say.

But what else is new?

From the text archives of Curved for her Pleasure and Polka Dot Panties

To Curve from Panties: Okay, spill. I have to know how you did it.

From Curve: Did what? Finally managed to create a trail you couldn't finish in less than ninety minutes?
Skill, Panties.
Skill and technique and a commitment to excellence.
And I checked out a book on tracking animals in the wild and tried to be smarter than a wild animal. It was tough, but I managed.

Panties: No, not that, though that was a nice surprise. I like it when you challenge me.
Excellence comes so easily that sometimes I get bored, you know?

Curve: *nose emoji* *beer emoji* *geyser emoji*

Panties: You just snorted beer out of your nose? Good. I hope the Holy Gail was there to see it and now understands that you are a mere mortal and borderline gross like the rest of the boys on campus.

Curve: Gail has a lifeguard certification test tomorrow. She's home studying and resting up, but she has texted me several times.
I'm not one to sext and tell, Red, but I think how "gross" I am is the last thing on her mind…

Panties: So I've heard. So how did you do it?
Every guy at this school has tried to hook up with Gail Goodnight, but for three years she's turned every one of them down. The Holy Gail, like her namesake the Holy Grail, is unattainable and mysterious and probably the secret to eternal life and happiness. But we all assumed no one would ever know for sure because of the unattainable part.
Now you've gone and proved everyone wrong.
How? I have to know.
What's your secret trick?

Curve: There has to be a trick? The fact that I'm a nice guy with a decent sense of humor who's easy on the eyes isn't enough?

Panties: Sorry, but no, it isn't. Better men than you, Curve, have stormed the Goodnight Castle only to be dismembered by its portcullis.

Curve: *drooling emoji* Me no talk big words so good.

Panties: Lol. You do, too.
You're just not up on your medieval battle armaments.
A portcullis was a rapid response defense mechanism in medieval castles— incredibly heavy doors with iron spikes on the bottom. So when they dropped on invading enemies they tended to gore people to death.
Limbs were lost. Tears were shed. Dreams were dashed.
Much like the situation with the beautiful, boobilicious Gail and the horny and heartbroken boys of Penn U.

Curve: You're not right, Panties.
There is something seriously messed up in that squirrely brain of yours.

Panties: Fine. If you don't want to tell me, just say

so.

But as someone who has a thing for an Unattainable, I could use some practical advice, and you're probably the only person who can tell me what I'm doing wrong.

Curve: Aw! Panties has a crush! That's so cute.

Panties: Shut up! I am not cute.

Curve: Precious little Panties is in lurrrvve! So who is he?

A fellow super-secret soldier spy?

A former Navy SEAL studying nuclear physics on the GI Bill?

The scary guy with the shaved head who runs the ROTC?

Panties: Ew. No. He walks like he has a pole up his ass.

Unattainable doesn't go to school here. We met our senior year of boarding school, before he was accepted to West Point. I've been angling for some one-on-one time ever since, but he never bites. And aside from him, I've never had trouble landing at least a first date with someone I'm interested in.

I know I'm not the hottest thing going, but I make up for that with entertainment value, and it usually takes people at least one date to realize they have no interest in my particular kind of crazy.

Curve: You are highly entertaining.
So what's wrong with this guy? Why is he too stupid to be into you?
And since he's obviously stupid, are you sure you want to bother with his dumb ass?

Panties: I do. There's just something about him…
But I've tried all my usual methods—insulting him, ignoring him, sitting on his lap when he least expects it, teasing him until he laughs so hard he pukes—but nothing is working.
He's an uncrackable nut, the Archie of the Covenant to your Holy Gail.

Curve: But his name's not Archie?

Panties: God, no. That would be a deal breaker right there.

Curve: Okay, so…
Though I agree that insulting people and ignoring them are usually excellent ways to show them you're interested in a meaningful connection, I'm going to suggest a slightly different tack.

Panties: *drooling emoji* Thanks. Me no flirt so good.

Curve: No, you do. But you only flirt one way. You have the Red method down pat, but people have different needs, different proclivities, different buttons that they need to have pushed to start thinking of a friend as something more.

Panties: Proclivities. Nice.
Are you showing off because you didn't know what a portcullis is?

Curve: Do you want an answer or not? Because I do have a game to watch and more beer to drink, and I was thinking seriously about whipping up some vegetarian nachos.

Panties: Sorry, sorry. I want an answer, but I'm confused…
So you're saying I need to change my entire flirting style to please this guy? Isn't that counter-intuitive? I mean, I want him to like ME, not someone I'm pretending to be.

Curve: You're not going to pretend to be someone else.
You're going to be Red, just Red focused on meeting the needs of her partner, instead of impressing him with her knowledge of medieval battle armaments or fucking with his head by running hot and cold with the insults and lap sitting.

Panties: Ouch.
Okay, first up I was kidding about my flirting style.

And secondly, I am all about meeting people's needs. Hell, I usually know what the person I'm with wants before they do—a side effect of being raised by a father who chewed my ass for fucking up first and explained how to avoid fucking up never.

I know how not to fuck things up, Curve.

And as far as I can tell, I'm giving Mr. Unattainable exactly what he needs.

Curve: Which is?

Panties: Someone who refuses to take his shit or pander to him because he's beautiful. Someone who praises him when he's the most wonderful version of himself—which is pretty wonderful—and refuses to let him off the hook when he's phoning it in.

Someone who makes him laugh, which he needs. I can tell he has some sad stuff in his past, even though he never talks about it.

And I know he likes me. A lot.

But only as a friend…

So maybe it's just…me? Maybe I have no sex vibe? OMG, I can't believe I just texted that. Delete it and forget it. Or if you can't delete and forget, at least please refrain from teasing me. I can't handle that on top of the Mr. Unattainable brush off.

This is why we should have stuck with notes in the hole! I would never have written something like that and put it in the hole.

Why didn't I respect the hole?!

Curve: Lol. Relax, psycho. I'm not going to tease you.
You definitely have a sex vibe. You're a little feral sometimes, but totally pounceable, and I hear some guys like the wild-girl-who-needs-to-be-tamed thing.

Panties: Thank you. And I think he would like it. If he gave it a try.

Curve: Great. Then assuming your guy is open to what you've got to offer, you just need to figure out what's holding him back, the way I did with Gail.
So I'm going to share my magic trick, but you have to swear never to tell anyone. Dasher oath of honor, spit in your beer and hope to die.

Panties: *spitting emoji* *beer emoji* *skull and crossbones emoji* Done.

Curve: Okay, so…I call her sweetheart.

Panties: Excuse me?

Curve: I call her sweetheart. And 'sweets' sometimes, when the moment is right. She likes the mushy stuff, so I supply the mushy stuff. I think she likes that I'm willing to let the way I feel

about her show.
You know?
Hello?
Panties…
Are you still there?
If you tell me you're leaning over the toilet because my sweetness made you barf, I will never share anything private with you ever again. Ever. So choose your next words carefully, kid…

Panties: I'm still here. Sorry. My roommate came in with her Bang-O-The-Month, and I had to move down to the study lounge.
So you call her pet names? That's it?
You whipped out a sweetheart or two, and she fell into your manly arms?

Curve: No. I don't just whip them out. I *mean* them.
She is a sweetheart, and I care about her, and I'm happy to do what it takes to make her feel special.

Panties: That's…really sweet.
So I guess you're a sweetheart, too.
The sweetest sweetheart ever, sweetie sweets.

Curve: Stop.

Panties: But I'm serious, sweets. You take the cake. You're so sweet the cake knows it's going to taste sour by comparison so it just gives up and lets you

take it.
Done. Mic drop. Cake out.

Curve: That's it. You just got taken off the No Bullshit list.
Now you only get surface conversation and insults. And I'm going to put forward a motion to have your Dasher name changed to Farts with Wolves.

Panties: NO! I'm sorry. I really am. I just couldn't help myself. You know I couldn't. It was too perfect a set up.
But I'm truly grateful for the advice and happy for you and Gail. You two are going to have amazingly gorgeous babies and make the world a better place. Or at least a prettier one.
Please forgive me?

Curve: *beady eye emoji*

Panties: Please. I swear I'm sorry, and I promise I'll take the sweetheart stuff to the grave.

Curve: You'd better. Or I will find a way to make you pay, feral squirrel.

Panties: Got it. My lips are sealed.
But for what it's worth, if you were my man, I'd rather be called feral squirrel than sweetheart. It shows some originality, you know?

And it doesn't make me want to barf. So, that's a plus.

Curve: I'll keep that in mind for the day I realize I've been secretly carrying a torch for your polka-dot-pantied ass.

Panties: You do that, Curve. You do that.
And maybe, if you're lucky, I'll have come around to a similar realization.

Curve: One can only hope…

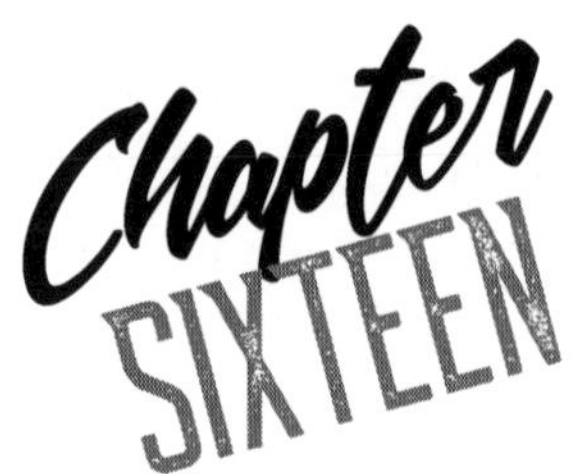

Cat and I face each other down across the island in her kitchen, which is large by city standards, as is the rest of her apartment, making me think she must do pretty well for herself, whatever kind of lawyer she is.

I'm not surprised, of course. It was clear from the moment I met her that Red could do anything she set her mind to.

Which is probably why this Nico thing is so hard for her. She's the kind of person who is used to calling the shots and solving her own problems. For her to have hired someone to help her out of a mess, any mess, is completely out of character. She's in unfamiliar territory, something I should have remembered before I lost my temper and control of my mouth.

"You ready?" I ask, doing my best to forget that I was talking dirty to her less than ten minutes ago.

But my cock doesn't want to forget. It doesn't give a shit

how unprofessional it is to be coming on to my client. It just wants to get Cat naked and make up for turning her down all those years ago.

"Ready as I'll ever be." Her tongue slips out to wet her bottom lip, and I pretend I'm not thinking about biting it.

There are six shots of tequila and two beers in frosted glasses lined up between us and judging by the intense expression on Cat's face she's ready to open the confessional.

"You remember how this works, right?" She brings her hand to her mouth and licks the back of it, holding my gaze as she reaches for the saltshaker. "After each confession, we drink. And everything we say from the time we open Religious Advice until the final words of the ceremony is top secret, never to be repeated to another living soul."

I nod. "I open this confessional in the name of the fox, the hound, and the brew that never lets them down. Let the truth be spilled, but never the beer. Hoo ha, hoo ha ha."

"Hoo ha, hoo ha ha," she echoes, reaching for her beer.

I reach for mine and we tilt our frosted mugs back. I take several deep pulls, until the cold starts to make my head ache, before dropping my half-empty glass back to the marble counter. Neither of us has eaten anything since the bag of pretzels we snagged on the way between trains earlier, and drinking on an empty stomach is never a wise idea. But a buzz sounds good right now. I need something to take the edge off, to make me forget that I'm breaking all the rules and risking my life for a woman who drives me crazy.

Apparently Cat feels the same way. By the time she emerges from her beer with a deep breath, only a couple inches of amber liquid remain at the bottom of her glass. "Remember that last night, before you left for Japan?"

"I remember," I say, grateful for the buzz I can feel creeping in to dull the sharp edges of her words. If we're going to talk about that night in the woods, I'm going to need all three shots of tequila and then some.

She swipes a hand across her upper lip before bracing both palms on the counter. "After you left to go put out the bonfire, I went for a walk around the lake with the joint you left behind. I smoked the entire thing. All by myself."

"Probably not the best idea. It was your first time, right?"

She nods. "Yes, and it was a completely shitty idea. I ended up wandering around the student union, high as a kite, shouting quotes from *The Art of War* at the owl statues on top of the building. I was caught by a city cop doing his campus rounds and spent the night in the drunk tank, crying my eyes out because it felt like my intestines were trying to crawl out of my throat."

I wince. "That wasn't good pot. I'm sorry your first experience sucked so hard."

"It really did suck hard. It sucked so hard I thought I was going to die. And if I'd known your real name, I would have given you up to the po po in a heartbeat. Because by two in the morning I was so high I was seeing gremlins on the ceiling and convinced you were trying to kill me." She reaches for the first shot of tequila. "Forgive me, friend, for I have sinned."

Following her lead—and the rules of our bastardized religious ceremony—I reach for my own shot. "I absolve you in the name of the fox and the hound and the brew that never lets them down."

We lick the salt from our hands, pound our shot, and reach for the tray of lime slices at the same time, our fingers brushing. Cat flinches away, watching as I pop my lime between my lips before reaching for hers.

"Anything to say?" she asks, sucking the wedge.

"Nope. Just that I'm sorry, and I'm sure that wasn't a great way to end your sophomore year."

"No, it wasn't." She shakes her head loosely, her body language already more relaxed than I've seen it all day. I don't know if the confession or the alcohol is responsible, but it's good to see her shoulders drop away from her ears. "And it only got worse from there. My dad found out—because of course he did; he always knew exactly what I was up to, especially when I was doing something I wasn't supposed to be doing it—and he acted like I'd murdered a flock of baby sheep for fun."

I snort, but Cat doesn't crack a smile.

"I had enough money saved to pay for my own rehabilitation class to get back in good graces with the school," she continues, "but Dad knew arrest for pot possession could keep me from getting into the FBI training academy. That had always been his dream, not mine, but he mourned the death of my career as a federal agent hard enough for the both of us."

"Sorry again. Truly. I feel you." I consider telling her that I know all about killing your father's dreams, but this isn't my confession.

"He never forgave me," she continues. "Not even on his deathbed. His last words to me were a depressing plea for me not to fuck my life up anymore than I had already."

I curse, and she finally smiles, though it's more rueful than amused.

"Not to fuck up any more than I had already," she repeats softly. "Even though I hadn't taken a single step from the straight and narrow for eleven years. Not one single step. I never even lied about my weight on my driver's license." She laughs. "But one mistake was all it took to make me a fuck-up for life. At least as far as Dad was concerned."

I reach for the second shot, but she holds out a hand. "Sorry, that wasn't my second confession. That was just additional information, stuff I left out of the story this afternoon when I told you things didn't end well with Dad."

I nod. "You left out the fact that it was my fault your relationship with your father was destroyed forever."

She shakes her head, sending her silky hair sliding around her shoulders. I have the sudden, powerful urge to drive my hand into all the red and let it slip through my fingers. I know it will feel like silk, but more alive, an entity with a will of its own that wants to touch and be touched.

Touch would be a lot less painful than hearing how one stupid night when we were practically kids wrecked her life for over a decade.

"No, it wasn't your fault," she says. "It was Dad's fault, but all the shit with him complicated the way I felt about you for a while."

"You were angry," I supply.

She skims her fingertips through the salt spilled on the counter. "I was. That's why I didn't email, even though we said we were going to keep in touch." She tips her head toward her shoulder with a lopsided grin. "Well, that and the fact that you never emailed. Or messaged. Or anything else. That was kind of a clue, you know, and I'm good with clues."

"At first I didn't have internet access. And by the time I did..." I shrug, not wanting to say more, but feeling like I owe her the truth, especially while we're under Religious Advice. "I thought a clean break would be for the best. For both of us. By that point, I'd had some time to think about things and felt like maybe I'd sent you some…conflicting signals over the years."

A huff of laughter escapes her lips. "You think? With all the flirty notes and texts and staring at my ass like it was your job every time we ran?"

I fight a smile. "Yeah, well, your ass was—and is—a hard thing to look away from. I'm only mortal."

She rolls her eyes. "Yeah, well, you definitely sent conflicting signals, and a clean break probably *was* for the best." Her smile fades as she reaches out to spin her next shot in a slow circle on the counter. "But it was also weird. And sad. You were such a big part of my life, and then suddenly you were gone. Like you'd never really been there to begin with."

"I was there," I say, feeling like shit. "But I was also twenty-two and full of myself and dying to get out in the world and do things."

She spins the glass faster. "And I was just another girl."

"No. You weren't." I want to reach out and take her hand, to still her fingers and thread them through mine, but I haven't earned the right to touch her like that. Not in private, when it would mean something more than a show put on to make another man jealous.

"You were just…complicated, and I wanted simple. I needed it," I continue in a firmer voice, as her lips twist in a knowing smirk. "Things weren't great with me and my dad at that point, either. He was really fucking disappointed in me, and every time I called to check in, he let me know it. So I stopped calling him or anyone else. I tossed my cell and travelled around Asia studying with artists I respected, and by the time I came back home, college seemed like another world. One I remembered with a smile, but…"

I chew my bottom lip, hunting for the right words. "By that time I'd learned to give fewer fucks about everything, and that meant not wallowing in regret over shit I couldn't change."

"So you regretted how things ended?" Her fingers pause in their relentless spinning.

"I did." I lay my hands on the counter near hers, almost close enough to touch. "I should have called. Or texted. Or at least written an email to let you know that my decision that night truly had nothing to do with you. It was all me."

She laughs, a breezy giggle that surprises me after the heavy tone of the conversation so far. "Well, shit. That sucks, Aidan. I'm glad you didn't call, then."

"Thanks," I say, scratching my beard.

"Seriously, that's the worst. The one time a guy said that to me, I almost punched him in the face. I settled for dumping a glass of wine in his lap and telling him my decision to do so had *everything* to do with him."

I shrug. "Then I guess it all worked out for the best."

"I guess it did." She lifts her chin, meeting my cool gaze with an even cooler one. "But I'm going to make my second confession anyway. There was never any Mr. Unattainable. Well, there was, but he wasn't a friend from boarding school. He was you. You were my Archie of the Covenant." She presses her lips together, turning her laughter into a wry hum. "I had it so bad for you, dude. So, so bad. It was fucking ridiculous."

"Why was it—"

"Forgive me, friend, for I have sinned." She plucks her shot from the counter, holding it between us.

"There's nothing to forgive," I say, my gut twisting. I feel bad for my part in leading her on when we were younger, but that's not why I feel like I swallowed a pound of buckshot. There's something more, something that lingers in the air between us as she brings the glass to her lips, something that reminds me of good food going to waste and kids being diagnosed with cancer.

"Say your part," she says in a husky voice. "And drink."

I take my glass, meeting her gaze over the rim. "I absolve you in the name of the fox and the hound and the brew that never lets them down." We drink, neither of us looking away, even when we set the glasses down hard on the counter.

This time, we don't reach for a lime.

"Seriously, Red, I'm not as dumb as I look. After the stuff in the woods, I figured out that you'd had a thing for me. Though, yes, I should have caught on a lot sooner."

"You should have." Her smile is hard, heavy. "You were a dumb boy, but I was dumb, too. I should have given up and dated someone who was interested instead of carrying a torch for you for two years."

She rolls her neck, a sensuous movement that's so sexy all I can think about is how much I want my lips on her throat, feeling the pulse of her blood beneath her pale skin. But between the fucked-up past and the fucked-up present, this island between us might as well be an ocean.

"But I'm still glad I confessed." She brushes her hair over her shoulder with a graceful flick of her wrist. "That's information I wanted to be sure you had in your possession before you started talking to me about my panties again."

Fuck.

Fuck me. Fuck me somewhere it hurts without lube.

"I'm sorry," I say, though I know it's not enough. "I'm an asshole. I didn't even think about—"

"No you're not an asshole. You were right." She blinks, her

green eyes clear and focused. "My panties were wet," she says in a voice that goes straight to my dick, sending my flagging erection surging back to life. "One kiss and I was ready to go at it against my ex-boyfriend's limo."

"Cat…" Her name is a warning, though I don't know if the warning is meant for her or me or both of us.

Or what I'm going to do if she ignores it.

"I wanted you to fuck me as much as I ever did," she continues, bracing her palms on the counter. She leans forward, granting me a view down the front of her dress and a glimpse of creamy lace against creamier skin, sending my blood pressure skyrocketing. "Maybe more. You were always good with your hands and your mouth, but you're even better now. You make me feel like I'm on fire. All over. In the best way."

I clench my jaw and fight the urge to sweep my hand across the counter and send the glasses shattering to the floor as I drag Cat across the marble and take her right here on the kitchen island.

"So yes, Aidan, I was wet this morning." The gleam in her eyes is diabolical, making me suspect she might be deliberately trying to give me a heart attack. "And I was wet when you were talking dirty to me a few minutes ago. And I could be wet again in a hot second if you said you wanted to take your next shot off my tits and fuck me on the floor."

I fist my hands so tight my knuckles ache. Sweat breaks out between my shoulder blades and a vein in my neck starts to throb. I am so fucking close to losing control, but I force my hands to remain on the counter.

She's not done torturing me yet—I can tell by the lilt in her voice. And, glutton for punishment that I am, I have to hear what she's going to say next.

"But I know that's a conflict of interest for you." Her gaze scans my face, honing in on my mouth, making me think she wants to be kissed as much as I want to be kissing her. "Though, you haven't seemed too stressed about keeping things professional thus far. So maybe all that 'no more than a kiss' stuff is just a front to keep on the right side of the law. Maybe you always fuck your clients."

"Never. Not a single time," I say in a voice too thick with lust to be convincing, even though I'm telling the truth.

I want to open a second location of my shop badly enough to play Knight With Scary Tattoos to deserving women in need, but not enough to fuck people for money. I'm as shameless as the next confirmed bachelor when it comes to getting laid, but I fuck who I want, when I want. Because sex should be about what two people want to do to each other, not what one of them has bought and paid for.

I'm about to tell Cat so, but she waves her hand through the air. "Seriously. It's not a big deal. Even if you have sex with women for money, I don't care." She reaches for another shot. "Which brings me to my third confession. Are you ready?"

"Shoot," I say tightly, deciding that convincing her I'm not a manwhore will have to wait until I don't have a hard-on.

She takes a deeper breath, but when she speaks, her words are a whisper. "I still want you. I want you more than I've ever wanted anyone, even Nico. And I want to do something about it."

"Something like…what?" I ask, though I have a pretty good idea.

"I think we should go for it," she says with a smile that's equal parts wicked and nervous. "Let's do it. Let's make fucking each other stupid part of our arrangement."

Before I can assure her that I absolutely will *not* fuck her stupid for money—I will fuck her stupid for *free* because I am not a whore, and I'm pissed that she has so easily assumed my dick is for sale—she pushes on.

"I have to know if you really will be the best I've ever had." She wags her shot back and forth, sending the liquid sliding from side to side. "Or if it's like Gail said, and you're all foreplay, head games, and nice-smelling cologne but nothing special between the sheets."

My eyebrows shoot up. "What? When did she say that?"

"My junior year," she says, her grin growing even more wicked. "After you left for Japan. I think she was just trying to make me feel better, but who knows? She could have been shooting straight. It was always hard to tell with her. The Holy Gail kept her cards close to her chest. You know she eventually became a nun, right?"

I blink. "No, I didn't."

"She did. So the Holy Gail bit really did fit." Her forehead knits. "Though I think her name is Sister Maria Faustus or Maria Faustina or something like that now. Something that reminded me of Dante's *Inferno* when I heard the news."

"Well, good for her. I hope she's happy," I say, not really surprised to hear that Gail's life went in that direction. Of all the girls I dated in college, she was the sweetest and the prettiest, but also the most devout and the least interested in learning if my reputation for delivering multiple O's in the bedroom was fact or fiction.

And a girl who has no interest in multiple O's clearly has a higher calling.

One I can't understand on a personal level, but…

"Don't worry," Cat says, a knowing look on her face, as if she can read every thought racing through my mind. "I'm sure it wasn't your lack of skill between the sheets that turned her to a life of celibacy."

I bend lower, dropping my elbow to the counter and propping my chin on my fist with a wry grin. "Thanks. I'm sure it wasn't, too. Especially considering we never slept together…"

Her eyes widen slightly. "Really?"

"Really. It never felt right. For either of us."

She hums thoughtfully. "So she *was* just trying to make me feel better." She shrugs, setting the tequila in her glass to sloshing again. "Well, that was nice of her. By that point everyone knew I'd begged you to punch my V card, and the Dashers made it their mission in life to fuck with me about it, so I was pretty demoralized. It was nice to get a kind word from someone who'd allegedly been there, done that, and wasn't that impressed by it all."

"How did everyone find out?" I ask, troubled by that part of the story. "I didn't tell anyone."

She shrugs again. "I think Empty Tool Box overheard something when he came to get your help with the bonfire. But he would never cop to it, not even when I let him do the honors and punch my V card himself."

"Tool Box?" I ask, lip curling. "God, Cat, why? Why do that to yourself? He's dumber than a box full of rocks."

"I told you, I was demoralized, damn it! And you don't get to judge me right now." She points a finger at my chest, making a snarling sound that causes Fifi—who has been resting in her dog bed on the couch in the other room, minding her own business—to lift her head and let out a curious "you okay in there?" bark.

"I'm fine," Cat calls back, making me smile in spite of the fact that she's still glaring at me as if she'd like to do the tender parts of my body serious damage. "What's so funny?"

"Nothing. Before you answered her, I was just thinking that Fang sounded like she was asking if you were okay."

Cat's frown softens. Just a little. "Yeah, well. She has very expressive barks. She has ever since she was a puppy."

"She really does." I glance pointedly at the tequila glass in her hand. "So is that all? Are you finished with your third confession?"

She looks up at the ceiling, seeming to search her thoughts as she taps her pointer finger and thumb together. "Um, I want you, I want to make getting naked together part of our arrangement… Yep," she continues in a breathy voice, nodding a little too long before she clears her throat. "I think that just about covers it."

"All right."

Her eyes flick back to mine. This time I don't try to hide the way her words affect me. I hold her gaze, hoping she really can read every thought flitting through my mind. Because they're all dirty, and they all involve me blowing her mind while I do wicked, wonderful things to her beautiful body.

"All right?" she says, her voice a half octave higher than it was before.

"Then say your part." I claim my shot glass.

"Oh, right." She swallows hard. "Bless me, friend, for I have sinned."

"I absolve you in the name of the fox and the hound and the brew that never lets them down, Religious Advice concluded," I say, adding on before she can take her shot, "On one condition."

She pauses with her glass an inch from her lips. "And what's that?"

"We lay down some ground rules, so we're clear on when I'm in charge and when I'm not."

She nods slightly. "Okay. So…when are you in charge?"

"Drink first. Then rules." I take my shot, the semi-oily tequila going down much easier now that I've got a buzz on, and place it carefully on the counter.

After a moment, she drinks, blowing air through pursed lips as she sets her glass next to mine. "Next time, make me get the good stuff out of my closet instead of the bargain basement brand I use for mixed drinks."

"Rule one." I circle around the island toward her, refusing to be sidetracked by talk of tequila or next times or anything else. "This is not part of our professional arrangement. You will not mention paying me for sex again. I'm not a gigolo, or a manwhore, or any other kind of whore, and I don't earn money with my dick."

Her lips part, but I don't give her a chance to speak.

"When I'm fucking you it will be because I want to fuck you." I continue stalking toward her. She begins slowly backing into the darkened living room, apparently not so sure of herself now that the time out provided by Religious Advice is over. "It will be because I need to get my cock inside you."

Her eyes widen as she nods. "Understood. And I'm sorry if I—"

"Rule two: We keep our working relationship and our fucking relationship separate. When we're working, we're working, and nothing I say or do can be taken out of context."

Her bottom collides with the back of the couch, and she lets out a shaky laugh.

"Understood?" I stop a foot away, giving her room to breathe, but not too much room. I'm enjoying the sight of Cat breathless.

She nods. "So if we're at a party and you tell me you can't wait to get me home and tie me to your bed because you know Nico's close enough to hear, that doesn't mean you're actually going to tie me to the bed."

"Exactly." I step closer until heat pulses in the air between us, and the potential energy of the moment makes my nerve endings hum. "Though, I might tie you up, if I think that's what you need."

"What I need," she murmurs, as if hearing something familiar but forgotten until this moment.

"Do you remember that time you asked me about my secret to success with Gail?" I ask. "The talk we had about giving people what they need?"

She nods again, watching me with this half-amused, half-mesmerized look that makes me want to get her underneath me right this fucking second. But this is important.

"I remember," she says.

"You said you were good at intuiting what people needed." I reach up, threading a hand into her silky hair and making a light fist. "I'm good at it, too. And when we're together, behind closed doors, I'm going to give you exactly what you need."

Her lips curve on one side. "And what is that, pray tell?"

"Right now, I think it's a good hard fucking." I tighten my fist in her hair, summoning a soft, hungry cry from her lips, which goes straight to my dick, making all nine and a half inches fight to dismantle my zipper with the force of lust alone. "A fucking that will get you out of your head and into your body." I dip my head until my lips brush the smooth column of her throat below her ear, inhaling the sexy as hell smell of her as I add, "And make you forget how important you think it is to stay in control."

"Speaking of control," she says, her pulse racing beneath my mouth. "You never said when you were in charge and when you're not."

"Because that's the easiest part, Red." I open my mouth, raking my teeth lightly over her cool, sweet skin. She shudders against me, making my erection swell to epic proportions. "I'm always in charge."

"Is that right?" she whispers.

"It is." I lick a trail from the base of her throat to her jaw, and her shudder becomes a sustained tremble. "When I'm working to keep you safe, I'm in charge. And when I'm working to make you come, I'm in charge. Because that's the way you like it, isn't it?" I let my free hand trail down to cup her ass, pulling her against me until there can be no doubt in her mind how badly I want her.

She moans, arching into me until her breasts are flush against my chest and her pubic bone rocks against where I'm so hard it's painful. "I don't know whether to say yes, or to tell you to go fuck yourself so you'll quit being such a smug bastard."

"You're going to say yes." I pull back to gaze into her flushed face. Damn, she's beautiful, with her eyes glittering and her full lips parted in a silent invitation to lay claim to her mouth. "Say yes, Cat. Say yes, and I will give you everything you want. Everything you need."

Her eyes flutter closed. "Damn you, Aidan."

"Say yes," I whisper, inches from her lips. "Say yes, and I'll kiss you the way you've always wanted to be kissed."

"Yeah? How have I always wanted to be kissed?"

"Like you belong to someone," I say without a beat of hesitation, digging my fingers deeper into the strong, muscled flesh of her ass. Her eyes open, her gaze crashing into mine as I promise, "I'm going to kiss you until your mouth knows who it belongs to, Red. And then I'm going to repeat the process until every inch of your body knows that tonight you're mine. Every kiss, every moan, every time you come on my fingers or my mouth or my cock, every minute of your pleasure belongs to me."

A pained expression flashes across her features. "It's going to be such a let-down if you're all talk. Because your talk is *really* fucking good."

"I still need to hear a yes." I hitch her leg around my waist and rock against her, making her moan as my erection rubs against her through the thin fabric of her panties. They're white. Lacy. And I can't wait to get them off of her, but we both need this first. She needs someone to take the load off of her shoulders, and I need permission to take it, to take *her*, to fuck her the way she needs to be fucked, with no holding back.

"Yes, Cat. Say yes," I murmur as I continue to fuck her through our clothes and her breath comes faster and I swear I can feel the molten heat of her through my jeans. "Say yes. Please, say yes."

I don't know if it's the please or the hunger in my voice or the erotic friction of cock against clit that finally persuades her, but her arms go around my neck and her fingernails dig into my skin like she's never going to let me go. "Yes. Yes, damn it. Make me yours. Show me, Aidan. Now. Please."

I intend to start slow, give us somewhere to go, but the moment my lips touch Cat's, the world catches fire all over again. Our second kiss is even hotter than our first, an erotic battle of lips, teeth, and tongue that makes my pulse thunder. Within seconds I'm drunk on her smell, her taste, rocked by the electricity that leaps between us like we were made to complete a circuit. Her fingers claw deeper into my shoulders, and I moan, a sound she echoes, vibrating my lips, a buzzing I feel over every inch of my skin.

And because I've never been one to make a lady wait, I start to guide her down to the soft carpet, so desperate to have her skin bared to my mouth that I can't imagine taking another step without disposing of her dress first. But before I can do more than bend my knees, a low growl sounds to my left.

I glance up, spying Fifi, still in her bed, watching Cat and I with an intensity that's unnerving.

When my eyes meet the dog's, she lets out an enthusiastic yap.

“No, you can’t watch.” I reverse direction, standing and scooping Cat into my arms with a scowl for her perverted pet. “Where’s the bedroom?”

“Through there,” Cat says, pointing to the back of the apartment. I head that way, but Fifi leaps down from the couch to follow. “Stay, Fang. Stay!” Cat adds laughter in her voice. “Go back to your bed. To your bed, right now!”

The dog barks, three times in rapid succession, a clear “come on, Mom, let me come,” plea that makes Cat laugh again.

A less confidant man would be cursing the dog and the ruined mood, but I had no doubt I’ll have Cat begging again in no time.

The only thing I’m worried about is how long I’ll be able to hold off before I have to have her. I want to make our first time last, to make this a night she’ll never forget, but I’m already so desperate, so wild, so fucking hard it feels like I’ll do myself damage if I don’t get inside of her soon.

She drives me crazy, this woman, but as I slam the bedroom door, set her on her feet, and strip her dress over her head, baring her to my gaze for the first time, I decide sanity is overrated.

I don’t need sanity.

I just need Red, in my arms, skin to skin.

Right fucking now.

My gaze glides from her softly parted lips to her breasts, encased in white lace, down to her matching panties and impossibly long, beautifully strong legs. For a long moment, I fight the urge to reach for her, doing my best to imprint this moment into my memory.

I want to remember her like this, with her pale skin curving in all the right places and light-brown freckles scattered across her chest like a constellation of stars.

She's perfect. More than perfect. She's completely fucking stunning.

Earthy and ethereal, familiar and exotic, and so sexy I can't believe that even an abundance of integrity and a hefty dose of early-twenties stupidity was enough to make me turn her down the first time I had her in my arms. I want to kiss her everywhere. I want to name every freckle while I tease her nipples through her bra, driving her out of her mind until she's trembling in my arms and so wet I can smell the sweet, salty scent of her filling the air.

But naming her freckles would make her laugh, and I don't want her laughter. I want her gasps and her sighs and her moans. I want her husky voice in my ear begging me to take her, screaming that I'm the best she's ever had.

But first I need to make sure we go into this more prepared than we were last time.

"I'm clean. I was tested last month." I strip my shirt slowly over my head and toss it to the floor, not missing the way her gaze drops to my chest then skims lower, down my stomach to the close of my jeans, making my cock weep a single tear of pain for the tragedy of still being separated from this woman. "What about you?"

"I haven't been tested recently." She looks hungry, starving, like she wants to nibble a trail from my neck to my navel, and I realize I would sell semi-vital organs for the pleasure of being her next meal. "But I've never had sex without a condom."

I bite my lip as I reach for the close of my jeans, slowly popping the button free and catching the tab of the zipper between my fingers. "Never?"

She shakes her head dreamily from side to side, her attention fixed on the close of my pants. "Never. Nico wanted to, but—"

"I don't want to hear about Nico." I drag my zipper down, letting the humming sound fill the silence between my words. "I want to hear whether you're on the pill. And, if so, if you want me to fuck you bare. Or if you'd rather I wrap up. Whatever you want, Red, I just want to know before this starts. If I remember correctly, last time I touched you I lost my damned mind and was ready to fuck first and ask important questions later."

"I have an IUD." Her breasts rise and fall as I shove my jeans to the ground, setting my cock free to strain against the front of my boxer briefs in a desperate play to get closer to Cat. "And no condom. You can be my first time bare. I…I still trust you."

"I'm glad. And I wish I'd been your first in every way. You deserved so much better than Tool Box." I pull her into my arms and back her toward the bed, a bolt of pure lust surging through me as I realize I'm seconds away from having her under me.

I lower my face to hers, kissing her cheek before I whisper, "I wish I'd taken you that night in the woods, and every night that summer. I wish I'd made love to you until making you come was the special skill on my resume. Until I could make you come so many times in a row you would beg me to stop so you could catch your breath."

"No, you don't," she says, breath hitching as her thighs hit the mattress. "And I would never have asked you to stop. Like my tolerance to beer, my tolerance for orgasms is unusually high."

"I didn't say you would have *asked* me to stop." I guide her back onto the bed, lengthening my body on top of hers, every place we touch catching fire. The chemistry between us is so hot it's almost painful, but I can't wait to see how much hotter things can get.

I cup her breast in my hand, letting my thumb whisper across her already tight nipple, balls pulsing as she moans softly in response. "I said you would *beg*." I lower my mouth to her breast, brushing my lips back and forth across her nipple through the lace. "Do I need to teach you how to beg, Red?"

"Yes, I think you do." She holds my gaze as I trap her nipple between my teeth, biting down with gentle pulses. Her eyes darken with a heart-stopping mix of hunger and vulnerability that makes me even more desperate to be inside her. "Teach me, Aidan. Make me beg you to fuck me." I bite her nipple, and she gasps, "Break me, just a little."

"I will, I promise," I swear, pulling my mouth away from her nipple and curling my fingers into the lacy fabric. "I'll break you, Red. I'll make you beg and cry and think you're going to die if you don't get to come. But then I'll put you right back together again, baby. I promise."

"Don't call me baby," she says, a gleam in her eye that assures me the battle has begun.

"I'll call you whatever I want, baby." With a sharp jerk of my hand I tug her bra beneath her breasts, baring her to my mouth, and set about showing her just how merciless I can be.

Bending low over her beautiful body, I flick my tongue across one nipple while I tease the other between my fingers, gradually increasing my pressure until her breath is coming faster and her hips are rocking against mine, seeking relief from the sweet torture. But relief isn't part of my game plan, not now or anywhere in the near future. And so I wait until her thrusts grow urgent, demanding, almost frantic. I clench my jaw and let her grind against my cock through what's left of our clothes until I feel like I might die from how much I want her.

I am suffering, aching, desperate. The slit at the top of my cock is leaking, and my balls are throbbing, and every cell in my body is crying out for me to fuck Cat now, fuck her hard, fuck her until she understands that no one will ever satisfy her the way I can, but I deny myself. I deny myself because this isn't just about breaking her; it's about breaking me, too.

It's about taking us both so far into the darkness that we're lost. Lost and crazed and so desperate for a break in the suffering that the pleasure we find at the end of the long, grueling road be all the fucking sweeter.

"So sweet," I murmur against her nipple as I slide my tongue around her slick, swollen tip. "You're so fucking sweet."

"I love the way your beard feels against my skin. I love that every part of you feels like a man." She threads her fingers into my hair and fists them there, tugging hard enough to send a flash of welcome pain down the back of my neck. A little bit of pain is perfect, just what I need to give me the strength to keep pushing us both closer to the edge of reason.

"I want you so much," she moans. "Inside me, Aidan. Please, I need to feel you inside me."

She bucks into my cock, and I let her go, let her grind her clit against my pulsing length until she's trembling and clinging to my shoulders and so close to coming from the friction of our bodies sliding against each other. Then, and only then, when I sense she's truly about to catch fire, do I pull away.

I sever the contact between us completely, sending a cold rush of air gusting between us as I sit on my heels, fighting the urge to smile as her eyes widen in shock, and then outrage.

Now, the battle is truly on, and I'm going to enjoy every wicked, wonderful second of it.

Cat props up on her elbows, glaring at me through narrowed eyes. "Not nice. Come back here. Right now."

I tsk softly beneath my breath. "Bossy, bossy."

"Come back, please," she says, teeth digging into her bottom lip hard enough to turn the plump flesh white.

"Please is good." I shove my boxers down around my hips, freeing my cock and dropping one hand to my engorged length. I squeeze the base of my shaft tight, hard enough to hurt, using that fresh pain to regain the control to keep pushing us further. "But I want you to beg, Cat. You're not even close."

"Fuck you. I am, too, close." She scowls, making a low, growling sound of frustration as her gaze drops to my cock. "You're smaller than I remember."

I grin. "Any bigger and I'd really break you, sweetheart."

"You're a bastard." Her hips shift restlessly against the mattress, and her eyes flash, but I can tell she's fighting a smile.

"You know I hate being called sweetheart." She sighs. "But I really like you."

"I really like you, too," I say, surprised by how true the words feel.

I do really like her. I like her brain and her body and her wicked sense of humor, and I fucking love seeing her squirm. I love watching this force of nature unravel and knowing I'm the reason for the hunger flashing in her eyes and the blush staining her creamy tits a pale pink.

"Please, Aidan," she whispers, holding my gaze. "I want you so much. I feel like I've been waiting forever. Don't make me wait anymore."

"I don't want to make you wait, Red, but I still don't hear any begging." I reach for the top of her panties, letting my fingers tease lightly across her clit as I move.

She flinches and arches into my hand with a gasp, and I have to fight the urge to rip the lace in two. I'm past ready to eliminate the barrier between the hot pussy beneath the soaked fabric and my hand, my mouth, my poor suffering cock. Instead, I strip the lace slowly down her churning legs and then bring my palms back to her thighs, spreading her wider, groaning in appreciation as I take her in.

She's a true red head, with a thatch of damp auburn curls above her slick peach of a pussy, and she's as turned on as I've ever seen a woman. She's swollen and wet and so beautiful all I want to do is drop my face between her thighs and devour her until I make her even wetter and hotter.

But it's not time for satisfaction just yet.

"Beautiful," I breathe, using my thumbs to part her outer lips, giving me a better view of the clit lifting toward me. "Smaller than I remember, but beautiful."

She huffs. "Well, it was dark back then. My clitoris is bolder in the dark."

"And we were young." I scoot down the bed to settle between her thighs. "Everything seems bigger and better when you're young."

"Bigger, maybe," she says. "Not better."

"I agree. I think it's better now." I bring my mouth closer to her wetness as I loop my hands around the backs of her thighs and dig my fingers into her hips. I pause, inhaling the smell of her, deciding I've never smelled anything hotter than how much she wants me. "Now, I'm old enough to appreciate every moment of this. And I like you softer, sweeter."

She bites her lip. "So, this isn't the time to tell you that there are better uses for your tongue than giving me compliments?"

I grin. "No, this is the perfect time. Keep using your pretty mouth to be a fucking smartass and we'll stay like this all night." I nuzzle her thigh with my nose, letting my breath warm her already hot pussy. "In limbo, a breath away from the satisfaction that could be ours if you would just tell me that you're going to die if I don't put my cock in your pussy."

"It would take more than that to kill me," she says, her breath hissing out as my tongue swipes a trail from her ass to her clit. Her back arches, her tits lifting toward the ceiling as she gasps. "Shit, I've imagined that so many times. But that was way too fast. Go slower, please. I want time to memorize what it feels like to have your mouth on me."

"I'm going to give you time. Lots of time. All the time in the world." I bring the tip of my tongue to her clit and lightly circle the swollen pink nub. "I could eat your pussy all fucking night."

"Oh, God, that feels so good," she pants, her thighs shifting restlessly on either side of my face as I continue my gentle, calculated assault. Around and around, back and forth, up and down, I explore every inch of her sweetness with that same not-quite-enough pressure until she's shaking and whimpering as her toes curl into the mattress.

"Please, Aidan, damn it! Please!" She arches into my mouth, trying to forcibly intensify the pressure of my tongue against her swollen flesh, but I grip her hips tight, pinning her to the mattress. "You can't do this!"

"But I can. I am." I press a gentle kiss to her thigh, pretending I'm not as close to the edge as she is. "I'm in charge, and I'm not giving you what you want until I get what I need, Red. Until I hear you beg. Come on, baby. Beg me to fuck you. Let me hear you lose control."

"Fuck you," she gasps, her words transforming to a tortured groan as I resume my whisper-soft assault on her body.

My hands smooth up her sweat damp skin to cup her breasts, rolling her nipples between my fingers as I continue to lick and tease and suck, driving my tongue inside her far enough to make her wild, but no further. I pin her legs to the mattress with my upper arms, relishing the feel of her muscles straining against mine as she bucks and twists and tries every dirty trick in the book to get me to give her more. But I refuse to give in. I focus on her taste and her heat and how perfect it feels to have her pinned beneath me, spread wide for my mouth, mine to torture and pleasure and worship.

I ignore the racing of my pulse and the leaden weight in my balls and my throbbing, miserable, wretchedly hard cock. Every cell in my body is howling that this is insanity, that playing power games with Cat isn't worth this level of pain and suffering, but I silence the voice of weakness and fight to stay in the moment. I focus on the way her body blooms beneath me, the flush between her legs darkening her sex, her breasts swelling in my palms as I make love to her with my hands. My attention narrows to the slide of her soft skin against my arms as I press against her thighs with a rhythmic pulse, mimicking the way my body will push her into the mattress when I'm finally able to fuck her.

God, I have to fuck her soon.

I need her so much. I'm so desperate, so ready, so wild for her that it takes a few minutes for me to notice that she's letting forth a soft, steady stream of curse words, calling me every dirty name in the book and a few I'm pretty sure she's making up on the spot.

But by that point, I can barely make sense of her words. I can't make sense of anything but her scent and her taste and the bliss of her hands fisting in my hair with a desperation that echoes through my entire body. All I can think about is how much I need to replace my mouth with my dick and ride her into orgasm after orgasm, to fuck her until we're both bruised with the force of our pleasure. But I didn't come this far to turn back now. I'm going to have what I need, what we both need, even though a part of me is certain my damned cock is going to fall off if we keep this up too much longer.

Red isn't the only stubborn cuss in this room. I am every bit as stubborn and determined and insane as she is. So I wait and suffer and twist in the hot wind of a lust unlike anything I've ever experienced in my entire godforsaken life, until finally I hear Red begin to sob.

"Please, Aidan, please," she begs, sucking in a ragged breath. "I'll do anything you want, say anything you want. I'll get down on my knees and beg you right now if that's what it takes, but please, fuck me. Please!"

I drive my tongue deep in her dripping, swollen pussy, groaning as the salty heat of her envelopes me and I realize I am seconds away from having her, from being buried balls-deep inside this paradise between her legs.

"I'm going to die if you don't." She bucks into my mouth as I fuck her with my tongue, driving the rigid muscle deeper with each bob of my head. "I'm going to die, and I don't want to die, not without having you inside me. It's all I want, Aidan, please! God, please!"

Her voice cracks as she begins to sob harder and some primitive part of me realizes that's my cue. I surge up over her, slamming my mouth against hers, kissing her with the taste of her arousal still thick on my tongue as my cock finds her entrance and glides home, driving forward all the way to the end of her without a single hitch.

And it's so perfect, so right, like we've made love a hundred times. A thousand. It's like the combination lock on a secret room deep inside me has clicked into place, the door swinging open to reveal my true purpose.

All this time my cock has spent fucking other women, or hanging out against my thigh, or sweating next to my balls as I do dumb shit like run naked across the Brooklyn Bridge has just been a way of biding his time until he found the place where he's always belonged—between Red's thighs. Sheathed inside her. Held in the most perfect embrace ever dreamed up by whatever benevolent force gave human beings the capacity for pleasure like this.

She is so good. So damned fucking good.

And this is the rightest thing I've ever done without clothes on. I want to slow down and make it last, but we're both so wild I can't do anything but take her. Take her hard, take her deep, take her without a thought more eloquent than "yes, mine, now, mine, mine, fuck yes, mine" as she bucks into my thrusts, giving as good as she gets.

I don't think about showing off the tricks I've learned with other lovers, I don't think about all the things I wanted to prove to her when we started this. All I think about is getting closer, closer, until there is nothing between her soul and mine but a few layers of pulsing skin.

And when I look into her eyes, I realize how very stupid I was to push her away. I spent years stubbornly refusing to acknowledge that the perfect-for-me girl was right under my nose and even more years convincing myself that the recollection of feeling effortlessly at home in a certain redhead's company were just idealized memories. They were moments frozen in time that my mind insisted were perfect because they were in the past, never to be recaptured again.

But maybe I was wrong.

"Yes," she says, as if she can read my mind, looking up at me with tears shining in her eyes as she chants, "Yes, yes. Oh, yes."

And I know exactly what she means.

Yes to more of this unbelievable pleasure. Yes to unguarded moments when there is nothing to fear and nothing to prove.

Yes to long days and longer nights and months and years or however long we can hold on to this because there is nothing better than realizing that everything you'll ever need is already in your arms.

"You feel so good, Aidan," she whispers against my lips, her fingernails digging into the mounds of my ass as she urges me closer, deeper, faster. "I'm so close. So close."

"Yes, come for me. Come for me," I pant, breath catching as her pussy locks down around my cock, squeezing me so tight my heart skips a beat.

I fight to hold back, to keep going so I can make her come again, but the feel of her molten heat gripping me tight is more than I can take. I come with a deep cry wrenched from the center of my chest, a pained, pleasured sound that echoes through the room as my balls clench and my cock jerks hard inside her pussy.

"God!" she cries out, her hips bucking hard enough to lift me several inches into the air. "Again. Oh God, I'm coming again."

"Fuck, I can feel you. You're so tight," I groan, rocking my hips, letting the curve do its work against her G-spot as I continue to come so hard it feels like the muscles in my lower body are being shredded by the force of my orgasm.

But I'm not going to complain. If I've pulled a muscle fucking Red, it will be the best injury ever, one I will brag about for years to come.

Finally, after riding the wave, coming and coming for longer than I'd realized the male orgasm could last, Cat and I finally lie still, our bellies pulsing against each another as we catch our breath. We've fucked our way to the far corner of the bed from where we started, sent the comforter sliding off the other side, and managed to knock every pillow to the floor, but I don't remember when any of that happened.

I was too lost in her. *Found* in her.

The cheese factor of the thought would usually send a sour taste flooding through my mouth, but right now it just feels true. I haven't felt this good after sex in years. There is no awkwardness or distance, just the sense of being where I'm supposed to be, with someone I can trust. It's fantastic, and I finally understand why some of my friends preach the holy gospel of the fuck buddy. There's a lot to be said for hot sex with a good friend. A whole lot.

"Damn," she whispers as I roll to one side and lie facing her on the mattress, admiring how pretty she looks with her cheeks flushed red from fucking me. "Shit."

My lips curve as I brush the hair from her face. "Damn and shit?"

"Damn and shit," she says, breath rushing out as she grins. "That was amazing. I came so hard my toes are still numb."

My smile widens. "And that's something to cuss about?"

"Yes! Absolutely." She nods seriously. "Because now that you know you're the best I've ever had, you're going to get an even bigger head than you have already. You'll be completely insufferable." She sighs. "I was really hoping you would be like stinky cheese."

"Stinky cheese," I echo, because my brain still isn't anywhere close to fully functional. I may have actually fucked some of my brains out. And it was one hundred percent worth it.

Her tongue sweeps out to dampen her lips. "You know. Overpriced and overrated and it leaves an unpleasant aftertaste unless consumed with ridiculously expensive wine."

I let my palm skim down her ribs to her waist and fold my fingers over the curve of her hip. "You did not hope that I was like stinky cheese. You wanted it to be good. But it was so much better than good."

"It was," she says with a happy sigh.

"That was the best I've ever had, too." I'm so fresh from being open and defenseless I don't even think about holding back. “I had no idea it could be like that.”

“Well, thank you.” Her muscles tighten beneath my fingers. “I do a lot of Kegels.”

I lift my gaze to hers, blinking fast as I see that the vulnerable Cat I was making love to a few minutes ago has vanished, replaced by a Cat who watches me with a wary look even as her lips curve in another grin.

“You know, Kegels, right? The exercises that make your—”

“I know what they are,” I cut in. “I wasn't talking about that. I mean, yes, your pussy is amazing, but—”

“And your dick is a revelation,” she says with an enthusiasm that should be flattering, but for some reason isn't. “I can now testify that Curved for her Pleasure isn't just an excellent Dasher name. It's scientifically sound. I wasn't sure I had a G-spot until a few minute ago, but that was…completely incredible.” She rolls onto her back, squinting up at the ceiling, as if she expects the secrets to the G-spot to be written on the blades of her fan. “I didn't know an orgasm could feel like that, like it's turning you inside out but you're loving every minute of it.”

“Well, good.” I sit up, smoothing my hand down both sides of my face, taming my beard into something resembling submission. “I'm glad it was good for you, too.”

And I am. I don't need her to tell me that she felt the safe, home, this-is-so-right feeling, too. I'm pretty sure she did—though she might never admit it—and that's good enough.

Is it? Really?

How right *can it be if she's not willing to talk about anything but Slot A and Tab B?*

Maybe she felt jack shit, jackass. Maybe you're the only one floating around in a big soggy vat of your own feelings.

“Can I use your shower?” I clear my throat, deciding it's

time to get the soggy feelings stuffed back under the hood where they belong. "According to a very bad man I met today, I apparently smell terrible."

She humphs as she reaches out to squeeze my arm. "Of course you can, but you don't smell terrible. You smell wonderful, like an Aidan who's been eating pussy, which is probably one of the most incredible smells in the world."

I glance over my shoulder at her, smiling at her stern expression. "I'm glad you're taking this seriously."

"I take smell very seriously," she says with a straight face. "I've always loved the way you smell."

"Thanks." I lean over to kiss her cheek. "I'll be right back." I slide off the bed and cross the room naked, heading for the entrance to the bathroom.

She loves the smell of me and confessed that I'm the best she's ever had. What more can a man expect from an old friend he hasn't seen in years and has only been back in contact with for one very strange, very stressful day?

Nothing.

I have no right to expect or want anything more, but as I step into the shower and start the water, I can't help wishing our walls had stayed down long enough for me to find out if Red might consider making this thing between us about more than hot sex and business. Maybe we could become fuck buddies, the way we should have years ago. Maybe even something more…

"She's getting out of a terrible relationship with a psychopath, and you've never made a relationship last more than a few months," I mumble to the water spraying over my face. "Sounds like a recipe for disaster."

It does. But that doesn't make me want it—or her—any less.

Chapter Twenty

From the note and text archives of
Curved for her Pleasure and Polka Dot Panties

Dear Panties,

Let's talk about your ass, and how it wasn't at conditioning for the past two weeks, or at our last Dash on Saturday. Add to this the fact that you haven't responded to my texts, or been seen getting your nerd on in the library, or loading up a giant soup bowl at the frozen yogurt machine in the cafeteria, and a few of us have started to worry. If I'm on your shit list for some reason, please make contact with someone else in the club as soon as possible and let us all know that you're okay.

Pissy Toes and Back End Bonus are especially worried since they haven't heard from you, either, and apparently, unbeknownst to the dick-possessing members of the club, the three of you have a secret, girls-only conditioning run every Monday night, followed by beer, pizza, and chick flicks.

Cliques within the club and private runs, especially those divided along gender lines, are against the rules, PDP. But I'm willing to pretend I don't know about your forbidden chick gatherings as long as you text me the minute you pull this note out of the soldier's ass.

While it's still warm from his cheeks, Panties. Still. Warm!

Kidding aside, I'm not a fan of the disappearing act. Really not a fan.

If I don't hear from you or of you by Sunday, I'm going to take whatever steps are necessary to make sure you're okay. If that means finding out your real name, where you live, and making contact with your dad or whoever else you have at home, I'll do it.

I'd rather you be pissed at me for invading your privacy than have you be in trouble somewhere and no one know about it.

Hoping you're okay,
Curve

Text to Curve from Panties: Just got your note. I'm fine. Back on campus and ready to run tomorrow.

Curve: Where the hell have you been? We've been worried.
Back End Bonus went by your dorm room, and your roommate said you haven't slept there for a week. I was headed to Student Affairs first thing tomorrow morning to report your ass missing.

Panties: I'm surprised my roommate noticed that I wasn't around, considering I spend most nights couching it in the study lounge while she's having the loudest orgasms in the world.
I'm going to buy a muzzle and give it to her boyfriend. Tell him it's to help protect him from long-term hearing loss. It can't be safe for him to be that close to her mouth when she starts going off.

Curved: Again, I'll ask: where have you been and why didn't you text me? You did get those twenty messages I sent asking if you were okay, right?

Panties: Let me see…
Yep. There they are.
I like the one where you pretended you were locked in the bathroom with a giant spider outside

the door and you needed me to come kill it.
I almost texted back—
Panties is gone. I ate her. You're next. Love, Spider.
—but I figured if I did, then I'd have to keep texting or you would get mad at me. So I didn't.

Curved: Yeah, I would have been mad, but at least I wouldn't have been scared for you. Or as fucking pissed as I am right now.
Vanishing for a week and not telling a fucking soul that you're okay is a dick move, Panties. I thought you'd been fucking kidnapped. Or something worse.

Panties: If I'd been kidnapped they would have brought me back. I'm too much of a pain in the ass to commit to a long-term torture or imprisonment relationship.

Curve: This isn't funny.
My freshman year, a girl in my sociology class hitched a ride home from a bar downtown. Her friends saw her get into a white pickup truck and drive away, and no one ever saw her again.
You realize that could have been you, right? Because I fucking do.
And I was sitting here texting you and writing you notes and trying not to freak out because I know you can usually take care of yourself, but this voice in my head kept saying—but what if this time she can't?

What if this time she's in trouble and you're wasting time trying to play it cool and not annoy her, and meanwhile she's tied up in a psychopath's basement?

Panties: I'm really good at getting out of ropes, too. You'd have to tie me with a constrictor knot to have a chance at keeping me cooped up in a basement or anywhere else.

Curved: Fine.
Fuck you very much, too.
Glad you find the fact that you scared people who care about you amusing.

Panties: Wait! I'm sorry. Really I am. Or I will be.
Honestly, I'm a little drunk right now.
Probably more than a little drunk. After six days with my dad, I needed all the beers to take the edge off. Now I'm feeling no pain and everything seems funny, but I know it's not.

Curved: What were you doing with your dad?

Panties: Helping him pick up my mother's body in Northern Ireland and bring it back to Washington to be buried. For some reason he thought that would be a great way to introduce me to the mother I've never met—by giving me the unique privilege of escorting her corpse across an ocean and through customs and to a depressing-as-shit funeral home outside of D.C.

Curved: Shit. I'm sorry. If I were you, I'd be drunk, too.

Panties: Thanks. Though, apparently my mom was an alcoholic. A high functioning alcoholic, but she really loved her Irish whiskey. So I guess I should cut back on the beer unless I want to die before I'm fifty-five.

Though, she didn't die of alcohol poisoning or liver disease—she died of getting run over crossing the street while she was one-hundred percent sober—so that really doesn't make much sense.

Like I said, I'm drunk.

But I'm getting lots of things done. In between pulls on my flask on the train, I managed to get caught up on my homework from all the classes I missed. Drunk Panties is amazing at doing homework. She's also great at texting without making spelling mistakes.

Are you fucking bowled over by how fast I'm texting right now, or what?

It's like my thumbs have a mind of their own.

Mind thumbs. Mind. Thumbs. Thumb minds. Mind over thumb.

I don't know what I'm saying, but the words "thumb" and "mind" together are cracking my shit up right now.

Curved: Where are you? I'll bring you a burrito

to help you sober up and we can talk Mom stuff.

Panties: I don't want to talk Mom stuff. I don't care about my mom.
I guess that sounds terrible, but it's the truth. She left before I could walk because she wanted to be a spy and a drunk more than she wanted to be a mother.
And that's fine. Whatever. I got over it a long time ago.
I'm more upset with my dad for making me go with him to get her. He should have let her friends cremate her body the way they wanted to because I'm never going to visit that grave.
Ever. I'd rather eat spiders. Live spiders.

Curved: Are you sure? I'm a good listener.
And I've got Dad and Mama drama in my past. Nothing like what you've been through, but enough that I can definitely lend a sympathetic ear.

Panties: Thanks, but no thanks. I'd also rather eat spiders than cry on your shoulder about my shitty life.
Are you really afraid of spiders? Even a little bit? Or was that bullshit designed to get me to text you back?

Curved: I'm not afraid of spiders. People are the only animals that scare me.

Panties: Me, too. So much.
I have a black belt in jujitsu and trained with the best self-defense experts in the world, but people still scare me. They just don't make any fucking sense, you know? I mean, I can beat just about anyone in a fight, but if some psycho decides to strap a bomb to his chest and sit down next to me on the train, what the fuck can I do? How do I prepare for that?
I can't. So spending ten years of my life learning to pin men twice my size to a sparring mat was a huge waste of my time.
I almost told my dad that this weekend. I almost told him that I wished he'd let me stay with my grandmother instead of taking me with him on his deployments and turning me into a freak as big as he is. But I didn't.
Because learning to fight might have made me strong but it didn't give me courage.

Curve: Where are you? You shouldn't be alone right now.

Panties: I'm a coward. I really am.
But Drunk Panties is less cowardly than Sober Panties, so I'm going to ask you why you thought I was mad at you.

Curved: I didn't think you were mad at me.

Panties: Yes, you did. You wrote it in your note. That if you were on my shit list for some reason I should contact one of the girls. You wouldn't have written that unless you had some idea why I might be mad at you.

Curved: I don't know. You seemed weird at the last party.

Panties: Weird, how?

Curved: You didn't want to try my beer. You always want to try my beer.

Panties: Well, yeah, because you bring the best beer. I never knew beer could have so many tastes until I met you.

Curved: So? What was up?

Panties: I thought I might be coming down with a cold. I didn't want to infect you. But I didn't want to tell you I might be coming down with something because I knew you would make me go home and rest.
You're very bossy.

Curved: But you like it. Admit it. You like it that I boss you around every once in a while.

Panties: I guess I do. As Drunk Panties I can admit

that, even though the Panties of tomorrow will be pissed at me for it.
But I do like it. It means you care, that I'm special enough for you to waste your time trying to tell me what to do.

Curved: I do care. So let me bring you burritos and be the bossy big brother type who insists you need food in your belly to go with all that beer.

Panties: Whiskey, actually. In honor of Mom. May she rest in peas.

Curved: And carrots.

Panties: Thanks for that. Dumb jokes are…good. Shit, now I'm crying…

Curved: Tell me where you are. Right now.

Panties: I can't. I don't want you to see me like this. I might say more things I'll regret tomorrow.

Curved: You don't have to regret anything you've said or will say. You get a free "my mom just died" pass to act like a complete fool. I just need to make sure you don't pass out, puke, and choke on your own vomit.
You're too good to go out that way, feral squirrel.

Panties: Aw, you remembered my pet name.

I love you, too, Curve.
See you at the race tomorrow. I'll be the one with the hangover, puking on her shoes on the switchbacks.

Curved: Take care of yourself, Panties. And call me if you decide you'd rather I take care of you, instead. There's no shame in needing people now and then, you know.

Panties: So I've heard. So I've heard…

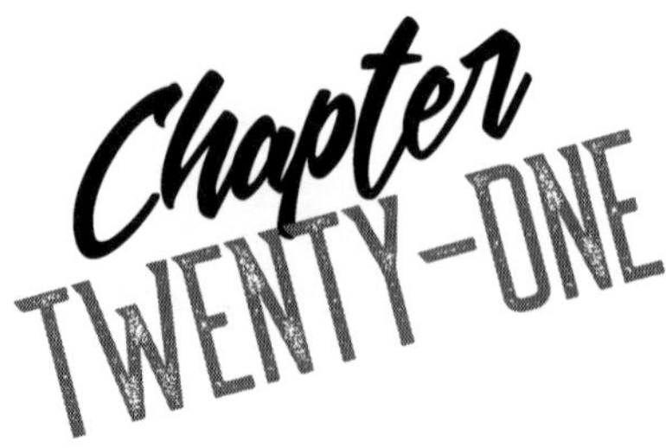

Chapter Twenty-One

I wake up a little after three a.m., going from sleeping deep and dreamless to wide-awake, ears straining, without knowing why.

Pushing up on one arm, I glance down at Cat, who has curled into a ball on her side with her cheek resting on her folded hands and a half smile on her face that makes me wonder what she's dreaming and hope it's something about me.

Or at least my cock.

She looks catlike and beautiful, and my heart does weird things in my chest when my eyes land on her face. But I don't give in to the urge to curl my body around hers and go back to sleep, or kiss her until she wakes up and gives me a second shot at finding her G-spot.

Something woke me up—I'm a sound sleeper unless I'm disturbed—and I need to figure out what it was.

Cat armed her security system before we went to sleep, and she assured me that Nico never knew the code to disarm it. The chances that someone is in the apartment are slim, and after several moments of listening, the air is still as quiet as it ever is in the city, with only the faint drone of late night traffic on the Avenue to disturb the peace. There are no drunks digging through the recycling on the sidewalk, or married couples screaming abuse at each other in languages I can't understand, proving Cat's neighborhood is significantly swankier than mine.

She has a very nice, security-system-protected apartment in an even nicer part of town, and by all rights she should feel safe. But she doesn't, and that's enough reason for me to slip from between the covers and reach for my clothes. I tug on my boxers and jeans and scan the darkened room for anything that might serve as a weapon.

My eyes have adjusted to the shadows, and light filters in through the lowered blinds, but there's not much to see. Aside from the brushed silver lamp on the bedside table, there's nothing remotely dangerous in the uncluttered space. Cat's decorating style runs to contemporary and minimalist. It's clean, efficient, and sexy, like the woman herself, but sorely lacking in heavy tchotchkes good for knocking intruders over the head.

"Fists it is, then," I whisper as I pad silently across the room in my bare feet. I grip the door handle carefully, cracking the door without making any noise.

I'm equally careful as I ease out into the short hallway, checking the bathroom on my left to make sure no one's lurking in the shower before moving on. My heart is beating faster than usual, and my senses are on high alert, but deep down I don't think I'm going to find someone snooping around in the living room or the kitchen.

If someone had broken in the alarm would have sounded. And even if Nico had somehow managed to shut off the security system, it would have beeped loudly as it was disarmed. It wasn't anything that obnoxious that pulled me out of my sleep. It was something softer, the dull thud of someone stumbling home drunk in the hall outside, maybe. Or the person's feet in the apartment above hitting the floor as they headed to the bathroom to take a piss.

Or maybe the dog. Fang could be in the living room working out her abandonment issues on the furniture. According to Cat, the dog usually sleeps with her, so the little pervert probably isn't thrilled to have been consigned to her dog bed for the night.

I'm already planning to take Fang back to bed with me if she's awake—I grew up sleeping with dogs, and I know I won't be able to resist the "why can't I come snuggle?" pup eyes if they're turned my way—when I see the tiny form sprawled on the kitchen floor in front of the refrigerator.

My mind registers that it's Fang, but something about the scene immediately strikes me as wrong. It takes a moment to realize that it's her position. I've never seen a dog sleep on her side with her head lolled awkwardly toward the floor like that. From there my mind clicks from one thought to the next pretty quickly. I jump from realizing Fang is hurt, to theorizing what could have hurt her, to understanding that one of those things could be a human intent on hurting me, too, in just a few seconds.

But my mental process isn't quite fast enough.

I've just started for the bottle of tequila, planning to arm myself before I check on the dog, when I'm hit hard from behind. The step I took into the kitchen makes the blunt object strike my shoulder instead of my head. I'm not knocked unconscious, but it still hurts like a son of a bitch.

I cry out and spin with a clenched fist, deciding to punch first and figure out who I'm punching later. My fist connects with the toned stomach of a shorter man, but the guy clearly isn't expecting my blow. He doesn't have time to clench his muscles, which means my fist goes in hard and deep.

He doubles over with a gagging sound just as the door to Cat's room flies open.

"Get back inside and lock the door!" I order, distracted from the intruder long enough for him to rush me.

He butts his head into my midsection like a battering ram, sending me staggering backwards. My back hits the edge of the island, sending a flash of pain through my spine. I try to knee him in the chest, but he's still coming, plowing into me with his head as his fists go to work on my ribs. I clench my gut muscles and reach for his shoulders, trying to pry him off of me. But before I can get a solid grip on the bastard, Cat's foot connects with his hip hard enough to send him tumbling to the floor.

"Get somewhere safe and call 911," I shout as I push away from the island, charging the guy as he jumps back to his feet.

"Let me help you," Cat says, but I'm already tackling the smaller man to the ground. We roll over and over, landing in a rectangle of light beaming in through the half-closed blinds, giving me my first good look at his face. I recognize Petey, Nico's driver, the man responsible for making his boss's enemies disappear, and my blood goes cold.

Cold, and then boiling hot, my vision blurring with rage

as I realize this man has come here to hurt Cat, maybe even kill her.

I aim a fist at his face, fully prepared to break a few bones, but the rabid little shit gets to me first. He's small, but he's insanely fast, and strong as fuck. I've barely caught the flash of movement out of the corner of my eye, when his fist rams into my right cheekbone, making cartoon stars streak across my vision. The blow connects with enough force to knock my weight to the left. Before I can shift back to the right and return the punch, the weasel wiggles out from under me and makes a break for the front door.

With a curse, I jump up to run after him, only to slam into Cat, who apparently had the same idea. We bounce off each other with twin sounds of pain and surprise. I hit the wall and recover my balance fairly quickly, but Cat, having collided with someone almost twice her size, falls all the way to the floor.

I move to help her up, but before I can take a step, she's bounced back to her feet with some back snapping ninja move that reminds me that she's a black belt in one of the martial arts.

"Stop him!" she shouts, starting for the front door.

I dart into the hallway just ahead of her, running fast, but the front door is already closing behind Petey the Disappearer. Skidding to a stop on the hall carpet, I wrench the door open in time to hear the door leading out to the street thunk heavily shut and footsteps pound away outside.

"Wait." I grab Cat's arm as she tries to push past me.

"I have to catch him," she says. "If I can prove Nico sent someone to break into my house, then the police will have to take me seriously."

"He's got too much of a head start," I say, holding tight as she tries to pull away. "And we have to check on Fang. He hurt her. She's unconscious…maybe worse."

Cat's face pales, and the fight goes out of her. "Oh, no." Her hand flies to cover her mouth. "Fuck, Aidan. If he killed Fifi, I don't know what I'm going to do." Her eyes begin to shine. "I'll have to kill him. Hunt him down and kill him with my bare hands."

"I'll help you," I promise, putting an arm tight around her shoulders. "Come on, let's go check on her together, then I'll start Googling twenty-four-hour vet offices."

"No, I've got a friend." Cat shuts the door and presses a hand against it for a moment, as if bracing herself for what we might find in the kitchen. "If Fifi is still alive, Shane will take care of her, any time of day or night."

"Then let's go get her and take her to your friend." I capture Cat's hand, holding tight as we move back into the apartment, praying that Fang isn't down for the count for good.

Thankfully, when Cat and I kneel down beside the fallen guard dog, it's immediately obvious that she's still breathing.

"Thank God." Cat's breath hitches as she scoops Fifi gently into her arms. "Come on, baby. Let's go get you fixed up."

"I'll get her bed and her leash just in case," I say, wishing I could do more.

Helping take care of the damage Petey has done is too little, too late. As Cat hurriedly changes out of her pajamas into a pair of black yoga pants and a grey tank top, I can't help thinking that it could have all too easily been her lying on the floor. It could be her unconscious in my arms, and me figuring out ways to kill the person who hurt her.

We're in way over our heads. It's time to make contact with Bash and get some professional help before someone other than Fang is hurt.

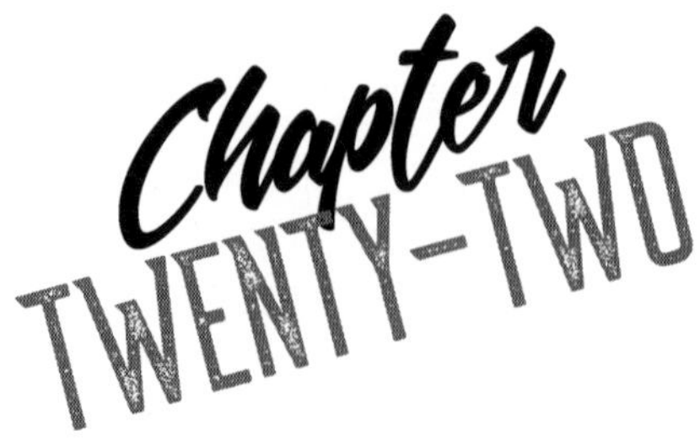

By the time we get out of the cab near Cat's friend's building on the Upper West Side, dawn has stained the sky above Central Park bright yellow with streaks of orange, and Fang is starting to whimper in Cat's lap. It's an encouraging sign, but I know Cat's not going to feel better until we hear from a licensed professional that her fur baby is going to be okay.

I won't, either.

This never should have happened. I should have kept it from happening. Or at least kept Petey from getting away.

Some bodyguard I'm turning out to be.

I follow Cat into the grand old building at the corner of 72nd Street and Central Park West, attempting to look non-threatening as the man at the front desk eyes the bruise on my cheekbone. Finally, after he calls upstairs to ensure that Shane is expecting a "large man with several tattoos," he adds our names to the guest register and motions us through to the elevators. I may have earned a battle scar—and done at least a little damage to Nico's thug—but it never should have come to this.

Neither my client, nor any of her nearest and dearest, should have been hurt on my watch. This is my fault. If I hadn't underestimated mobster security system hacking abilities, and ignored Cat's warning that her ex would lose his shit if he found out I was spending the night at her place, Fifi wouldn't be shivering and crying, and Cat wouldn't be so pale that she blends in with the white elevator walls as the lift zips skyward.

I'm so busy mentally ripping myself a new one, and thinking of all the things I could have done better, I don't realize we've stopped on the penthouse level until we step out into an apartment so enormous it reminds me of the museum on the other side of the park. The Met is the only other place I've ever been that has rooms with twenty-foot ceilings and artfully lit paintings on the walls.

The museum vibe continues in the rest of the space. Heavy couches with carved wooden arms, draped with blankets from at least a dozen different countries, create a welcoming conversation area in the center, while floor to ceiling bookcases with a sliding ladder lend gravitas to the far side of the room. To our left, a galley-style kitchen long enough to fit in a luxury cruise ship, filled with stainless steel appliances and dominated by an island larger than my entire apartment, gleams in the early morning light.

Sitting cross-legged on top of the island is a plush woman in pink harem pants and a tight black tank top with a white towel folded in half in front of her. As soon as we step through the elevator doors, she motions urgently to Cat with both hands.

"Bring the little love over here, Sweet Pea," she says, her blue eyes kind and compassionate behind her black horn-rimmed glasses. "We're going to make it all better, I promise."

"Thank you so much." Cat sniffs as she lays the trembling Fang down on the towel in front of the woman I can only assume is Shane. The gentle way her fingers probe Fang's belly speaks of a vet's comfort with animals. "She seems to be coming around," Cat says, staying close. "But she hasn't opened her eyes yet."

Shane hums thoughtfully, her gaze fixed somewhere in the distance as she continues to run her hands over the dog. "Well, that makes sense," she says softly. "She's so little. Even if that worm only gave her a tiny bit of sedative, it would knock her out for a good long stretch. I *could* give her something to help her come to. But considering I don't know what was used to put her out, I'd rather wait and let her wake up on her own."

"But she *is* going to wake up." Cat nibbles anxiously on her thumb, clearly in need of reassurance. "It's just the sedative that's keeping her knocked out, right? They didn't hurt her?"

"I'm not seeing any evidence that she was injured." Shane lifts Fang's head and gently examines her teeth. "I imagine the sniveling coward slipped into your place with a treat, Fang gobbled it up like the terrible little guard dog that she is, and then laid down for a long hard nap."

With a final nod, she sets the pup down and folds the towel in half, covering Fang in the fluffy white cotton. Only when she's finished with the exam does she reach out to grab Cat's hand and look her friend fully in the face. "Feefs is going to be fine. And, thank God, so are you!" Shane turns, holding her free hand out toward me. "You must be Aidan. I'm Shane. Thank you so much for keeping my stubborn friend safe."

"Good to meet you." I take her hand, surprised by the strength of her grip.

Now that I've looked her full in the face, I'm struck by how much she resembles one of those English rose Victoria's Secret models, or maybe a Persian cat. She looks like a creature accustomed to being petted and pampered and served delicacies on sterling platters. Even without makeup on, she has an over-the-top beauty that's a little mind-numbing at first glance. But she's also got a firm hand and no shortage of fire in her belly when it comes to defending a friend.

Shane releases my hand and turns to Red with a pointed look. "Maybe now Miss Catherine will finally listen to reason and come live with me until the Nightmare in Human Form can be convinced to leave her alone."

"It's weird when you talk about me in third person when I'm standing right here." Cat sounds as tired as she looks, and her usual smartass tone is noticeably lacking.

"Well, if a girl weren't so stubborn," Shane says in a decent English accent, "a girl wouldn't drive her friends to appealing to total strangers for help in making her see sense."

"*Game of Thrones*," Cat says, seeing my confused look. "She watches too much of it."

"There is no such thing as too much *Game of Thrones*. It's like cats and chocolate and orgasms." Shane smiles up at me, apparently amused by my continued confusion. "Things that are better in bulk. I had ten cats before I moved to the city. And as soon as I can convince the HOA committee to let pets in the building, I plan to bring all of them to live with me and acquire three more so I'll have a baker's dozen."

Shane gives Cat's hand a final squeeze and then slides off the island to land lightly on the kitchen floor. "I'm going to put the kettle on and make a hot water bottle to help keep Fang calm as she starts to wake up. Anyone want tea? Coffee? Children's chewable morphine for the huge bruise on his face?"

"Now she's talking about *you* in third person." Cat leans wearily against me. "That means she likes you."

"Does she really have chewable morphine?" I whisper.

"Possibly. She has a surprising collection of weird shit."

"Which is why I like *you* so much," Shane says, turning back from the sink with a red kettle in hand. "But sadly, no, I don't have morphine. I do have ibuprofen and those gigantic Tylenol that make me sleepy, but always knock out my backaches. Either of those sound good?"

"Thanks, but I'm okay," I say. The throbbing pain on the right side of my face is the least I deserve for doing such a shit job of handling Cat's intervention so far.

"Nonsense. Of course they sound good." Shane puts the kettle on the range beside the sink—as opposed to the other range located on the island near Fang, making me wonder if I've ever been in a kitchen with two stoves. "I'll bring both, and you can decide which you prefer. No need to suffer. And if you get sleepy, you're welcome to take a nap here. I have two guest rooms, though I'm guessing you two would prefer to share."

Cat stands up straight, shrugging off the arm I've wrapped around her shoulder. "I don't know what you're talking about."

"Right." Shane's full lips twist in a smirk as she circles around the island. "Why don't you join me in my bedroom while I fetch the painkillers, Catherine Elizabeth, and we'll see how long you can stick to that story."

"I can't leave Feefs," Cat says, holding her ground as Shane loops an arm through hers. "Seriously. Someone needs to keep an eye on my puppy."

"Luckily Aidan appears to be someone," Shane says. "Are you someone Aidan?"

"Last time I checked," I respond dryly, wondering how long I'll be able to hold my own against these two.

"Perfect." Shane's grin widens. "And sweet baby Fifi isn't going to be awake for another half hour at least. Now that she's warm, she's gone back to sleep, which is probably for the best. The longer she sleeps it off, the less disorientated she'll be when she wakes up. But you'll keep a close eye on Precious, just in case. Right, Aidan?"

"Of course. I'll be right here."

"Perfect." Shane winks at me like we're coconspirators in some mission I don't understand as she tugs Cat toward the other side of the room. "We'll be right back with pills. After I get Cat to confess how long you two have been sleeping together and share the most interesting details."

"Jesus Christ, stop it," Cat whispers as she takes the lead, urging Shane more swiftly toward a pair of double doors framed by the bookshelves. "How are you this meddlesome at six thirty in the morning?"

"Morning person," Shane chirps. "I'd already done yoga, watered the orchids, and was sitting down to make my list for the day when you called."

"Bet you put yoga and watering orchids on the list anyway, didn't you?"

"Absolutely." Shane stretches her arms overhead, wiggling her fingers happily as Red opens the door to what looks like an obscenely enormous bedroom. "There is absolutely nothing in the world more satisfying than marking things off lists."

"Then you won't need to hear any details of what Aidan and I have been up to," Cat says with a smug grin. "We haven't marked a single item off of a single list. We haven't even made a list."

Shane waves a hand through the air, ignoring the arm Cat extends pointedly between them, encouraging her friend to precede her into the other room. "That's okay. I can make a list of the things I *think* you've been up to, and then I'll mark off the guesses that are right. As someone who hasn't dated in over a year, I need to live vicariously through my girlfriends, and none of my other girlfriends have big sexy lumberjack boyfriends." The kettle begins to whistle, and Shane starts toward the stove only to be stopped by Cat's arm through hers.

"He's not my boyfriend," Cat snaps as I turn off the burner and shift the kettle to the other side of the stove. "We're old friends, and he's currently my employee. Aidan is the bodyguard type person I told you I was going to hire to help Nico get the message that things are over between us."

Shane's nose wrinkles. "Well, he's clearly not getting the message."

"I know," Cat says through gritted teeth.

"And you probably shouldn't be sleeping with your employees," Shane adds, shooting me a "sorry about that" look.

Cat's arms flap up and down at her sides. "I never said I was sleeping with anyone, you psycho!"

"It didn't need to be said. You guys have 'recently been banging' written all over you. Might as well make matching 'We Just Banged and All We Got Was Some Orgasms' tee shirts and wear them around town. I mean, I hope you both had orgasms. I don't like to assume, but you both give off an 'I know what I'm doing in the bedroom' vibe."

"Inside." Cat points a stern finger into the bedroom. "Now, before you say anything else that makes me want to blush or muzzle you."

Shane giggles. Cat pushes her into the room before turning to me with a pained expression. "I'm so sorry."

I force a smile. "It's no big deal."

"No, it is. I don't want you to feel uncomfortable," Cat says. "I'll explain everything and be back in a few minutes. I promise I'll have her dialed back to embarrassment Threat Level Blue by then."

"Good luck, Sweet Pea," Shane calls out from inside the bedroom. "Better women than you have tried and failed."

Cat huffs and rolls her eyes before closing the doors with a firm *thu-dud.*

And then I'm alone with only one chatty female, who is presently still asleep.

Figuring it might be the only peaceful moment I'll have for a while, I tug my phone from my pocket and turn it on. I take a deep breath, bracing myself for an onslaught of textual abuse from Bash and the unpleasant task of telling my best friend that I'm the first consultant in Magnificent Bastard history to sustain blunt force trauma while on duty.

As expected, the moment my phone comes online, the texts start dumping onto my screen.

There is one from my stepmother offering her cutest guest cottage if I can make time for a summer visit, one from a girl I took for tofu burgers last week and decided not to call again due to irreconcilable, I-Refuse-To-Become-A-Vegetarian differences, and two from my front desk guy at the shop, Gus, letting me know one of my appointments for next week had to cancel, but that he's already moved a wait-listed client into her place.

The rest are from my very irate best friend/boss—

> *Don't you dare turn off your phone, Aidan! You don't have that option right now. We have things we need to talk about.*
>
> *Turn your phone back on, asshole!*

You fucking arrogant, stupid, passive-aggressive punk...

Well, fuck you, too, shit stick. Fuck you very much. Or fuck me, I guess, since I'm the one who's apparently to blame for you deciding to risk your life for some girl you had a two-week stand with.

I'm assuming it was a two-week stand, since I haven't noticed you keeping a girl around for longer than that lately. But maybe this woman is a blast from farther in your past?

Either way, why didn't she mention that you two had a history, Aidan? Why be sneaky and give me a fake name and lie like a liar who lies?

I'll tell you why—because she is taking perverse, revenge-y pleasure in putting your life in danger. She's getting revenge on Nico and you at the same time, buddy, and you're falling for her evil plan hook, line, and sinker. And, sure, you'll get paid if you complete the job, but you might be dead or in protective custody by the time payday rolls around.

And maybe that's exactly what this psycho bitch wanted from the start—you dead, or with your life permanently fucked up beyond recognition.

Think on that, asshole.

Think on it long and hard, and then Call. Me. Back.

I let out a measured breath, determined not to let Bash piss me off. He will say—or text—anything when he's angry. I know this. I've known this since sixth grade when we got into a fight and he told all the kids at the skate park near his grandmother's house that I thought I'd grown a hair "down there," but then I peed out of it and realized it was just my tiny, tiny, sad excuse for a dick.

In his defense, I had just picked him up with one arm on a dare from another pre-pubescent asshole—Bash didn't start getting taller until eighth grade, and I was already gunning for six feet by the time I turned thirteen—but that afternoon taught me that my best friend isn't himself when he's angry. Chances are he doesn't believe a word he texted about Catherine and her revenge plans.

But even if he does, it doesn't matter. I know the truth. I know that Cat is an old friend who is in over her head, who turned to me because I'm one of the few people in her life who has never let her down. Or who didn't let her down more than once. And hopefully I made up for that bad call in the woods with the delivery of several mind-numbing orgasms earlier tonight.

My irritation soothed by the thought, I return to the dozen Bash texts that I haven't read yet. There are several continuing to dish out abuse to me and to Cat and to himself for letting things slide while Penny was gone.

There are also a couple from Penny apologizing on Bash's behalf…

> *Don't pay too much attention to those last texts, Aidan. (This is Penny, btw).*
> *Bash says things he doesn't mean when he's upset, but he's only upset because he loves you and he's scared for you. So please call us, okay?*
> *You can call my cell if you feel that Bash took things too far with the name-calling. He's sorry about that, though. I can tell.*

And then there are a few more cuss-filled lines from Bash un-apologizing on his own behalf…

> *I'm not fucking sorry.*
> *I'm fucking angry as fuck, and I will never fucking forgive you if you don't*
> *CALL ME BEFORE THE SUN GOES DOWN YOU FUCKING FUCK-FACE FUCKER, JESUS FUCKING CHRIST JUST CALL ME ALREADY!*

After that, there is a lull of several hours with no texts before the final string, sent around ten p.m. last night.

> *I just got back from a meeting with your detective friend, Lip, and I have some amazing news. Seriously, my heart is out of my throat for the first time today.*
> *Everything is going to be okay.*
> *Catherine is going to be safe, you're going to be safe, I'm not going to have a stress-induced stroke, Penny won't have to follow through with that spanking she threatened to deliver if I didn't stop texting you in all caps, and everyone will be able to go back to their regular boring lives.*
> *Call me as soon as you read this. I'm not mad anymore, but I do have things to tell you that I promised I wouldn't send in a text or share over a cell phone.*
> *Shit is happening, Aidan. Big shit.*
> *Get to a landline and call my office phone. I'll be waiting for your call.*

Needless to say, I'm intrigued.

This could all be a ploy from Bash to get me on the phone—he's smart and very good at manipulating people when he's not too angry to control his mouth and thumbs—but my gut says he learned something from Lipman, aka Lip, my friend with the NYPD. I've tattooed at least of third of Lipman's body and talked him through a divorce, the death of his partner, and a cancer scare. I'm practically his therapist by this point, and I know if there is anything he can do to help me out of a sticky situation, he'll do it.

I'd intended to call him last night as soon as Cat and I were settled at her apartment, but drinking, confessions, and sex got in the way. Yet another sign that I didn't have my head in the game the way I should have. But all of that's over. From here on out, I'm one-hundred percent focused on Cat's safety until this mess is behind us.

Then, we'll see…

Maybe she'll be interested in exploring something beyond the intervention; maybe she won't. Either way, that's not something I can afford to be worried about right now.

After a quick check on Fang, who is still asleep, and snoring a very cute Chihuahua-sized snore, and a glance at the door to Shane's bedroom—still closed—I look for a phone. I find one on the other side of the kitchen, near a pantry large enough to house a few NFL linebackers and their groceries for the week.

Despite the early hour, Bash answers after the first ring. "Are you all right? Tell me you're all right."

"I'm all right, and Cat's all right," I say softly, not wanting to disturb the dog or the women in the other room. "But a man broke into her place last night. I fought him and he ran off, but not before he drugged her dog and used my face as a punching bag."

Bash sighs heavily before repeating everything I've said to someone on the other end of the line that I can only assume is Penny. "So, you're not all right is what you're saying," he says, voice tight.

"No, I'm fine. Just a few bruises and sore ribs."

"What about the dog?" Bash asks. "Penny looks like she's going to cry, so the damned dog better be okay."

"Fang is fine. She's been checked by a vet and should be good as new once she sleeps off whatever drug the jerk gave her. But this guy, Petey, who works for Nico, is a scary motherfucker. He fights like an animal," I say, fingers curling into a fist at my side. "I don't want to think about how things could have gone down if Cat had been there alone. She knows how to hold her own in a brawl, but this guy was playing dirty. He would have knocked me out if his first blow had hit my head instead of my shoulder."

Bash curses softly.

"Exactly," I agree. "It was too close, and I blame myself for it. I underestimated her ex and his thugs, but I'm not going to make the same mistake again. If I can't figure out a way to keep Cat safe myself, I'll convince her to go to the authorities. I know witness protection isn't anyone's idea of a good life, but at least she'll be alive to feel shitty about it."

The thought of Cat in the witness protection program, forced to give up the career she's worked so hard for, and to hide from all the people she loves, makes me feel like I've swallowed something rotten. To say I'm grateful when Bash says—

"No one's going into witness protection. Nico and his people will be warming cots in prison by the end of the week."

—is an understatement.

"You're serious," I say, throat tight with hope. "They have enough to put him away?"

"For life and then some," Bash confirms, making the tension behind my ribs release with a spasm of relief that's almost painful. "Lipman said that come Friday morning Cat should have nothing to worry about. He wouldn't share the specifics on when the raid or whatever is going down, but he promised me that as long as Cat stays away from her ex for another forty-eight hours or so, she'll be in the clear. He's waiting for your call to give you instructions on where to take her. He's going to get her set up in a safe house with an armed guard to wait this out."

"Thank God." I let out a rush of breath. "She'll be so relieved. This feels like waking up from a nightmare for me, and I've only been in Crazyville for a day."

"Good. I'm glad," Bash says. "But speaking of Crazyville, Lip said he thinks you should lay low for a while, too, since you might be on Nico's radar. He offered to put you up at the safe house, but if you want to wait it out at my place, feel free. I can go stay with Penny so you'll have the entire apartment to yourself. I've got a security system and Bob downstairs manning the desk to keep you safe."

Penny says something in the background that I can't understand, to which Bash replies. "No, he's not a slacker. Bob's great. He won't let anyone up who's not on the list." Penny murmurs again, and Bash grunts. "You slipped by him with a mixture of diabolical cuteness and boobs. Bad guys who work for the mob are not known for either cuteness or boobs."

"Thanks for the apartment offer," I say, wisely not commenting on Penny's cuteness or her boobs. "But if Cat doesn't want me to stay at the safe house with her until Friday, I may get out of town for a while." I glance over my shoulder, making sure I'm still alone and the Fearsome Fang is asleep. Luckily, both things are still true. "I feel like I could use some time to think."

"Oh, yeah? To think about what?"

I stretch my head to one side, wincing as my sore shoulder sends a flash of pain shooting up my neck. "You know, just… life."

"Life. Yeah. That's a good thing to think about. And maybe think about how much it sucks to turn off your phone and blow off your friends when they're worried about you. That's a good thing to think about."

"This from the guy who blew me off for most of the past two months?"

"Do as I say, not as I do," Bash says. "Besides, you're supposed to be the levelheaded one. That's the arrangement we made in fifth grade, and you know I don't embrace change."

I hum low in my throat, a sound that's echoed from the bundled up pup on the counter behind me. I turn to see Fang squirming beneath her towel. "I've got to go. The dog is waking up."

"Okay. Call me when you decide what you're doing," Bash says. "And erase my texts from yesterday. I'll erase yours, too, and we can start our bromance fresh, with no fuck-yous in it."

"I'll call," I promise and hang up.

No way am I deleting any of his texts, though. I'm saving them for evidence in case I need to talk him into taking an anger management class. Though, now that Penny's back, I doubt I'll be seeing as much of Bash's cranky side. He's a better man with her in his life.

It makes me wonder how I would change if I had someone like Penny, someone who brought out the best in me and muted the worst.

As I uncover Fifi, who greets me with a sleepy tail wag and a few exploratory licks of my hand, I have a feeling I might like that person—like him better than the man I've been lately, a man who has mastered excusing his own bullshit and running away while standing perfectly still.

"Come here, Ferocious. What a good girl you are." I lift the wiggling dog into my arms, smiling as she nuzzles closer to my chest and her tail wags faster. "Yes, you're a good girl. Such a good girl. Who's the sweetest dog I know?"

"I think you win that award," a feminine voice says from behind me. "Hands down."

Face flushing hotter, I turn to see Shane and Cat standing in the doorway to the bedroom watching me get my puppy-talk on with Fang.

Thank God I didn't use the baby voice. I haven't talked to a dog—or a baby—like that in my life. But with my luck lately, the first time would be in front of two women perfectly capable of eviscerating me with their sharp tongues and sharper minds.

But Shane and Cat look more touched than mocking, proving just how glad we all are to see Fang awake and seemingly no worse for wear.

"Seriously," Shane continues, interlacing her fingers beneath her chin. "You two are so sweet I think my ovaries just exploded." She elbows Cat gently in the ribs. "What about you?"

"My ovaries are still intact. For now." Cat's eyes meet mine in a long, searching look before she blinks and drops her gaze to the ground.

Shane sighs wistfully. "Well, big men holding tiny dogs are my personal ovary kryptonite. And Aidan is on my good list from here on out. I'll get Fifi some water and examine her again, but from the look in those sweet eyes, I think someone is on her way to being as good as new."

"Thank goodness." Cat crosses the room toward me, her attention fixed on Fang. "I am so excited to hold this little girl." She reaches for the dog with a soft, cooing sound that might be *my* personal kryptonite. There's something completely compelling about seeing one of the toughest people I know melt into a love puddle over her fur baby. "How are you Feefs? How are you feeling, sweet thing?"

Fang goes eagerly into her mistress's arms, lifting her face to lick Cat's cheek like it's her job, something I make a note to remember later. I love dogs as much as the next man, but I don't want to get Fang's sloppy seconds.

I'll kiss Cat's other cheek. Or her mouth. Or any other part of her body she'll let me get my lips on.

I don't want this to be good-bye. I want to stay with her, make up for letting her down, and convince her to melt a little with me, too. I know I'm not as cute as Fifi, but I care about Cat, and I'd like to get back to that place we found while we were naked together last night, that place where it felt like everything I needed was right there in my arms.

Maybe spending a few days holed up together hiding from their world is the perfect way to show her that she doesn't have to hide when she's with me.

"Thanks." I nod to Shane as she sets two pill bottles onto the counter next to me. I share the good news about the sting that will close down Nico's organization and Lipman's offer to provide protection, then add in a casual tone, "I'd like to come with you to the safe house, if that's all right. You know, stay on duty until we get word that Nico and his people are no longer a threat."

"I would love that," Cat says, the relief on her face making her look like she shed a couple hundred pounds of nasty mobster from her shoulders. "If I were going to go to the safe house, you could absolutely come. But I'm not."

Her bright smile confuses me for a moment. I experience the odd sensation of smiling with half my face while frowning with the other before I process what she's said. "What do you mean you're not going to go?" I ask, frown taking over.

"She's going to stay here with me, instead," Shane supplies as she bustles around, fetching a dog dish from beneath the sink. "And we're going to stay in PJs until Friday and order tons of takeout and watch all the romantic comedies and—"

"I can't stay with you, either." Cat kisses Fifi's head, her next words muffled against the dog's fur. "I would never put you at risk like that. I wouldn't have come here this morning if it hadn't been a puppy-related emergency. I just had no idea where else to go to find a vet at six in the morning."

Shane props a hand on her hip with a frown, but before she can give Cat a piece of her mind, I jump in. "You *are* going to the safe house. I'm not risking your life again."

"I am *not*," Cat insists in a calm voice that is somehow more infuriating than her pissed-off one.

Anger tightens my face. "Yes. You are."

"No, Aidan. I'm not." She looks up, meeting my gaze with her signature "I'll do what I damned well please" glare. "I know all about those death traps. Most of the city's safe 'houses' are actually nasty old hotels infested with bed bugs and black mold. The NYPD arranges for a floor to be set aside for their use and then sticks a single guard at one end of the hall." She holds up an emphatic finger. "One guard. *One* to watch out for all ten or twenty traumatized people in protective custody at a given time."

I'm about to assure her that I'll pull strings with my friend on the force to get her booked into the least disgusting safe house available, but she's not finished with her rant.

"And ninety percent of the guards are new recruits so green they spend most of their time flirting with the housekeeping staff or fucking around on their phones," she says, rolling her eyes. "Meanwhile, the people they're supposed to be watching out for overdose in their rooms or go out for pizza and never come back or get tracked down by the creeps who sent them into protective custody in the first place."

Shane huffs. "Now, Cat, please, they can't all—"

"Yes, they can," Cat says, cutting her off. "I've visited clients at these places for my pro bono work. They're gross, unhealthy, and, most importantly, dangerous. If Petey could disarm my security system and drug my dog without waking Aidan or me up until he was already in the house, he'll take out a baby policeman before he can look up from his copy of Busty Boobies Monthly."

Shane's mouth flattens into a thin line. "Doubtful. Men glance up pretty damned fast when they're looking at porn while they're supposed to be working." Her words are flippant, but her tone is strained, and when she turns to me, it's clear she's as concerned as I am. "Talk to her, Aidan. Tell her that holing up in a safe house with a hunky, tattooed man who gave her the best sexing of her entire life is where she needs to be."

"Shane, you promised!" Cat barks, inspiring a hoarse yip of outrage from Fifi, who apparently agrees that everyone should back off and let Cat do as she damned well pleases.

"Quiet." I point a finger at Fang. "You haven't been awake long enough to weigh in on this situation."

"Yeah," Shane says, wagging her own finger at the dog. "And you're not old enough to be hearing about your mama's sex life. Cover your ears."

"And you, behave." I shift my finger to point at Shane. "No more talk about what Cat and I have done or will do when we're alone behind closed doors. Believe it or not, we're both private people, and embarrassing us isn't helping anything right now."

Shane bites her lip, looking legitimately penitent. "I'm sorry. Teasing is the way I handle stress. And I'm really stressed. I don't want to lose my best friend because she's too stubborn to let you help her stay alive until Friday."

"I'm not stubborn," Cat says, inspiring twin "yeah, right" sounds from Shane and me. "I'm not!" she insists. "I'm willing to let Aidan help me stay alive until Friday morning, just not at a safe house or a friend's house. Maybe we could get a hotel or something?"

"Lip isn't going to like this." I bring my hand to my chin, scratching at my beard as my wheels begin to turn. "Or Bash either, but…I may have an idea."

"What's that?" Cat puts Fifi down on the island as Shane sets out a dish of water. The dog hurries over and daintily dips her head to drink.

"Why don't we get out of the city for a few days?" I say, thinking of my stepmother's text, offering the use of one of her cottages. "Go somewhere Nico won't expect you to go."

Red's eyes light up. "You mean a road trip? You know I love a road trip."

"A short road trip," I clarify. "Just five or six hours."

Cat bounces lightly on her toes, apparently just the thought of being on the road infusing her with a shot of energy. "Five or six hours is more than enough time to eat an entire package of Red Vines and overdose on Dr Pepper. And where do we end up at the end of this journey?"

"I was thinking my parents' place in the Finger Lakes." I smile as Fang finishes her drink and comes to sniff my hand instead of Cat's. "My stepmother owns a winery and bed and breakfast. She uses her maiden name, so on the off-chance Nico figures out who I am and starts looking for family connections, there's no way he'll trace me to Julie. We should be safe lying low there for a few days, and I know she'd be thrilled to meet you. I used to talk about you a lot back when I was on break from college."

Cat's eyes narrow on Fifi as her lips press thoughtfully together. "This is an excellent plan, but I think Fang should stay here with Aunt Shane. If that's okay with you, Shane."

"Of course it is," Shane says, clapping her hands lightly together.

"But I thought you couldn't have pets in the building." I rub my new best friend behind the ears until her tongue lolls out of one side of her mouth. "It's no problem to take Fang with us. My parents love dogs and I—"

"No, that can't happen," Red says with a firm shake of her head. "I need her to love me best. She's already starting to like you better. If we take her with us, she'll break up with me and convince you to buy a man purse—the better to tote her around Manhattan on your motorcycle—and let her be the live-in mascot for your tattoo shop."

"Only service dogs are allowed in the shop."

"But the man purse is still on the table?" Cat asks, amusement in her voice.

I shrug. "A man has to carry shit, and sometimes my wallet gives me a cramp in my ass if my jeans are too tight."

"Shane, save me." Cat leans across the island to squeeze her friend's hand. "You have to watch Fang so she'll still love me when this is all over."

Shane laughs. "She will always love you, crazy pants, but yes, I can hide Feefs from the mean old HOA for a week or so. She's such a good puppy. She'll know not to bark when the grouchy man downstairs is at home. We'll have an amazing time and get all rested up to celebrate your new lease on life when you get home."

"Perfect," Cat says, turning back to me. "I hope you're not too sad that it will be just you and me."

I shake my head. "Not at all. I like just you and me."

And I do. In fact, I can't wait to be on the open road, zooming away from the dangerous men, dark memories, and bad habits of the city, looking forward to a few days with Cat all to myself.

From the text archives of Curved for her Pleasure and Polka Dot Panties

Panties: Where is he, Curve? Where are you hiding him?

Curved: Red! Good to hear from you. I was just about to call you to talk about this. I'm—

Panties: Don't try to placate me, Curve. Tell me where Hole in the Ground is. I know you're with him. I just went by his dorm, and his roommate said that you'd been there a few minutes ago.

Curve: That doesn't

Panties: The roommate also said he'd overheard something about Hole's life being in danger. He didn't seem very impressed when I told him that I'm the one who's going to kick Hole's ass so hard his anus is going to pop out through his left nostril.

Then he mentioned that I looked familiar.

If he had said anything about the picture, I would have kicked his ass just for being in the wrong place at the wrong time and having eyes.

You need to hand over Hole before I vent my rage on innocent people.

Curved: Where are you?

Panties: I'm crossing the quad, scanning dark corners for signs of a snake and his handler hiding in the grass. Where the fuck are you and that shitty piece of shit is a better question.

Curve: I want you to take a deep breath, Panties. Uncurl your death mittens and find a place to sit down in the shade. It's a beautiful day.

Panties: It is *not* a beautiful day. It is a shit day! This day is a diaper full of green baby diarrhea.

Curve: How about I send you some of that soothing, pan flute music you like to listen to? I'll gift it to your Music Monster account right now. You can pop your ear buds in, relax in the

shade, and let yourself be lulled by the pan flute for fifteen minutes while I deal with Hole.
And as soon as I'm done I'll come get you.

Panties: No, you're not dealing with Hole! I'M dealing with Hole. It's my ass that he plastered all over the Internet, so it's my ass that's going to make HIS ass sorry that it was ever born.

Curve: I made him take it down, Red. That's the first thing I did when I got to his room. He's erased all the posts, and I made sure he wiped it from his phone and his computer, too.

Panties: That's not good enough!

Curve: He's also going to be on disciplinary leave from the Dashers for the next month and have to perform a trial by fire to get back into the club's good graces.
And you can decide his trial by fire. Does that sound fair?
I was thinking of making him run up and down the street on pub-crawl night wearing nothing but a pair of polka dot panties. That would be fitting revenge, right?

Panties: No it wouldn't. Because he enjoys running around half-naked, making a fool of himself. Remember the lingerie he wore to the cross-dressing event last year?

Everyone has already seen his junk. No one had ever seen mine.
But now the entire school has seen me squatting to pee in the grass, and the only way to make this better is to kill Hole with my bare hands.

Curve: First of all, not everyone has seen you squatting to pee. The post on the message board only had five hundred hits by the time I heard what happened and made him take it down.

Panties: Five hundred! Is that supposed to make me feel better?!
That only five hundred people have seen me peeing with a dumb look on my face?!
Oh my God, I'm never going to be able to show my face on campus or in Pennsylvania or anywhere else for the rest of my life!

Curve: Secondly, your "junk" as you so delicately put it, was not visible in the shot, just your ass. Your junk is still your private business and your ass is completely stunning.
Yes, I understand that the picture was taken and shared without your knowledge or permission, and believe me, that pisses me off as much as it does you.

Panties: I sincerely doubt that, you patronizing jackass.

Curve: But you have nothing to be embarrassed of, is what I was going to say. And I'm not being a patronizing jackass! I'm trying to make you feel better, while also making sure you don't get kicked out of school.

If you kick his ass, you will get kicked out of school, Panties. Assault is grounds for mandatory expulsion.

Yes, if you tell the disciplinary board about the picture, Hole will probably get kicked out, too. But will that really be worth it? I know you love it here, and your dad is a hardass who will not be happy about his daughter getting kicked out of university for fighting. Do you really want to fuck up your whole life just because an asshole thought it would be funny to take a picture of you while you were peeing?

And Hole is sorry, by the way. He really is.

I don't think he realized how upsetting this would be to you. He wanted to prank you, not shame or enrage you. He's as dumb as a sock full of rocks, but he's not cruel. You know that. If he were, then I would be beating the shit out of him myself.

But you should see him. He feels terrible. He's all sniffly and sad, and so scared he's about to crap his pants.

Panties: Then he should.

Curve: Should what?

Panties: Crap his pants. Tell him to crap his pants and then take a long slow walk around the quad so I can watch people's faces as he goes by.

Curve: You're serious?

Panties: The walk needs to last at least fifteen minutes.
The quad is packed, so that should be enough to make sure five hundred people see him wandering around with his pants full of his own feces.

Curve: Jesus Christ. That's really nasty, Red.

Panties: Those are my terms.
Communicate them to Hole. Should he choose to accept my offer, I promise I won't lay a hand on him.

Curve: All right.

Panties: All right, you'll communicate my terms? Or all right, he'll do it?

Curve: He'll do it. He's already done it, actually, and it smells like shit.
Imagine that.
We're starting toward the quad right now. He wants me to tell you that he's sorry, and that this is worth it to earn your forgiveness.

Panties: I didn't offer forgiveness. I offered him the chance not to get his face smashed in with my foot.
If he wants forgiveness he's going to have to change his Dasher name to Shit Pants for Brains and write Panties is My Master on the back of his lucky hat in puffy paint.

Curve: Done. Name change official as of now, paint to be applied after he's finished his walk of shame.
But if you have any more messages for him, you'll have to convey them yourself. He's on his own from here on out. I can't stand the smell of him a second longer. It smells like he had rotten tacos for breakfast.
I see you, by the way. Can I come over and watch with you?
Am I forgiven for the sin of trying to keep you from getting kicked out of school?

Panties: Yes. You're forgiven.
And yes, you can come watch with me. Public shamings are always more fun when shared with a friend. Even the Pilgrims knew that.
I'm still too pissed to thank you, but I probably will later. Sometimes my anger at the injustice of the world gets the better of me.

Curve: Like that time in Kathmandu?

Panties: You know we do not speak of Kathmandu.

Curve: Are you ever going to tell me whether anything really happened in Kathmandu, or if you've just been fucking with my head for almost two years?

Panties: Probably not. We women have to maintain an aura of mystery, you know. And I have to work harder to maintain mine now that you've seen my bare ass.

Curve: I have not. A picture isn't anything like the real thing. I consider us still on a no ass-information shared basis.
But if it really bothers you, I can show you my bare ass later so we'll be even.

Panties: Make me that offer later tonight, when I'm drunk enough to take you up on it without blushing my face off.

Curve: Will do. ;)

Panties: Now hurry up and get over here. People are starting to notice that Shit Pants for Brains has shit in his pants, too. I want to laugh at their horrified expressions with you.

Curve: *putting down phone* *running straight to you*

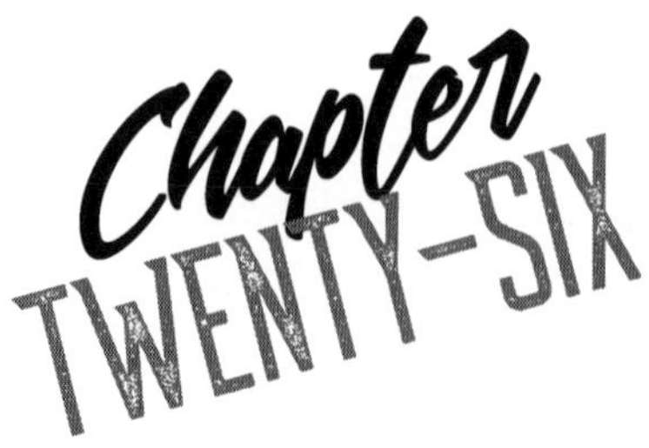

We get on the road fast, and by mid-morning, Manhattan is a distant memory as we wind through lush green hills toward the Finger Lakes region. We stop only for gas and snacks and by unspoken agreement refrain from talking about anything that will remind us of why we're on this impromptu road trip.

And eventually, my jaw relaxes, and I'm able to enjoy the drive and, of course, the company.

"Why on earth did you buy these?" Cat pulls a package of bright blue coconut snack cakes from the bag of road munchies I bought at the last gas station. "Ew. You know these are made of rat feces, radioactive food coloring, and armpit shavings, right?"

I snatch my package of Glo Balls from her fingers and drop it between my thighs before returning my hands to the wheel.

"Give them back! I wasn't finished reading all of the

disgusting ingredients." Cat reaches for the snack cakes, but I slap her hand away and point a warning finger in her direction.

"Stop. Right now. No messing with me while I'm driving."

She huffs. "But I wasn't finished examining your Glo Balls!"

"I never let women examine my Glo Balls on a first date."

"That's a dirty lie," she says, walking her fingers up onto the console between us. "I examined your balls last night. And that was basically a first date. A weird first date, but still…"

"We were friends for years, so last night was nothing like a first date. And you did not examine my balls. You didn't even roll them around in your fingers, let alone get up close and personal."

She hums beneath her breath. "All right. Point taken." She walks her fingers back over to her own seat and starts digging through the snack bag again. "I'll make a memo to do a thorough exam at my earliest convenience."

"Don't you mean my earliest convenience?" I ignore my thickening cock, which is insisting he's way more interesting than my balls, and should be examined as soon as I can find a smooth place to pull over onto the shoulder. "I mean, I'm the one who's going to have to get naked."

"Not necessarily," she says, a husky note in her voice that does nothing to help the increasingly uncomfortable situation below my belt. "I could always lean over and do an exam right here. I've never given road head before, but I'm willing to give it the college try."

My cock strains the fabric of my jeans, insisting that is an amazing idea, but I shake my head and warn Cat, "Behave," as I rip open my Glo Balls.

Shane didn't seem overly stressed about loaning Cat

and me her late aunt's vintage 1960s Rolls Royce, but I'm determined not to get so much as a ding on this car, which means no veering off onto the shoulder because I'm getting head while driving.

Though now, thanks to Cat, I can't shake the image of her kneeling at my feet, her gaze holding mine as she swirls her tongue around the tip of my cock. I try to replace the visual with something else, but not even imagining that my snack cake is actually made of all the gross things Cat said it was made of is enough to completely kill the fantasy.

I need conversation and quick.

"Remember the road trip to the Death Valley marathon?" I ask, inspiring a hungry moan from Cat.

"Yes. Oh my God, I ate so many Lemon Heads on that trip." She bites into a Red Vine and chews with a sigh. "Red Vines are good, but you can't beat a good Lemon Head binge. I ate those things until my tongue had first degree acid burns and it hurt to swallow."

I nod. "I can't believe so many stores stopped carrying those. They're so fucking good."

"So good." She hums again, wagging a fresh Red Vine toward my side of the car. "But they did make me drink a ton of water, which made me have to pee every hour, which led to us stopping the bus at the grossest rest stop ever."

"I remember." I take another bite of my Glo Ball, talking around the sponge cake disintegrating in my mouth. "Was that the place where you said it looked like a giant butt had been stabbed in the women's room?"

"Yes!" She slaps me on the leg, clearly pleased with my recall. "It was the nastiest thing I've ever seen. There was crap all over the walls. Seriously, all the way up to the ceiling in some places. It was like a giant butt had walked in there and been murdered all over the women's room, in every stall, all over the sinks. Just nasty butt murder everywhere the eye could see."

A burst of laughter constricts my midsection, making me fight to keep from spitting out my last bite of cake. When I've managed to swallow, I say, "You are so fucking gross sometimes."

"I am not," she says, but I can hear the smile in her voice and know she's pleased with herself. "I'm just trying to accurately describe a horrific situation, Aidan. It's called commitment to communication."

"I figured it had to be pretty bad for you to decide to squat behind a bush instead."

Cat makes a growling noise. "That's right. That's when Hole in the Ground took the infamous picture. I forgot about that."

"How could you forget?" I cast a surprised glance her way, before turning my eyes back to the road. "You almost murdered the kid."

She leans her seat back, propping her bare feet on the dash. "I did not. I was mad, but I got over it. Hole was actually a pretty sweet idiot. Dumb as rocks, but sweet." She takes another bite of her candy. "And I've had much worse things happen to me since then."

The words banish my smile, reminding me why we hauled ass out of Manhattan as fast as Shane's Rolls could carry us. We didn't even take time to go home to pack. Shane loaned Cat some clothes, I insisted I could grab a couple pairs of jeans and some T-shirts on the way upstate, and we bought toothbrushes at the last gas station.

We're not on an adventure; we're on the run, and I can't afford to forget that for a second.

I only talked to Lip for a few minutes before we left—he was on duty and up to his armpits in work—but our conversation made it clear Cat's not out of the woods. There is some concern that Nico may have found out about the upcoming sting operation and be making plans to leave the country. There are also rumors that he refuses to leave without a certain redhead, a fact that has enraged half his family, some of whom may be willing to take drastic measures to remove what they see as a threat to their golden boy's safety.

When I told Lipman about the break-in at Cat's place, he insisted we come down to the station to file a report and allow him to personally escort us to the safe house afterward. He wasn't happy when I explained our alternative plans, but once I assured him that no one knew where we were headed—I didn't even tell Shane the name of my stepmother's bed and breakfast—he grudgingly admitted that we'd probably be okay. He refused to give his blessing, but he did wish us luck and assured Cat that he would contact her as soon as the danger had passed.

He also urged us both to keep our cell phones close for the next few days, hinting that maybe the timetable for the raid had been moved up. This could all be over in less than forty-eight hours, a fact that makes me simultaneously relieved and strangely…sad.

"It's going to be weird," Cat says softly, dropping her half-eaten Red Vine back into the snack bag.

"What's that?" I check our rearview mirror for the tenth time, but the road behind us is as empty as it's been since we left the highway in favor of a back-road route to Ithaca, New

York.

"Not being worried all the time," she says, setting the bag near her feet. "Being able to laugh with a male friend or colleague without worrying that Nico is spying on me and getting nuts about it. It's amazing how quickly being afraid can become the new normal."

My jaw tightens. "I wish you'd never met the son of a bitch."

"I don't. I'm glad I met him." She tucks her legs beneath her as she shifts to face my side of the car. "As scary as it's been, it's also been a wake-up call. It wasn't until I became a statistic myself that I truly understood how horrific the statistics are. I mean, a third of the women who are murdered in the U.S. are killed by men they were romantically involved with. That's over a thousand women every year losing their lives to men who are supposed to love them."

"That's insane." I blink hard, trying to wrap my head around a number like that. "I mean, I knew things were bad, but not that bad."

"I know," Cat says. "And on a national level we're doing absolutely nothing to make things better. In fact, most states are cutting funding for shelters and assistance programs even as the need for those programs increases." She crosses her arms more tightly across her chest. "So, yeah, I'm glad I met Nico. And as soon as this is behind me, I'm going to find a way to make things better for women who don't have the money to hire a Spectacular Rascal to watch their backs."

"You should start a charity, or help fundraise for one. You lawyer types are great at fundraising, right?"

"I've done my share of raising funds," she says, nodding thoughtfully. "Though Shane is better at that. That's what she does for a living. She runs her late aunt's charitable trust."

"Or you could run for office," I say. "I'd vote for you."

She grunts. "As long as you promise not to tell anyone that I inhaled."

"My lips are sealed," I promise, reaching out to take her hand.

Her fingers curl around mine. "What's this for?"

"For being you. For being strong and taking a shit sandwich and turning it into the need to make the world a better place."

"Taking a butt murder and turning it into a butt ballet?" she asks with a laugh.

I squeeze her hand. "You can joke, but I'm serious. I'm proud of you, and I'm… I'm glad we're friends again."

"Me, too," she whispers, returning the squeeze. "I've missed you."

"I've missed you, too." I take a deep breath, trying not to read too much into her words. It's been a hell of a twenty-four hours. We're both exhausted, and taking anything said right now too seriously could be an emotionally damaging mistake. But I can't help hoping this means she'll be up for more than friendship in the future.

"And I meant that part about running for office," I continue. "Though you'll probably have to clean up your language. You've got a dirty mouth for a politician."

She smirks. "Again, I remind you of the diseased orangutan with the Brillo Pad wig that became a GOP nominee."

I nod, taking my set-down like a man. "Again. You're right."

"I usually am," she says with a yawn. "God, I'm tired. Can I nap, or will you take that as a sign of desertion? I know you didn't get any more sleep than I did last night."

"No, go ahead and nap." I release her hand, but can't resist squeezing her thigh before I return my fingers to the wheel. The urge to touch her gets stronger with every passing minute. "I'll wake you up if I need to."

"Are you sure?" She yawns so hard her jaw cracks before she adds, "Because I can totally stay awake and poke you with Red Vines."

"I'm fine," I insist. "One of us should be rested and ready to gossip with Julie. My dad isn't much of a talker, so my stepmother gets pretty excited about company."

I wait a moment, but Cat doesn't respond. When I glance over again, she's already asleep, her lashes fanning out across her pale cheeks and her lips slightly parted, all the sweetness she does her best to hide while she's awake on display. She's beautiful—so beautiful a crazy part of me wants to pull over and stare, just for a little while.

But we have hours to go before we reach my parents' place. And hopefully, if I play my cards right, I'll have the chance to watch Cat sleep again in the not too distant future.

Cat wakes up when we stop for gas outside Ithaca, and insists on dragging me into the mall by the interstate to get some clothes to throw in the duffle bag Shane loaned me.

As we wander around the men's department of a store that smells like a cologne factory jizzed all over it, she hooks her arm through mine. Together, we pick out a couple pairs of jeans, two tee shirts, a button-up in case Julie insists on one of her big sit-down dinners, and two packages of boxer briefs because, "you can re-wear jeans, but you don't want to get in a wearing-dirty-boxers-inside-out situation."

"My parents do own a washing machine," I say, even as I let Cat tuck a third package of underwear beneath her arm.

"We don't want to waste time doing laundry," she says, leading the way toward the checkout counter. "We'll be too busy day-drinking. I haven't had a solid, midafternoon wine buzz in way too long, and I love wine tasting. It combines three of my favorite things—day-drinking, nature, and shopping for weird crafts made out of used corks."

"We're supposed to be laying low. We'll have to keep the wine tasting confined to the private tasting room at my parents' place."

She smiles and lifts her brows. "Maybe not. We could be cleared to resume business as usual any minute, Aidan. And the minute we're cleared, I'm renting a limo and taking you wine tasting to celebrate."

"Sounds good," I say, though a selfish part of me likes the idea of lying low with Cat for a few days, of having her all to myself before the real world comes crashing in. But she's right—the sooner Nico is behind bars and we're cleared to go back to our old lives, the better.

I pull out my wallet, doing my best to ignore the tight, unsettled, unsatisfied feeling building in my chest, but she's already slapped her credit card down on top of my pile. "Don't fight me," she warns. "I owe you after nearly getting you killed last night. I owe you more than clothes, but this is a good place to start."

Reluctantly, I put away my wallet, saving my response until she's signed the credit card slip and we're walking out of the cologne fog toward the sun shining beyond the glass double doors.

"You don't owe me anything. I'm the one who let *you* down," I say softly. "I should have stayed up to stand guard instead of going to sleep. Or I should have insisted we find somewhere to hide where Nico wouldn't be able to find you. If I'd taken the threat more seriously—"

"If you'd taken the threat more seriously, you wouldn't have taken the job," she says, cutting me off. "So, again, I'm glad things worked out the way they did. And I'm glad to be here with you." As we step outside, she lifts her face to the sun and sighs. "I feel like I can breathe for the first time in weeks. This trip may be the best idea you've ever had."

"I don't know." I open the passenger's side door for her. "I've got a history of having really good ideas. There was the marathon party bus, and you remember the Dasher T-shirt contest."

"That *was* brilliant! I was so sad when mine finally fell apart in the wash."

"Which design did you have, again?" I ask, grinning because she's grinning, and when she's happy her smile is completely infectious.

"Run Like You're Being Chased by a T-Rex," she says, laughing. But her smile fades as she wraps her arm around my waist and leans into me. The moment her body fits against mine I'm instantly warm all over, making me wonder if it would always be like this, if Cat and I are like a spark and tinder, destined to ignite whenever we touch. "So what are we going to tell your parents? Do they know that you're a professional Spectacular Rascal?"

"No, they don't." I toss the bag of clothes onto the seat so I can hold her properly. I haven't had the chance to hold her since everything went down, and I want to fully appreciate the miracle of her—warm, safe, and close, looking up at me like she's thinking about letting me in.

Assuming I don't screw shit up, of course.

I search her eyes, choosing my next words carefully. "I could tell them about the business and that you're my client. But I can guarantee that my father will think I'm crazy, fucking with him, or both."

She winces. "Your dad and my dad would have gotten along great. Both kind of stuffy and old-fashioned, aren't they?"

"My dad has devoted his life to making wine barrels exactly the way his ancestors made them in medieval France. So yes, he's behind the times. He still uses a straight razor to shave and is incapable of responding to a text." I shrug. "I don't really care if he thinks I'm crazy. I'm used to that by now. But I thought, maybe, if it's okay with you, we could just tell my parents that we're…dating."

"Dating." She turns her head, studying me out of the corners of her eye. "It would have to be a pretty serious dating for you to bring me home for a visit, wouldn't it? I know people change, but you never used to be the 'bring her home to meet the folks' kind of guy."

"I'm even less that guy now than I was back in college," I confess. "But I don't think we'll have a problem convincing them that we're serious."

"And why's that?" She goes still, motionless, even as her gaze sharpens to a knifepoint. That gaze is dangerous, capable of severing my connection to Cat with a single slice, and my only defense against it is the truth.

"I like you. I've always liked you." I pause, summoning the guts to put it all out there and risk hearing her tell me the Cat ship has sailed all over again. "I used to think you were just one of those friends who stay with you even when they're not in your life anymore. But now that I'm not a twenty-two-year-old idiot, I realize it's more than that. It was always more than that."

"More?" she asks softly.

"More than friends," I say. "And I'd like to find out how

much more. How about you?"

I thought her gaze was sharp before, but now it narrows to a surgical blade. I swear I can feel that look probing at my insides, looking for rotten places in my story, but she doesn't pull away from our embrace.

"If it's too soon after all this stuff with your ex, I get it," I say. "It won't make my day, that's for damned sure, but…" I swallow, and it's not easy, because I've suddenly realized just how unhappy it would make me to lose the right to touch her like this. "But I'll wait until you're ready. If you think you might be interested, that is."

She remains frozen for another long, gut-twisting moment during which my palms start to sweat a stupid amount, making me feel like I'm fifteen instead of thirty-fucking-two. I'm about to remove my sweaty mitts from her waist long enough to discreetly wipe them on my jeans when she says, "I'm interested. And it's not too soon. Eleven years is long enough to wait, don't you think?"

"I do." My grin breaks across my face like an egg cracked up the middle, sending all my happiness spilling out in a messy, very uncool flood.

But Red has never given a shit about playing it cool. In fact, I'm pretty sure she likes me better like this.

She confirms that suspicion when she grins and says, "I'm so hungry I could eat your face without even bothering to shave the beard off first."

I hug her closer. "I told you we needed something more than candy for breakfast."

"You were right," she says. "Take me somewhere pretty and feed me? Bonus points if there is greasy diner food involved."

Pressing my lips together, I lift my gaze to the clear sky.

"Pretty and greasy… That's a tricky combo, but I think there's a place in the town square that fits the bill. It's got killer potato pancakes and matzo ball soup."

"Perfect."

And then, before I realize what's happening, she's pushed up onto her toes, wrapped her arms around my neck, and kissed me.

Right away I can tell this kiss is different. It's still combustible, but it's also sweet, unguarded, and so addictive I can't seem to stop kissing her back. So I don't. I stand in the middle of a mall parking lot and make love to Red's pretty mouth until I lose all awareness of space and time, until there is nothing but her lips, her taste, her heat, and the feeling of being exactly where I'm supposed to be.

Chapter Twenty-Eight

After lunch, we walk around the square, collecting more very important overnight items like deodorant, mouthwash, and light brown mascara Cat insists she needs to keep her eyelashes from disappearing. I tell her she looks perfect with or without eyelashes; she tells me I'm a beautiful liar and makes me wait outside the drugstore while she finishes buying girl things. I stand on the sidewalk and smile like an idiot because turns out I like being called a beautiful liar when Cat is the one doing the name-calling.

We finally head out of town around one-thirty and pull up to the winery in the hills outside Ithaca proper a little after two, rolling slowly down the gravel road to keep from getting dust on the vines growing on either side of the drive. I keep one eye on the road and one on Cat, not wanting to miss the moment she sees The View.

Even when I was sixteen, obsessed with dirt bike culture

and pissed as hell at my dad for getting remarried, I was secretly glad when we moved in with Julie. I could never resist this view.

Almost every summer afternoon, I would take my drawing pad and pastels out into the fields at the edge of the vineyards, climb a tree, and spend hours sketching the curves of the hills down to Lake Cayuga, the sailboats on the water, and the sunset suffusing everything in a gauzy, dreamlike glow that reminded me of Italian frescos I'd seen in museums.

Before The View, I hadn't been much of a landscape person, but those afternoons spent capturing slices of everyday magic helped set the course for the rest of my life.

At sixteen, I wasn't sure if I wanted to be a painter, a professional BMX biker, or a cooper like every other Knight back to the days when Knights actually were knights, as well as barrel makers. But after a couple of summers in my tree, I realized that those hours spent alone, growing as an artist, were the ones that meant the most to me. Those were the times when I was most alive, most in tune with myself and satisfied with my place in the world.

After high school, I convinced my dad to let me pursue a degree in fine art, with the unspoken understanding that I would return to Ithaca when my four years were through and complete my training in the ancient art of molding oak into barrels. Instead, at the beginning of my sophomore year at Penn U, when I was really getting into the idea of tattooing as a career, I got a job working part time with a building crew who appreciated my way with wood. I saved my pennies, and by my senior year I had enough stored away to pay my way to Japan to apprentice with one of the tattoo world's living legends.

To say my father was pissed would be the understatement

of the past several millennia.

He was a devastating mixture of disappointed and enraged. We didn't speak a word to each other for two years. He hated me for betraying him, I hated him for refusing to let me choose my own path, and we both hated apologizing too much to make any meaningful effort to mend the rift between us.

We might have stayed estranged forever—or at least a decade or two—if Julie hadn't been diagnosed with breast cancer. Being faced with the possibility of losing someone we both loved is what it took for us to pull our heads out of our asses and get back to being family. I was there for him, he was there for Julie, and a new normal—a normal where we enjoy each other's company without ever discussing coopering or tattooing—was established.

Which reminds me…

"Just FYI, my dad and I never talk about my work or his work," I say, pulling to the side of the road to make room for a bus packed with drunk tourists. "It's part of our truce agreement. So if talk turns to professional stuff, don't be surprised if I don't chime in."

"Got it." She nods, leaning farther out the window and inhaling deeply. "It smells so good here."

"It does." I study her blissed-out expression, not certain she's understood me. "But I'm serious, Red. I don't talk work with my father. Ever. It gets ugly if we even start."

She nods again. "I get it. My dad and I never discussed religion, gays in the military, Ronald Reagan, my mother, my father's family on his dad's side, sex, gun control, pot, feminine hygiene, or Elvis Presley. I'm very good at avoiding family trigger topics."

"Why Elvis? What did he ever do?" I pull back onto the road, satisfied that she does indeed get me. I should never have doubted her.

"I had a crush on him when I was little," she says, letting her fingers play through the wind as we drive. "I made Dad perform a wedding at sea between me and my teddy bear, who was playing the part of Elvis in Blue Hawaii. Dad had one of his friends film it and brought the video out every Christmas to torture me." Her tone grows wistful. "It was actually one of our favorite times of the year, but I pretended to hate it because I was a teenager and that's what teenagers do, you know."

"I do," I say. "I pretended to hate the winery when we first moved, but it's the most beautiful place I've ever lived. Hell, one of the most beautiful places I've ever seen."

"I'll say." Cat's jaw drops as we turn the corner and the money shot comes into view. "Wow, Aidan, it's gorgeous. It's paradise with a side of Tuscan countryside."

And even though I've seen it a hundred times before, the panorama of the rolling hills with the lake far below and the neat, ordered rows of vines spiraling away from the big red barn that serves as the tasting room, pings pleasure centers deep in my brain. But it isn't the landscape that takes my breath away. It's the redhead leaning forward with her hands on the dash to get a better look, an awed expression on her face that makes me want to arrange to surprise her with wonderful things at least once a week.

Her gaze is still glued to the scene unfolding before us as we wind down toward the tasting barn, and she reaches over to take my hand. "Thanks for bringing me here. I love it already."

"My pleasure," I say, threading my fingers through hers. "Hopefully my parents won't change your mind."

"No worries. I love parents and parents love me. I know how to put on my best manners. I was raised by a general, remember?"

"Just know that my stepmom talks all the time, and my dad hardly ever talks at all. It's nothing personal. She never listens to what other people have to say, and Dad gives everyone the cold shoulder. That's just business as usual."

She tilts her head, staring at the entrance to the barn, where my father's mounted fish trophies and my stepmom's collection of antique road signs serve as eclectic decorations. "I'm not worried."

"Good. You shouldn't be," I say, trying to hide the fact that I'm worried for her. The closer we get to my father, the more certain I am that he'll be a cranky bastard to Cat and make me want to smash a fist into his grouchy face for the first time in years. I've come to terms with the grouch factor, but Cat has been through enough. She doesn't deserve to be forced to humor a fractious old fart on top of it.

But there's no turning back now. As we circle the barn and pull up into the driveway in front of the Mediterranean style villa overlooking the lake, Julie and Dad are already out in the flowerbeds, up to their elbows in dirt.

Julie stands immediately, waving an enthusiastic arm. She's talking before Cat and I can shut off the engine.

"There you are!" She pulls off her gloves and tosses them onto the sun-warmed driveway, the skin around her blue eyes crinkling as she smiles. "Oh look at you! Aidan, I swear you're even taller than I remember! And you must be Cat. Look at that hair! Oh my God, you're like a pre-Raphaelite model from a painting. Isn't she, Jim?"

My father, predictably, says nothing, but he does stand

and step out of the flowerbed with a semi-civil nod in Cat's direction. He's wearing khaki pants and a button-up shirt because Jim Knight refuses to wear jeans, even to garden, because jeans are undignified.

"Just gorgeous, and such beautiful skin." Julie floats toward Cat with her arms outstretched. "I'm so glad you're here, love. You are so welcome and warmly received." She pulls Cat in for a hug that lasts a little too long because Julie's hugs always last too long, but thankfully Cat doesn't seem to mind.

She returns the embrace with a smile. "Thank you so much for having me. I can't wait to see where Aidan lived as an angsty teen."

Julie chuckles, releasing Cat from her embrace, but still clinging to her hand. "Did you hear that, Jim?"

My dad grunts in response, which is actually a lot from him. But then he always enjoys it when other people give me shit.

"He *was* angsty, especially at first," Julie whispers to Cat with a wink for me. "But sweet, too. There's a heart of gold in that big furry body. I'll tell you all the embarrassing stories over a glass of wine or three. You drink?"

"Yes," Cat says, grinning. "The sooner the better. I can't wait to hear embarrassing Aidan stories. I'll tell you mine, and you can tell me yours."

Julie laughs. "Oh good! Finally someone willing to tell on you, Aidan! I love this girl already."

"Now, come on, Red," I say, popping the trunk to grab our bags. "I've never told your embarrassing stories to anyone."

"That's because you're a gentleman." Cat detaches herself from my stepmother and crosses to claim the small roller suitcase Shane loaned her this morning. "And I really do like that about you."

"Yeah, well, just remember how much dirt I have on you, Panties," I murmur as we start toward the front door. "Push me too far and I might forget my manners."

"I hope so," she says for my ears only. "I like that side of you, too."

The sexy, suggestive lilt in her voice would usually have been enough to get my blood pumping faster, but at that moment we draw even with my old man, who falls in beside us.

"How's the garden?" I ask, nodding toward the decorative cabbages, one of the many weird things my father collects. "Cabbages are looking good."

He grunts again. "Good enough."

"Are those your fish mounted above the door to the barn?" Cat asks pleasantly, kindly ignoring the fact that my father is a terrible host and hasn't said so much as hello to her. Lucky for him, Julie handles everything to do with the guest cottages on the other side of the property, or the business would have failed years ago. "That tiger fish is impressive. I pulled a three-footer out of Lake Tanganyika on a fish safari with my dad, but I've never seen one that big."

As the words leave her mouth, my father lights up. He literally turns a lighter shade of tan as some cranky-old-man filter is lifted from his features by the pure joy of meeting a fellow angler and fish aficionado. Of all the things Cat could have said to this man, she picked the absolute perfect thing, the one guaranteed to un-mudgeon the curmudgeon.

"Four feet, ten inches, and eighty-eight pounds," Dad says, his barrel chest puffing out. "And that's no fish story. Biggest striped waterdog our safari guide had ever seen that wasn't a goliath."

"Jesus," Cat breathes, the proper degree of awe in her tone. "That must have been one hell of a fish fight. What kind of tackle were you using?"

My father launches into the war story of Jim versus the Striped Waterdog with Teeth as long as a Man's Finger, one of his favorite stories in the world, and by the time we've dropped our bags inside the door and joined Julie on the back patio for wine, my father has arranged to steal the seat next to Cat's. But I don't mind.

I've only brought three women home in my entire life, and never in the course of my dating career have I given two shits what my father thought about the girl I'm with. My father doesn't care much for me, his own son, and I've learned not to have feelings about *that*. I'm so far beyond caring what my father thinks of my taste in romantic partners it's laughable.

Or so I'd thought…

But as I watch my father smile—smile, like a normal human being capable of being amused and not grunty and scary—at Red, I can't help hoping the spell won't wear off. I like that Jim realizes that she's something special. I like hearing Cat talk fish and African safaris and old cars with my father and realizing that this is the way she must have talked to her own dad. It's a part of her I've never seen, and it makes me like her even more.

"Good job, big guy," Julie whispers as she refills my glass with her latest pinot noir. "I'm so happy for you, sweetheart. You deserve love with a wonderful girl."

She squeezes my shoulder and moves away to refill the other glasses before I can respond.

And I'm glad. Because I don't know what to say.

I'm not ready to name what I feel for Cat—certainly not something as big as love—but as she meets my eyes across the table with a smugly triumphant look that clearly says "see there, Curve, told you I'd make them love me," I can't help but smile.

She's a pain in my ass.

She's always been a pain in my ass.

But I'm beginning to think it's a pain it would be terrible to live without.

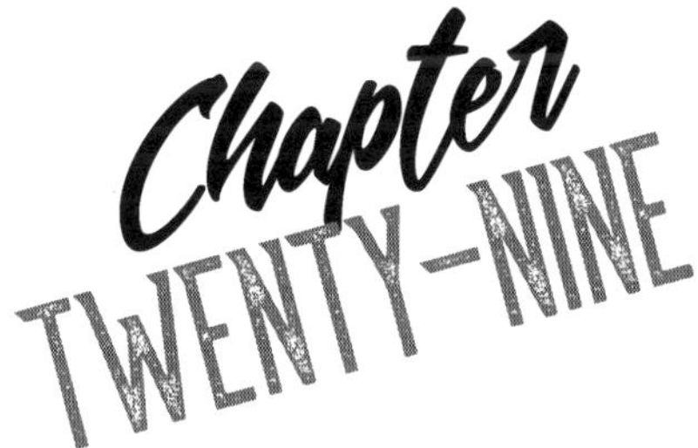

Chapter Twenty-Nine

By the time we drink wine, eat dinner, and drink some more wine while watching the sun set over Lake Cayuga, it's almost nine o'clock, I'm feeling no pain, and Cat is flushed and giggly.

"I'm fading fast," I finally whisper just after nine-thirty. "If we don't find our way to the cabin soon, I'm going to pass out on a lounge chair."

"Oh, thank God." She laughs again, a rich, round sound that sends happiness bubbling through my blood. "I'm so drunk and *soooo* tired. I'm going to pass out the second my head hits the pillow. I don't see how you're still awake. At least I had a nap in the car."

"Awesomeness," I say, or try to. The word is so badly slurred it inspires another giggle from Cat, attracting Julie's attention.

"Are you two ready to turn in?" she asks. "I made up the guest room for you upstairs."

“I thought you had a cottage free,” I say. The thought of sleeping down the hall from my father and stepmother, where they will be able to hear everything I say or do to Cat, is enough to sober me up pretty quickly.

“I do.” Julie stands, stretching her arms over her head. “But that was before I knew the friend you were bringing home was a *girl*friend. I had you two in one of the kid cabins, the ones with the bunk beds. It’s the only one I have free.”

“Oh, that’s fine,” Cat says, clearly not liking the thought of being under the same roof with my parents any more than I do. “We love bunk beds. It will be like the hostels we stayed at back in college.”

“Yeah. It will be great.” I nod enthusiastically, glad my father headed up to shower an hour ago. As smitten as he is with Cat, I’m sure he’d lobby to have us stay here so he could talk fish with her over coffee in the morning.

Julie shakes her head. “Are you sure? I mean, those mattresses are narrow and you’re—”

“We’re sure,” Cat and I both say at the same time, before she adds, “Yes, ma’am, we’re sure. And if it isn’t too rude I would love to head over to the cottage now. I’m starting to feel like the walking dead.”

“Of course.” Julie sets her glass of water on the deck table—the wise woman stopped after two glasses of wine, like the professional she is. “I’ll give you a ride over in the golf cart. It’s on the far side of the glen, so you should have privacy. The other cabins are full, but it’s a quiet crew. They turn in early, but they’ll be up early, too, so you two should get your rest.”

I pull her in for a hug, giving her an extra squeeze of thanks. “Will do.”

Fifteen minutes later, after driving Cat and I over and

giving us a brief guided tour of our cottage—a kitchenette, sitting area, bathroom, and a bedroom with two sets of bunk beds on either side of the cozy space—Julie waves good-bye and zips away up the hill.

Cat and I stand in the doorway, watching her go, silent for a moment.

A moment in which my exhaustion vanishes in the wake of the knowledge that I am alone. With Cat. And there's a bed less than ten feet away.

She glances up at me, her eyes glittering in the dim light. "Are you thinking what I'm thinking?"

I pull her inside, locking the door to the cottage before bracing my hands on either side of her face. "If you're thinking you're not ready to go straight to sleep anymore, then yes. I am."

"Right?" Her lips part as her hands come to my waist, trailing up under my shirt. The second her cool fingers brush across my hot skin, I'm hard. Hard, aching, and desperate to have her. "How could I even *think* about sleeping without taking a shower first?"

"A shower?" I bite my lip as her hands drift higher, molding to my chest. "You're sure a shower is all you want?"

"I haven't showered in over a day, Aidan," she says in mock horror as she brushes a thumb across my nipple, adding another item to the list of things on my body that are hard because of her. "That's disgusting. I'm a disgusting person."

"That's not the word I would have used." I move in closer, dropping my hands to her waist.

Her eyes darken, and her fingers curl until her nails dig into my chest. "It's not?"

I lower my head, bringing my lips inches from hers. "I was

thinking…delicious. That's the word that comes to mind when I think of you."

"Which makes *you* disgusting," she whispers in a husky voice I can feel in all the places I desperately want her to touch. "Can't you smell me?"

"I can." I inhale, humming in appreciation as her hands smooth around to my back, urging me closer. "You smell like sunshine and that sweet white wine you spilled on your shirt and…buttered popcorn." My lips curve in surprise. "When did you eat buttered popcorn?"

"I didn't." Her palms find my ass, and I flex my muscles beneath her grip, loving the way she touches me—without hesitation, without any doubt that every part of me is hers to explore. "That's what my sweat smells like at first, before it transforms into a more funky popcorn smell."

"That's amazing." I smooth my hand up her ribs, cupping her breast in my hand and finding her tight nipple through her tank top. "Your body is a fucking miracle of sexy evolution."

"So, buttered popcorn turns you on." Her breath rushes across my mouth as I intensify the pressure on her nipple. "Good to know. I'll invest in a popcorn machine for my living room and crank it up before you come over."

"Fuck buttered popcorn. *You* turn me on. Everything about you." I curl my fingers into the top of her shirt, tugging it low enough to bare her breast, drawing a soft gasp from her lips. "I need to get my mouth on you, Red. I need every part of you pressed against me."

She arches into my fingers as I find her nipple again, this time with nothing between us to mute the electricity that leaps between bare skin and bare skin. "Then you're going to have to get what you need in the shower, Mr. Knight."

"I'll fuck you in the shower." I reach for the bottom of her tank top, ripping her shirt and bra over her head in one smooth motion before pulling her back into my arms. "I'll fuck you anywhere, anytime. Dirty or clean, sweet or kinky, any way you want it, as long as I get to feel you come on my cock."

"How about sweet and dirty?" she asks, as I lift her up and turn to carry her into the bathroom, my hands braced beneath her fantastic ass and her legs wrapped tight around my waist. "I don't want too kinky tonight. I just want to make love to you."

My heart does a hard flip in my chest. I pause in the doorway to the bathroom, staring deep into her eyes. "I want to make love to you, too. So don't hide from me, okay?"

She blinks, but she doesn't tell me I'm crazy.

Instead she leans in, kissing me softly, deeply. Kissing me until my pulse races and I start feeling drunk all over again. But this time, I'm drunk on her, this woman who makes me feel things I've never felt with anyone else, who makes me want to stand still and dig deep and tell the truth.

"I mean it," I mumble against her lips as I set her down by the shower. "You ran away too fast last night."

"I was just taking precautionary measures," she says, working her words in between kisses as we dispose of the rest of our clothes as quickly as possible. "Running before you could beat me to it."

"Do I look like I'm running?" I reach past her to start the water, but keep my eyes on hers. "Even a little bit?"

She shakes her head slowly. "No. You look…beautiful. Have I told you that just looking at you makes me feel like I won some kind of lottery? How lucky am I? That I get to be with you, even for a night?"

"It's going to be way more than a night," I promise, heart skipping another beat as she steps close, pressing her warm skin to mine. "And you're the most beautiful thing I've ever seen, Red. Especially like this."

"Like what?" Her breath comes faster. "Naked and willing?"

"Naked and willing. And looking at me like there's nowhere else you'd rather be."

"There isn't." Her gaze softens the way it did for Fang, but better, because she's looking at *me,* and she's turned on, and I know that I'm going to get a lot more from her tonight than a scratch behind the ears. "Don't you know that by now? That you've always been one of my favorite people?"

"And you're one of mine." My cock throbs, hot and hard, against her belly, and I want her as much as I did last night, but it's not my dick that aches the most. There's a fiercer, painfully sweet ache spreading through my chest.

It hurts, but it's a good hurt. A hopeful hurt.

Maybe there has always been a girl out there who was made for me. And maybe I've found her again. And maybe now I'm going to be smart enough to hold on tight and give this one-in-a-million woman a hundred different reasons to stop running away.

"So stay with me," I whisper. "I promise I'll make it worth your while, feral squirrel."

She smiles, a big, beautiful smile that turns to a laugh as I take her hand and pull her into the spray. She's still laughing as I cup her ass in my hands and lift her off her feet, drawing her up my body until our lips are level.

"Be careful, Knight," she says, pressing a kiss to the tip of my nose. "Or I might just have to start falling hard for you all over again."

"Good," I say gruffly. "It's about time you caught up."

Her smile fades, and her eyes search mine for a long moment, while the warm water beats against our shoulders and my heart beats out a rhythm that's probably Morse code for her name, and I pray that she sees there's no reason to hold me at a distance.

In the end, I'm not sure what she sees, but she must like it, because pretty soon her smile is back, bigger and brighter than ever. "Then kiss me, sexy. And fuck me against the wall of the shower like you mean it."

"I'm always going to mean it," I promise, crushing my lips to hers.

And pretty soon I've got her pinned between the cool shower tiles and my burning skin, and I'm soaping up her breasts like it's my job. I let my fingers tease over her slick flesh again and again until she has the cleanest nipples in the Tri-state area and she's so wet I can feel the difference between the hot water splashing against my thigh and the hotter, stickier heat of her pussy as she grinds against my cock.

I wait until her breath is coming fast and she's moaning into my mouth as we kiss, but I don't hold out for begging tonight. I don't want to wait, and I don't want to make her wait. I just want to feel her tight and slick around me and know that I'm as close as I can be to the woman in my arms.

"Oh, God, Aidan. I love this. This moment, right here." Her head falls back against the tiles as I slide inside her, pushing deep until I'm buried to the hilt and she's pulsing around me, every throb of her pussy assuring me I'm welcome, wanted, wonderful.

I am enough, more than enough, and she is…perfect.

I want to tell her that—that's she's perfect, flawless, the best thing I've ever felt—but I know she won't believe me. Because back when we were younger, I was an idiot in a hurry to get the first peek at the glossy magazines hitting the shelves, too stupid to realize I was breezing right by a work of art without a second look.

Cat is a work of art. She's the real thing, the kind of person who gets better, smarter, funnier, more fascinating with age. And I missed out on eleven years of her. Eleven years of Red growing and learning and changing, but also staying the same because she is a diamond in a world full of people made of glass.

I want to tell her that, too, that's she's a diamond—strong, clear, unbreakable, timeless—but I don't because she starts coming and all I can think is—

Yes, God, yes. More, more, please, more, let me feel you like this forever, baby. My Cat. My Red. Mine, mine, mine.

Stay with me. Stay...

And maybe I say a few of those things as I come inside her, my cock jerking so hard I see stars. I don't know for sure.

I only know that by the time I come back to my body, she's cupping my face in her hands and looking up at me with a soft, sweet, wonder-filled look that makes me feel like the entire world has gone sideways and she's the only thing still standing on solid ground.

And for a second I'm scared because, *fuck* this is happening fast, and I'm not even sure I know how to do the couple thing, at least, not the way I want to be able to do it for her.

But then she whispers, "Hey, Aidan," as she brushes her thumb across my lips.

"Yes, Red," I say, my voice rough, my throat tight.

"Do you want to push the beds together and make a blanket fort?"

I smile and nod, unable to speak for a minute. But when I can, I don't take the easy out she's given me. "How do you always know what to say?"

"Because I know you," she says, kissing me softly before whispering against my lips. "But you don't have to be scared. I don't think either of us has to be scared. Not anymore."

I nod gently. Because she's right.

What is there to be scared of as long as she's here? As long as I know that I get to wake up and do this entire day-into-night thing with her again tomorrow?

"Is it okay that I'm a little scared of fucking on the top bunk?" I ask, sensing it's time to lighten the mood. At least a little.

She pulls away, a wicked glint in her eyes as she gazes up at me. "No, it's not okay. You're going to man up and fuck me on the top bunk tonight, and wake up tomorrow knowing that you've got what it takes."

"What it takes for what?" I ask, grinning.

"To be a top bunk fucker, the best kind of fucker there is," she says, grabbing the shampoo bottle and spraying a glob of amber liquid onto my chest. "Now get your ass cleaned up, soldier."

I give her a mock salute and run my hand down my chest, dragging the glob of shampoo to my dick and getting things sudsy. "Give me ten minutes and the captain and his crew will be ready for duty."

She smiles as she watches me work the soap around my cock. "Perfect."

As promised, ten minutes later, I've helped her push the

bunk beds together and drape the extra sheets into a tent and joined her on the double top bunk. There, I kiss her into an orgasm on my mouth, fuck her into yet another on the top bunk, and then threaten to have her again on the bottom bunk, but she falls asleep before I can coax her down the ladder.

And so I curl my body around hers and drift off to sleep, determined to get my rest so I can wake up and do it—and her—all over again tomorrow.

From the **UNSENT** draft emails of
Catherine Elizabeth Legend

To: Curved4HerPleasure
From: RunPantiesRun
Re: Me After You

It's been six months without any word. From you or of you.

I don't know where in the world you are, or if you're even alive, but I assume you are. I feel like I would know if you were dead. That's probably crazy, but I guess I'm a little crazy. Or at least a complete failure when it comes to reading other people.

That's something I've had to come to terms with

now that you're gone and all I have left are the things you left behind.

I've been over every saved note, every text, and every piece of Dasher memorabilia that was ever touched by your hands, Curve. My dorm room is an archeological dig of words and raunchy tee shirts and an eclectic collection of beer coasters.

But mostly words. So many words, but nowhere in any of it is there a promise of anything more than friendship. It lurks beneath the private jokes, and whispers from the careful curves of your letters in the notes I've read so often the ink is beginning to fade, but you never said anything outright. Never brought the truth out of the shadows or gave it a name.

But it had a name for me.

I was in love with you.

Maybe that makes you laugh, or roll your eyes.

Most likely it makes you feel sorry for me, the pathetic underclassman who took two years of friendship way too seriously. But I don't care. I loved you. And not in the silly way the girls in my dorm "love" boys. You weren't a crush, or some good-looking jock I put up on a pedestal and worshipped without knowing who you were. You were flesh and bone, laughter and secrets, beautiful and messed up in ways I knew I could help you fix if you'd let me.

The way you always fixed me. You helped me and changed me in a dozen different ways from the day of that first run to the day you left without saying good-bye.

And we both know I'm not crazy. You gave me a hundred reasons to think you might love me, too. Last summer there was no doubt in my mind…

But now that I've gone so long without seeing your face…

I miss your eyes the most, I think. I miss looking into them and watching the world fade and blur until you're the only thing in perfect focus.

Or maybe it was *me* that was in focus.

You made me feel like someone had finally seen me. Seen me and found no reason to be disappointed. When we were together, I forgot that I've spent my life letting down the only man who ever loved me. You knew all my secrets, and you liked me anyway. You knew what it was like to wander through a world of two-dimensional people without ever finding anyone real enough to hold onto until a September morning two years ago.

Or so I thought. I knew you were scared—I was, too, or it wouldn't have taken me two years to kiss you—but I was certain you'd get up the courage to admit that you loved me eventually.

I sound pathetic, don't I?

And I was. I was sad and pathetic for a long, long time.

But now there are days when I don't miss you at all. Days when I don't think about you, or wonder where you are, or care if you're thinking about me. And on those days, I know I'm better off without you. Because I deserve someone brave enough to care, brave enough to give all the fucks because that's what fucks are for. To give them away to people smart enough to treasure them.

But now it's too late. Now I know I'm better off alone than wasting my time trying to convince a coward to be brave. I used to think I could be brave enough for both of us. But there's no such thing as a courage transplant, and I need my courage to make my other dreams come true.

And those dreams no longer include you.

If you were thinking about contacting me, don't. If you weren't, take a minute to feel like shit—you deserve it—and then go back to forgetting me.

I'm already back to forgetting you.

Good-bye and good luck,

Catherine Elizabeth Legend

(Because after all this, for some stupid reason, I still want you to know my name.)

The next day dawns bright and beautiful, but Cat and I pretend it's raining and stay in our bunk bed fort all morning. She makes coffee wearing nothing but a tiny apron she finds beneath the sink, while I fight to keep my hands to myself long enough to enjoy the show.

She's fucking gorgeous padding around the kitchen, her pale skin glowing in the morning light and the dark red strawberries on the apron matching the red of her hair. I maintain control until she leans over to add sugar to my coffee and a nipple slips free and then, well…

Let's just say my stepmother wouldn't be happy to know what I had for breakfast on her table.

Later, after I've made Cat come loud enough to trigger a round of irritated honking from a pair of geese outside our window, I grab the scones Julie's cook left on the front step. We crawl back into our fort to eat, because food in a fort is always twice as much fun, and make love on the crumbs before adjourning to the bathroom to wash the mess away.

We intend to wash quickly and head up to the main house to say hello to my parents, but washing the crumbs from Cat's back turns into washing her hair and washing her hair turns out to be an unexpectedly sexy experience that ends with her palms braced against the slick shower wall while I take her from behind.

By the time we're finally ready to interact with the world outside our love cottage, it's lunchtime. We head up to the barn to find Julie enjoying lunch on the patio with two of her five tasting room workers, and my father thankfully out working on the grounds. Julie has brought extra pasta and vegetable salad and bread for Cat and I—just in case—and hands over a picnic basket without even asking us to stay and eat with her crew. She simply warns us that there will be "fancy dinner among the vines at eight" and that we're expected to attend, and waves us on our way.

Cat and I take our picnic up to one of my favorite trees, climb it, and eat while watching the sailboats drift across the azure surface of the lake.

"This is the most magical place," she says, lifting her face into a breeze that blows her hair over her shoulders. "I think I want to live in this tree."

"It's the best," I agree. "I used to come up here to draw when I was a kid."

"So those landscapes in your dorm room were yours," she says with a smile. "I always wondered."

"I can't believe you remember them." I tear off another hunk of bread and pass it over to her.

"I remember just about everything about Curve," she says,

using the old nickname. “I really liked him. Though, I have to confess, I like Aidan even more.”

“I’m glad.” I lean closer. “Because Aidan is pretty crazy about you.”

She tilts her head to the side, but when I try to kiss her she moves just out of reach. “Is this real, Aidan Knight? Because I can’t help feeling like I’m going to wake up any second and all of this will have been a beautiful wine buzz dream, and then I’ll be sad.”

“It’s not a dream, Catherine Elizabeth,” I say, dizzy from a hardcore sex hangover and the smell of her, so sweet and close. “The only thing you have to be sad about is that I’m taking you back to the stinky city on Sunday. But I promise to bring wine and a landscape painting or two to your place Monday night if that sounds good to you.”

“I would love that.” Her breath sighs out, warming my lips. “I can’t wait to have a Knight original on my wall. It will be my most treasured possession.”

“No, my cock insists that he should be your most treasured possession.”

She laughs softly. “So he belongs to me now?”

“From curve to balls,” I say, threading my fingers through her hair. “He’s all yours, beautiful.”

And then I kiss her, and it’s not long before I want to be doing so much more. But we’re in a tree, and though Cat is probably coordinated enough to pull off sex on a tree limb, I am not. So we pack up our lunch and hurry back to the cottage where I have her in our bunk bed fort, making love to her until the pleasure is so intense I’m pretty sure I’m going to die.

But I don’t die; I fall. I fall into her eyes and into her heart, deep down to the center of this person I don’t want to live without. And as I hug her close and she falls asleep on my chest, I wonder if this is a moment we'll talk about later, when we tell the story of us. The moment when I knew I was falling in love with Red and she—hopefully—knew she was falling in love right back.

Everything is perfect.

So perfect, that a part of me worries that something is going to come along and spoil it. But after a moment, I force myself to dismiss the ominous feeling.

We're safe at my parents' place and soon all the bad stuff is going to be behind us.

I sleep the afternoon away and wake up in time to get dressed to take Cat to Julie's fancy dinner without a care in the world. We hold hands as we walk through the vines, and I pretend not to stare at her, memorizing how beautiful she looks in the sunset, with her hair catching fire, her skin glowing, and her eyes glittering just for me.

We meet my parents' friends, help uncork way too many bottles of wine, and settle in for four courses of decadent food. By the time we're finished with our salad, we're deep in conversation with the couple across from us and the older woman to my right. Cat's so good with people, charming everyone, including my uncharmable father, but she's only pure Cat with me. I get her unfiltered, which makes me ridiculously happy.

I'm so happy that I forget to hide it.

I let it show in a dozen ways, from the hand I place at the small of her back during the main course to the kiss I can't help pressing to her cheek when she has a slip of the tongue that sends our end of the table into uncontrollable laughter. She's stunning and mine, and I'm so high on her that all my defenses short circuit and shut off.

So when my father pulls me aside before the dessert course—while everyone else is visiting the porta-potty on the other side of the road or taking in the sunset—I go without a fight. Not only without a fight, but without bracing myself for conflict or worrying about what the hell he wants.

It's stupid. But love makes people stupid. Bash and Penny's insanity in Prospect Park should have taught me that, but apparently I didn't learn my lesson.

Therefore, I'm completely unprepared for my father to pull me in for a tight hug and say, "This makes me happy, son."

I fight the urge to flinch in surprise and then awkwardly close my arms around Jim, not wanting to admit that it feels kind of nice to hug the grouchy bastard. "Well, thanks, Dad. It's been a good visit."

"I'm not talking about the visit," he says, never one to mince words. "I'm talking about Catherine. I never thought I'd see the day, but you made a damned good choice, son. She's good people. She's going to be a beautiful bride, a strong partner for you, and a wonderful mother to your children."

My eyes go wide. I'm so shocked, I can't think of a thing to say. I simply stand there, numb and blinking like an idiot as my father thumps me solidly on the arm.

"So how long, do you think?" he asks, a twinkle in his eyes. "How long before you two give me my first grandson?"

A grandkid.

A grand*son*, in particular, someone to carry on the Knight name, the Knight cooper legacy, and to make my father's dreams—the ones I killed years ago—come true.

That's why my father is so happy. That's why he hugged me for the first time in years and smiled at me the way he used to before I committed the unforgivable sin of choosing to live my life my way.

It's enough to make me ill. Physically ill. My flank steak turns to lead in my stomach, acid pushes up my throat, and for a second I'm worried I'll have to make a run for the bushes on the other side of the tree.

But I've spent my entire adult life learning not to care what my father wants or how much I've disappointed him. So I swallow the wave of sickness and return the shoulder thump, smothering the spark of caring before it can become a flame. I will set him straight, get back to Cat ASAP, and forget that for a moment I thought Jim and I might be on the road to being close again.

I have no fucks left to give Jim; I haven't for years.

"Julie and I want you to have it at the winery," he says, a happy shine in his eyes that I note distantly. Dispassionately.

So what if my dad looks like he's about to cry from happiness overload. That's on him. That's the price he pays for sinking all his fucks into continuing our three-hundred-year-old family business.

"But if Cat has her heart set on somewhere else, that's fine, too," he continues. "I'll cover the cost, either way."

"That's nice of you Dad," I say coolly, slipping my hands into the pockets of my jeans. "Very generous."

He rolls his shoulders, shrugging off my gratitude. "I know the bride's family usually pays, but it doesn't sound like she has any." He glances back toward the lamp lit table, his gaze softening. "And I don't see that it matters. She'll be our family soon enough."

The words slip past my defenses, sending a sharp stab of hurt flaring behind my ribs. "You really like her, don't you?"

Jim's lips push forward, and his brows pull closer together. His thinking face. "Catherine?"

"No, the other woman you think I should marry."

His eyes narrow, and the thinking face becomes his "Don't fuck with me" face. "So you two haven't talked about what comes next?"

"No, Dad," I say, "we haven't. I don't even know if she wants kids, let alone if she—"

"Then you should find out," Jim says, frustration creeping into his tone. "You're not getting any younger, Aidan. By the time I was your age I'd been married for six years and had a two year old. If you're not careful, you're going to fuck around and waste your entire life."

"So my life is a waste?" It's a purely rhetorical question. I know exactly what my father thinks of my life choices so far. "I decided not to spend a few decades bending wood into barrels, so therefore my entire life is a waste?"

"That's not what I said. This isn't about the work; it's about a lack of respect for things that matter. Things like tradition and family and—"

"Family didn't seem to matter to you when I came back from Japan. You put 'return to sender' on my Christmas card for fuck's sake, Dad," I say, fighting to keep my tone calm and even. "If Julie hadn't gotten cancer, you would have been happy to pretend you'd never even had a son."

"You cut me out of your life first." He meets my glare with his own. "You ran off to Japan without telling anyone where you were going. For three days after we got home from your graduation ceremony, I had no idea where you were. Did you ever stop to think Julie and your mother and I might have been scared for you?"

"I sent an email as soon as I could, but I—"

"I cried, you bastard," he says, cutting me off before I can apologize for the sins of my twenty-two-year-old self. "I thought you'd gotten drunk and driven your car into a lake, or gotten into a fight and ended up buried in some monster's back yard."

"I'm sorry, Dad," I say, anger and shame making my throat tight. "I never meant to upset you. It was just the only way I knew how to leave."

"Bullshit," he barks softly, obviously trying to keep our

argument from the rest of the party. Judging by the laughter drifting through the night air, everyone else is still having a great time. “You were raised better. You can find fault with me all you want, but your mother and Julie taught you some goddamned manners.”

“They did.” I clench my jaw and press my tongue tight to the back of my teeth, ordering my mouth to stay closed. But the damn thing isn’t in the mood to take orders. “But *you* taught me to be terrified of letting you down, and when I was on my way to Japan that lesson was the only one that mattered. I knew if I told you what I was doing, there was a chance you would be able to talk me out of it, and then I would have hated you. And I didn’t want to hate you, Dad.”

I swallow and it feels like I’m forcing a human fist down my throat instead of my own spit. God, I just want to shut up—to shut up and walk away before this gets any worse.

Instead, I say, “I still don’t want to hate you. And I don’t want you to hate me. Or decide to hug me for the first time in I can’t remember how long because you like my date and think she’d be a good breeding mare for a couple of grandkids.”

“Catherine is a lovely young woman. I would never—”

“And even if I wanted to marry Cat,” I cut in, “which is honestly nowhere on my fucking radar right now, I—”

“Why not?”

“I barely fucking know her!” I shout. “We weren’t officially dating until yesterday, and before Monday I hadn’t seen the woman in eleven years. Eleven fucking years, and back when I used to know her, she was a lunatic half the time.”

“Stop it, Aidan,” Dad snaps, mouth going tight around the edges. “There’s no need to insult Cat because you’re angry with me.”

"I watched her pick up a rattlesnake with her bare hands, Dad," I barrel on. "Twice! And I spent hours keeping her from doing shit that would land her in the dean's office or worse. I just want to get to know her again, see if she's the kind of crazy I can deal with, and see if we work. Marrying her and squeezing out a kid for you to saddle with your impossible expectations is the last thing on my mind."

My father doesn't respond or meet my gaze. His eyes are fixed on something in the shadows over my shoulder. Even before he speaks, I know what—or rather, *who*—it is.

I smell Cat's sweet, spicy, mysterious smell a second too late.

Fuck.

"I'm sorry you had to hear that," my father says to her, his eyes soft and sad. "It's my fault. At my age I should know better than to assume things. Especially where my son is concerned."

I curse beneath my breath as I turn, gut twisting as I see Cat standing in the dim light at the edge of the lanterns' reach, watching me with an unreadable expression. Unreadable because she doesn't want me to read it, because she's shut the door to herself and left me on the other side.

"I'm sorry," I say, holding my hands out, palms up. "I didn't mean to—"

"It's no big deal," she says, her gaze shifting to my dad. "And don't apologize, Jim. It's nice to hear what people are really thinking. I *was* pretty crazy back when Aidan and I knew each other before. I was a teenager most of that time, but still…"

My breath rushes out. "Please, Cat, I'm sorry."

"I'll leave you two alone." Dad retreats, rejoining the rest of the party, leaving me alone with the mess I've made.

I prop my hands on my hips and hang my head, waiting

for my old man to be out of earshot, wishing I could rewind time and never stand up from the supper table. I was so angry I can barely remember what I said, but I know it was shitty and untrue and hurtful to the one person I never want to hurt.

And as I stand there, starting to sweat because I don't know how to make this better, I realize that forever with Cat *is* on my radar. I haven't thought about marriage—mostly because I've assumed for years that I would never get married—but I have thought about what it would be like to wake up next to her every morning. To make love to her every night. To know I'm never going to run out of reasons to laugh because the person who makes me happiest has agreed to share her life with me.

To share *herself* with me.

Last night she trusted me enough to let me in, all the way in, and I rewarded her by running my mouth like an asshole. And now that mouth, the one that was so eager to spew stupid shit out into the world a few minutes ago, can't think of a single thing to say.

"I got a call from Detective Lipman," Cat says, her voice soft in the strained silence. "But the reception was bad and the call got cut off. I got up to see if the signal was better over here on the hill. I wasn't trying to spy on you."

"I know you weren't." I run a hand through my hair. "You should call him. This can wait."

She holds up her phone, wiggling it back and forth. "No reception at all up here. I'll call him when I get back to the cottage. I think everyone is almost done with dessert."

Again, I wish I'd stayed at the table. If I had, I'd be having a second helping of strawberry shortcake instead of trying to weather the first rough patch in my barely day old relationship. "I really am sorry," I say again. "I didn't mean any of the shit I said. I was hurt and talking out of my ass."

"Why were you hurt?" She crosses her arms, wandering closer, but not too close. She stops when there are still several feet between us, proving everything is not okay.

I shake my head. "Nothing. I just forgot not to give a fuck what my dad thinks for a few minutes. But I'm better now and I'm..." I clear my throat, looking for something more meaningful to offer than another lame apology, but coming up empty. "Fuck, I'm just sorry."

"Are you?" she asks, crossing her arms tighter.

"Sorry? Yes, I am. I swear I am."

"No, not sorry." Her eyes close for a second before squinting open again. "I meant, are you better? Is it really *better* not to care what your dad thinks? I mean, he is your dad."

"Yes, it's definitely better not to care." I tamp down a flash of irritation. Cat has no idea how bad things were with Jim and I at one point. I deliberately gave her the glossy version so she wouldn't think I was crazy for bringing her up here. "Caring about Jim Knight only leads to getting angry and saying stupid shit. He's never going to change his mind, and I'm never going to change mine. It would be stupid to invest any more time, energy, or caring into that man. He made his choice about what matters to him a long time ago, and it sure as hell isn't me."

"That's not true," Cat says. "Your father absolutely cares about you. You should see the way he looks at you when you aren't paying attention, Aidan. He loves you so much."

I tilt my head toward my shoulder, but my neck muscles remain whip tight. "I don't want to talk about this."

"Well, I do," she says. "I think it's past time for you to stop pushing your father away and give him a real second chance."

"What the hell," I say with a strained laugh. "You two bonded pretty fucking quick, didn't you? You realize people usually don't like Jim, right? He's not a warm and fuzzy, friends-at-first-sight kind of person."

"Yeah, well neither am I," she says in a harder voice. "But you still brought me home and consented to fuck me half a dozen times between last night and this evening. Even though I'm a lunatic you only started dating yesterday."

"Come on, Cat. I told you, I didn't mean any of that." I reach for her, but she steps away, a stiffness through her shoulders that makes it clear my touch isn't welcome.

I interlace my hands behind my head and press my skull back into the basket of my fingers, fighting the urge to pull her into my arms, haul her back to our cottage, and make her come until she forgets all the stupid shit I said. "Please, Red. Can't we just forget the last ten minutes ever happened?"

"Sure thing." She smiles, a brittle curve of her lips that makes me feel even shittier than I did a second ago. "I've had three glasses of wine, so I'm sure most of tonight will be blurry by tomorrow. But I do need to return the detective's phone call." She backs away, jabbing a thumb toward the party still in progress. "Tell everyone good night for me? I think I'll head to bed after I make my call. I'm not used to drinking wine two nights in a row."

"Let me walk you down." I start toward her, but she stops me with a shake of her head.

"No, Aidan." She runs a hand through her hair, wrapping the silky strands tight around her fist. "I said things will be blurry by tomorrow, but right now I remember every word you said. And I don't really want to walk anywhere with you."

My eyes squeeze closed as a wave of regret punches me in

the gut and the throat and a few places in between. "Fuck, Cat, I'm sorry." I open my eyes, searching hers. "How many times do you want me to say it? I'll say it a hundred times if that's what you need me to do. Because it's true. It's the only true thing I've said in the past—"

"Seriously, Aidan," she says, cutting in with a wave of her hand. "We're fine. I just want to be alone for a while. I don't need any more sorrys."

"Then I'll keep my sorry to myself," I say, my feeble attempt at a joke falling flat. "Just let me walk with you so I know that you're safe."

"I'm safe. I'm sure that's what Lipman is calling to tell me. Besides, there hasn't been a car down the road for hours." She takes another step back, casting her features into almost full darkness. I have no idea what expression is on her face when she says, "All the other visitors are sleeping tight, and soon I will be, too. I'll see you in the morning. You're in charge of coffee this time. No apron, though. I don't think that apron would even come close to covering the subject in your case."

"All right." I smile, but it tastes sad on my lips. "I'll take the bottom bunk tonight? Give you the top?"

I wait for her response, praying that she'll say I should join her on the top bunk and prepare to properly atone for my sins. But instead, she says, "That sounds good. Good night, Aidan."

"Good night." It's just good night, but as she turns and starts down the path leading between the vines, heading toward the lights of the cottages, it feels like good-bye.

I ball my hands into fists at my sides and watch her go, hating that I've fucked things up. Why couldn't Jim have kept his plans to turn my future kid into his barrel-making slave to himself—at least for another week or two? By then I would have been back in the city, and I would never have answered a phone call from my dad with Cat in the room. Because I fucking know better. When my guard is up, I know not to leave any cracks in my defenses for crap that makes me feel like shit to crawl inside.

But then there are no cracks for the other things, either. For the good shit. For hope and happiness and all the things she makes you feel.

Can it really work this way?

Can you shut out the bad without shutting out the good, too?

I don't know. But I know I have to make things better with Red. I'm not even close to being done with her, with us, with whatever we're going to be to each other.

"I'll make it up to you," I whisper to her retreating shadow, silently sending another apology her way before rejoining the party

Back at the table, I make Cat's excuses to Julie, ignore my father, and promise the adorable couple who brought dessert to take the extra strawberry shortcake back to the cottage so Cat can have some in the morning. I help finish off a bottle of blush wine Julie opened to pair with the strawberries and then take charge of gathering all the recyclables into the wheelbarrow and the compost into an empty salad bowl to be added to the pile in the back yard.

I force myself to go through the usual "post dinner party" motions, ignoring Julie's probing stares and my father's artic shoulder, reminding myself that this could be worse.

Cat's hurt and disappointed, but she's safe and sound and will be sleeping in the bunk above mine tonight, close enough for me to hear her breathe and for my silent "forgive me" vibes to hopefully penetrate her outer layer of defenses. Really, in the scheme of things, she's being pretty damned cool about this.

Pretty damned cool…

"Shit," I curse, pressing the salad bowl in Julie's hands.

"What?" She blinks up at me in the glare of the motion-activated floodlight by the barn. "What's wrong?"

"Cat's never this cool when she's mad," I say, breaking into a run.

"What?" Julie calls after me. "Aidan, what's wrong? Did you and Jim have another fight? I told him not to say anything about weddings yet, but he never listens to me."

"I'll explain later," I throw over my shoulder, knowing there's no time to waste.

Cat and I are both older, wiser, and generally more sane and rational than when we were in college. We've grown up, settled fully into our adult skins, and learned our lessons from the mistakes we made in the past. Hell, after eleven years we're practically different people.

Except that we aren't. Not really.

My dad still gets under my fucking skin like nothing else, and I'm betting money Red still only plays it cool when she's truly devastated.

I run faster, hoping I'm wrong, but when I get to the cottage, I'm not surprised to find no sign of Cat. I check the main house and the barn and then do another check of the cottage and the back seat of Shane's Rolls just in case, but Cat's nowhere to be found. She's vanished, like an animal slinking away to lick its wounds, the way she always has.

She's still the same Panties I knew in so many ways.

Exactly, genius. Which is why being with her feels so right.

You say you've never been in real love, but the truth is you've never fallen out of it. You've been in love with that girl since you were both kids, and now you've gone and fucked things up one day into the rest of your life.

With another curse, I double back toward the main house again. I'll tell Julie what's happened and get her advice. I think I've searched everywhere Cat could possibly be, but another woman might have a better gut instinct. And in any case, I need Julie to keep an eye out for Cat, to promise me she'll take care of Red if she shows up on her doorstep in the middle of the night, needing a glass of water and a place to crash.

Cat may not want anything to do with me, but I still need her to be safe.

I need it like I've needed few other things in my life. As long as she's safe, there's a chance she'll forgive me, that she'll see I'm flawed and clueless at times, but that I'll make up for it by loving her. Loving her all the ways she needs to be loved, ways only I can love her because I'm hers and she's mine.

But even as I hope for the best, something deep in my gut insists that Cat is gone. Maybe for good.

And then, halfway to the main house, I get a call from Lipman, and I learn that Cat never called him back. I learn that the sting operation was a success except for one thing, one detail, one person who wasn't where he was supposed to be tonight.

One Nico Mancuso, who has left the city and is suspected to be en route to Ithaca, New York.

And now Catherine Elizabeth Legend calls a Time Out.

Hey, you. Yes, you.

The one flipping the pages of this novel.

You're probably thinking this is the chapter where we get a brief glance into the heroine's POV as she runs back to her cottage, devastated by the stupid, hurtful things the hero said. Maybe you're expecting tears or anger or a tormented interior monologue about how stupid it was for her to carry a torch for the one who got away for so long, when she knows damned well that the man in question isn't capable of forming a lasting relationship.

But that's not happening.

I refuse to go there. There's no point in going there. Aidan is who he is, and I am who I am, and if we were meant to be, we would have come together the first time around.

But we didn't. And that's just fine.

More than fine. I *like* who I am without Aidan Knight. I have a great job, wonderful friends, the most adorable dog in the universe, and the rest of my life ahead of me to get over the nightmare with Nico and a certain big, stupid, beautiful idiot who made me think that dreams could come true. Even crazy romantic dreams.

But I don't want to play the romance game anymore.

I would rather be in a women's fiction story. Maybe Julie and I can band together, kick the stubborn, pigheaded men out of her house, and run the winery ourselves. She'll be the mother figure I've always wanted, I'll be the daughter she never had, and we'll be so, *so* happy.

At least for a few chapters.

Until it's revealed that Julie has early onset dementia. Then I'll have to spend the rest of the book taking care of her as her health worsens, all while learning valuable lessons about the fleeting nature of time and the mercurial disposition of Fate. And maybe somewhere in there, right before the black moment, when we learn Julie isn't responding well to her treatments, I'll have an affair with the guy hired to run the harvest.

But that won't be part of the central plot, and he definitely *won't* break my heart.

Yes, we'll all end up crying at the end of the story when Julie walks into the lake—choosing suicide during a lucid moment in order to be the architect of her own death—but there will be hope, too. There will be kittens born in a corner of the barn, or a new grape clone named after Julie. Or maybe I'll find out I'm pregnant with the harvest drifter's baby, and the book will end as I realize that Julie has taught me how to be the mother I want to be. I'll stand with my hand on my belly as I gaze out over Lake Cayuga and wish for a girl so I can name her after the woman who was my chosen family.

Or if that's too depressing, we could go with some speculative fiction.

Maybe Aidan and I wake up in the woods eleven years ago with no idea how we got there, but with all our memories intact, and we have to sort out the mystery of our future-past. Or maybe we come home from work one afternoon to find that we've both metamorphosed into giant insects. We have a huge argument about who has to make dinner now that we both have feelers instead of hands and end up ordering pizza and eating the delivery boy.

That could make for some compelling book club discussion.

Is our transformation a statement on the current socio-political state of the Western world? Or maybe it's representative of the author's growing sense of alienation from the romance genre. Or maybe it's just a really creepy way of saying that love is hard, and sometimes it turns perfectly decent people into nasty, acid-spewing insects who lash out at those around them instead of examining their relationship and making positive changes.

Or maybe we should just stop this story right now.

Before I cry.

Before I start to hate myself for jumping straight into the deep end of the emotion pool after less than forty-eight hours with the best friend I never thought I'd see again.

Stop before a man steps out from behind the door to the cottage and clamps his hand over my mouth, whispering, "Did you miss me, Catherine?" as he jabs something sharp into my neck.

I flinch, pain flooding through my shoulder, and my muscles going limp. I lose consciousness in the middle of a thick-tongued call for help.

And to be perfectly honest, as I black out, my last thoughts aren't of giant bugs or book club questions or mother figures. My last thoughts are of Aidan and how much I wish I'd stayed with him and fought for us instead of running away. Because I'm in love with him, of course I am, of course I always have been, from the moment I saw his stupid, furry face.

So I guess this is a love story, after all.

And I guess we should get back to it before it's too late to prove that, with enough love, it's possible to find a way back to the precious things you lost.

Nico knows she's here. He knows. He knows. He knows…

The knowledge squirms through my head like a flesh-eating worm devouring my sanity. I should never have brought Cat here. I underestimated her ex a second time, and now she might not live long enough for me to make up for my mistake.

Not even the police suspected that Nico was tracking Cat's credit card purchases, or that our stop at the mall would tip him off that she was with me upstate, but that doesn't matter. I should have stayed glued to her side until I knew without a shadow of a doubt that she was safe.

Now my only shot at making this right is to get to her before Nico hurts her.

I turn on every light at the main house, grab a flashlight from the cupboard for good measure, and search the ground around each exit for clues. Thanks to Cat, I know a little about tracking and how to read the story of footprints in the dirt.

But the footprints leading to Dad and Julie's place all belong to dinner guests and a coyote who circled the gate around the chicken coop in the backyard several times before running into the woods between here and the lake.

"The police are on their way," Julie calls from the deck overlooking the back yard. "They've got cars coming from Ithaca and down the highway in the other direction and they're setting up roadblocks. They're going to find her, sweetheart. I know they are."

"I'm going to go look around the cottage," I say, cutting through the yard.

"The police said we should stay inside, Aidan," Julie shouts after me. "That's why all the guests are in our basement, honey. The people who took Cat could still be close by. It isn't safe for you to be out here."

"At least not unarmed." My father's voice is closer, but when I turn it takes me a moment to see him. He's standing in the shadows leading to the storage area under the house. As my eyes adjust to the darkness, I see my old shotgun case in his hands.

He crosses the damp grass and holds it out between us. "You remember how to use this, right?"

I take the case. It's lighter than I remember, but when I thumb the combination lock to the old numbers, it pops open smoothly, revealing my familiar Remington 870 pump twelve gauge.

It's the third gun I ever owned, the one I used to take on hunting trips with my dad when I was in junior high. We would spend long weekends shacked up at his friend's cabin in the woods north of Watkins Glenn, hunting and re-reading our favorite battered paperbacks—the ones that lived on the shelf at deer camp all year round, the pages bloated from exposure to heat and humidity—and eat venison for every meal. Back then, we actually enjoyed spending time together. We've never been the sort to have long heart-to-heart talks or share private jokes, but we both looked forward to weekends of shared solitude.

I haven't shot this particular gun since I was fifteen, the last time I was on good enough terms with my father to willingly subject myself to three days of nothing but his company.

"I cleaned it a couple of months ago," Dad says, holding out a box of shells. "It's in good shape, but don't take a shot if Cat's close to whoever took her. They're slugs, but it's dark, and you're out of practice. It isn't worth the risk."

"I know." I pocket the slugs before taking the shotgun out and handing the case back to my father. "But I can't just sit here."

"I know." Jim puts a hand on my shoulder. "Be careful. And if you have to shoot, shoot to kill. You wound a man like this and he'll make you sorry you showed mercy."

I nod, my throat tight, and reach for the ammo in my pocket, deciding it's best to load the gun here while I have enough light to see. Better to be locked and loaded and not need the weapon, than need it and be fumbling with shells and a flashlight in the dark.

As I load, my hands aren't as steady as I would like for them to be. I've never shot at a human being before. I've shot deer, ducks, and the occasional squirrel back when I was first learning to use my gun. But I ate those things, even the squirrels.

Part of the philosophy of hunting in our house was that it was done for food, not sport. Everything we killed was eaten and every part of the animal was used or passed on to someone else who knew what to do with it. Back when I was very young, my dad and I would squat down beside whatever we'd killed and take a moment to show our gratitude before we touched it. It was part ceremony, part show of respect, and part prayer of thanks.

But gradually, as I got older, we let the ritual go, the way we let so many other things go.

"I love you, Dad," I say softly, not wanting to head out into the dark without saying the words.

"I love you, too." He gives my shoulder a final squeeze before letting me go. "And I'm not ready to lose you. Remember, if these people are on our property, threatening the safety of our family, the law entitles you to use deadly force."

"I wouldn't care if it didn't." I sling the loaded gun over my shoulder. "I just found her again. I can't lose her now."

My father nods as I back away toward the cottage. "I'll be praying for you, Aidan, the way I do every night."

"Thanks, Dad," I say, my throat tight as I turn and hurry down the dirt road toward the cottages. Once again, it's taken a woman we care about in mortal danger to bring us back together.

As I reach the cottage and circle it with an eye on the ground, I send up a prayer of my own: that I won't be stupid or pigheaded enough to need a disaster to get through my Jim issues next time. And that I will get to Cat before the bastard who took her hurts the woman I love.

Though I might already be too late for that.

Now that I'm looking for it, the trail is as clear as a ransom note scrawled on paper and pinned to the door. One man, about my size, wearing hiking boots, entered the house alone and emerged with his footprints sinking much more deeply into the damp earth. Deep enough for him to be carrying the woman who made the sandal prints leading from the vineyard into the cottage.

Cat went into our cabin on her own two feet, but she left in the arms of a psychopath who left a trail in the gravel beside the road for a dozen feet before veering off into the woods, down the hiking trail leading to the boat dock.

I click off my flashlight and pick up my pace. I don't know how much of a head start Nico has, but I know this is the only path to Lake Cayuga. I also know that all the land from here to the shore belongs to my parents.

The person who took Cat has trespassed on private property and assaulted an innocent woman, and if I get a clear shot I'm going to make sure he regrets it for the rest of his life, however brief that might be.

Chapter THIRTY-FIVE

And now for something from Nico Mancuso

It's cold in the woods, cold enough I'm concerned that Catherine is going to be chilly on the way across the water. She's wearing a light sweater, but her legs are bare. If I'd known it was going to be this cool at night upstate, I would have brought blankets and warmer clothes.

"We'll get you warmed up soon enough," I murmur. She's still unconscious, but it's good to talk to her. After the madness of the past several days, I need this, need *her*, more than ever. "We're going to Cuba. It's all arranged. We have new names, new passports, even a new home beside the ocean. There's a plane waiting on the other side of the lake that will get us there before morning." I move faster through the moonlit trees, feeling freer with every step I take with Catherine in my arms. "By tomorrow afternoon we'll be drinking mojitos on the beach and wondering why we ever wanted to take over the world."

I smile. My dreams of becoming mayor of the city I've left behind are amusing to me now. I should have known better. Men like me don't go straight. Men like me go to hell and have one heck of a party on the way there.

"Who needs the world? Let the world burn and we'll roast marshmallows over the ashes. Isn't that right, love?" I hug Catherine closer, eager for the moment when her clever eyes will open again.

Her head is heavy on my chest and her body limp in my arms, but she should come around soon. I used the smallest dose of sedative possible. I just needed her quiet long enough for me to get her away from the thug who's latched onto her, and someplace safe, where we can talk.

Catherine is one of the smartest women I know, but she's in a vulnerable place. Her father, her only living family member, recently passed away. That, combined with the abrupt ending of our engagement—a situation caused by an abundance of fear, not a lack of love—and she was primed to fall under the spell of any man with a firm hand.

My Catherine likes to be taken to the edge and held there with her feet hovering over the fire. She craves the extremes of passion and emotion that can only be achieved with a power exchange.

"But the person with the power should be someone who loves you, someone you can trust," I say, lifting her higher as I step over a branch blocking the path to the lake. "I kept things from you for your own protection, *cara mia*. But in every way that mattered I was an open book. No man will ever love you the way I love you. That caveman isn't fit to lick your feet."

Though he did far more than lick Catherine's feet, and I know it.

Thanks to the surveillance equipment I had installed in her apartment, I know that Aidan Knight fucked my Catherine. He made her come and beg and cry out his name again and again until all I could see was red. Blood red, streaming down the walls, washing over my hands, flooding my mouth until I couldn't think straight.

All I could think about was that bearded Neanderthal shoving his tongue, his fingers, his dick in *my* woman's pussy.

I don't remember exactly what I told Petey when I ordered him to fetch Catherine from her apartment, but I wish I'd told him to kill that muscle-bound fuck. Mr. Knight deserves to die for standing between me and what's mine, to die the way Petey is going to die for double-crossing me and making plans to murder Catherine on the flight to Cuba tonight.

It will be harder to get to the little shit now that's he's in police custody, but I'll find a way. The detectives who took down my family may have destroyed one of the greatest criminal dynasties in the United States and wrecked my chances at a future in politics, but they won't take my vengeance away from me.

Petey will pay for his betrayal, and Aidan Knight will pay for trying to take what's mine. As soon as Catherine and I are safe in Cuba, I'll start making the arrangements.

I emerge from the woods with a surge of renewed energy, but when I reach the boat dock, I pause, the reptilian part of my brain insisting that something is wrong. Something has changed since I tied up the boat an hour ago. I haven't survived nearly forty years in a family like mine by ignoring the predator-prey instinct.

I'm immediately on high alert, searching for signs of enemies lying in wait.

I scan the rough boards of the dock, where the boats are moored on either side. My speedboat is still tied between two smaller, older boats on the left and nothing appears to have been disturbed. On the right are three blue paddleboats and a pink swan with a long fiberglass neck that bobs lightly as the waves lap against the shore.

My gaze narrows on the swan, honing in on dark shadows shifting back and forth on the boat's floor. Whoever it is isn't making much of an effort to be quiet, making me doubt that they're here for me, but I'm not taking any chances. I barely escaped the sting tonight without being taken into police custody. From now until the moment Catherine and I land at a private airstrip in Cuba, I can't afford to let down my guard.

Setting her down gently on a bench beside the shore, I pull my gun from the holster in my belt and move slowly down the dock, my feet silent on the boards. The moorings continue to creak lightly as the waves roll in, but aside from the wind and the faint chirp of crickets in the weeds, the air is silent.

Even when I get close enough to see who—or rather, what—has climbed aboard the paddleboat, the night remains quiet.

As I pause beside the swan, the two giant raccoons raiding the open cooler between the seats look up at me with challenging expressions. I can almost imagine the one of the right asking, "What are you looking at, buddy? Move along," as he pops half a Twinkie into his mouth.

I make a note to remember to tell the story to Catherine. It's the kind of thing she would love, the sort of observation that used to make her look at me with laughter dancing in her eyes.

She loved me then and she still loves me now. It doesn't matter what she said, or that she ran away and fucked another man. What we have is real, and soon our relationship will be even stronger than it was before. I just need to get her out of the country and everything will go back to the way it was.

I tuck my gun into its holster and turn back toward shore, only to find the bench where I laid Catherine empty.

Too late, I remember her unusually quiet step.

Before I can turn to search the dock, small hands shove hard between my shoulders, sending me toppling off the boards into the water between the paddleboats.

I smile as I fall, sucking in a breath and holding it as I plunge beneath the surface of the lake. I enjoy the smooth execution of a plan as well as the next man, but there's something to be said for fighting to get what you want.

And Catherine always did enjoy a fight.

I pull hard toward the surface, already imagining how good it's going to feel to wrestle Catherine to the ground beneath me and promise her this is the last time she'll ever take me by surprise. Soon, she'll see that I'm all she has, all she'll ever have, and realize it's time to start making amends.

Maybe we'll even start on the boat on the way across the lake. If anyone can take a woman from behind while steering a speedboat, it's Nico Mancuso, esquire, former consigliere, and the last free member of the greatest crime family New York has ever known.

From my hiding place behind the tiny boathouse near the lake, I watch Cat creep silently up behind Nico.

He's distracted by a pair of raccoons that have crawled up on the seat of the swan paddleboat—a fact I'd planned to use to my advantage to shoot the gun out of his hand—but before I can disarm him, Cat moves into the line of fire. Normally I wouldn't doubt her ability to take down a man Nico's size, especially with the element of surprise on her side, but she's not in top form.

As she walks, she weaves unsteadily from side to side, at one point coming way too fucking close to falling into the water.

I want to call out that I've got a gun on Nico and that she should turn and run. But I'm not sure she's steady enough on her feet to get out of reach before her psycho ex grabs her. So I bite my tongue, ignore my racing pulse, and pray that whatever she's got planned for Nico will put him out of commission long enough for me to get us both to safety.

A second later, she circles around him, slipping out of his line of sight just as he turns back to the shore, nearly giving me a heart attack in the process.

Nico stiffens as he sees the empty bench beside the water, and Red springs into action. Lunging forward, her palms slam into Nico's shoulders, sending him tumbling into the lake beside the paddleboats.

The moment his head goes under the water, I sprint out from behind the boathouse, shouting, "Run, Cat! Run! Now!"

"Aidan?" She spins toward the sound of my voice, the sudden movement sending her tripping over her own feet. She weaves unsteadily to the side, crashing into the swan's neck, sending the raccoons leaping back to the floor of the boat. Normally, she would have recovered her balance in a second, but now she bounces off the fiberglass and falls to the dock just as her ex-boyfriend breaks the surface of the lake

"You should have told me you wanted to fight, *cara*," he says, laughter in his voice as he pulls himself onto the dock beside her. "You know I live to please you."

"Stop!" She rolls onto her hands and knees and crawls back toward shore. His hand whips out, barely missing her ankle. "Leave me alone, Nico. Just leave me alone!"

With a growl, I run faster, determined to make sure Nico the Nutjob never lays a hand on Cat again. I'm still several feet away when I drop the rifle and hurl myself at the crazy fuck, tackling him before he can stand or get an inch closer to Cat.

He hits the dock first, grunting as we slide across the boards, the water from his clothes soaking through my shirt as I lock an arm around his throat and reach for his elbow with my free hand. I'm planning to wrench his arm behind his back and pin the motherfucker to the dock, but before I can get a good grip on his wrist, the air between our bodies and the deck explodes.

Despite the ringing in my ears, it takes me a moment to realize the sound was a gunshot, and a beat longer to feel the burning sensation coursing through my forearm. I cry out, cursing as the burning becomes fire surging in scalding waves from my arm into my shoulder, but I don't let go. I tighten my grip on Nico, dropping my full weight on top of him, pinning him to the ground.

As long as I've got the bastard clutched tight to my chest and trapped between my body and the dock, it will be harder for him to shoot me again. And even if he manages to get off another shot, he won't be able to hit anything vital without sending the bullet through himself first.

"You're bleeding," he grunts, straining to throw off my hold. "You're pissing blood all over my shirt."

"If you were so worried about your shirt, you shouldn't have shot me, you piece of shit." I force the words through a clenched jaw as sweat breaks out on my forehead.

The agony of the bullet buried in my arm is unlike anything I've felt before, but I know a thing or two about how to deal with pain. I have tattoos in all the most excruciating places—the back of my neck, top of my foot, and the elbow ditch where thin skin made the mermaid I got in Thailand hurt like a son of a bitch. That stubborn, sustained, six on the pain scale suffering is nothing compared to the sharp misery throbbing deep in my forearm now, but it's taught me how to ignore the primitive part of my brain that's screaming for me to let Nico go and run from the thing that hurt me.

"If she gets away because of you, I'll kill you." Nico's fingers bite into the wrist of my good arm, digging deep into the tendons. "Let me go and I won't cut your dick off before I put a bullet between your eyes."

"You're not in a position to be cutting anyone's—" I break off with a scream as he bites my hand hard enough to send fresh suffering blossoming through my thumb.

My fingers spasm and my grip loosens on his neck. Before I can get a better hold on him—one that would prevent his fucking teeth from making contact with my skin—he's grabbed my arm and flipped me over his head to land flat on my back on the dock. I hit hard enough to knock the air from my lungs, but manage to kick my leg toward his weapon, knocking the gun into the lake.

I gasp for air, making big plans to jackknife to my feet and slam my bloodied fist into Nico's face as soon as I can breathe. But before I can do so much as roll over, his boot connects with my ribs. I groan and roll away, but he keeps coming, kicking the shit out of me again and again until lightning bolts of pain electrify my torso.

I curse myself ten different ways to Sunday, wishing I were less of a lover and more of a fighter. I'm quickly realizing that my lift-heavy-things-and-run-fast muscles are no match for men who are accustomed to using their strength to hurt other people. It doesn't matter that I'm bigger and stronger, I'm unskilled at kicking ass, and at this rate I'm not going to live to log time in the sparring ring.

I've got to get the fuck away from Nico's boots and back on my feet.

I stop rolling and scuttle across the dock in this weird ass sideways crab squirm that allows me to bat the bastard's leg away with my good arm. The entire process is incredibly painful, but not as painful as the psychopath screaming bloody murder while he does his best to kick my ribs into my lungs.

"You never should have touched her," he shouts, spit flying from his lips. "I'm going to cut your hands off, and then your dick, and then watch you bleed out with a smile on my face." He goes for my throat with clawed hands, clearly intending to strangle what breath I have left out of me.

I ball my wounded hand into a fist to defend myself—the arm with the bullet in it has decided to stop listening to my brain's helpful suggestions and is pulsing miserably on the ground, begging for a time out—when Nico's features freeze in an almost comical grimace. His eyes bulge, his nostrils flare, and the middle of his tongue lurches out from between his lips just before he slumps to the dock, barely missing my legs.

"He needs his hands, you psycho piece of shit," Cat says, her voice slurred. "And his dick."

I look up to see her holding my shotgun by the barrel with both hands, weaving slightly back and forth. In the moonlight, the blood on the walnut stock, Nico's blood, looks black.

As black as the masks of the raccoons that leap from the swan paddleboat and make a break for the woods, clearly deciding it's past time to leave this party.

Chapter Thirty-Seven

I turn back to Nico, making sure he isn't getting back up, but his eyes are closed, his mouth slack, and his spine slumped in an uncomfortable-looking position that suggests he's truly down for the count.

"Are you okay?" I groan softly as I push into a seated position and lift a hand to Cat. "Did he hurt you?"

"I don't think so." She sits down hard beside me, the shotgun still clutched tight in her fingers. "But I can't feel my legs or feet. He injected me with something that made my whole body go numb for a while." She blinks hard, making a visible effort to focus on my face. "But there was a gun shot, right? I didn't imagine that? Are you okay?"

"I'll be fine." I reach for her with my bullet-free arm and pull her into an awkward hug, wincing as the movement sends pain ricocheting through my bones. Now that the immediate danger has passed, my nerve endings are doing their best to make sure I understand how fucked up I am, but I need her close too much to pay attention. "He shot me in the forearm, but I'll be fine."

"Oh my God." Cat pulls away, laying a gentle hand on my shoulder. "We have to get help, Aidan, I have to—"

"It's okay," I insist. "The bleeding is already slowing, and the police should be on their way. I texted my dad on the way down the trail and told him I was pretty sure the man who'd taken you was headed for the lake."

"Then we have to hurry." Cat shifts onto her knees, swaying hard as she moves. She braces herself with a hand on the dock, managing to stay upright as she says, "We need to push Nico into the water before the police get here. That way he'll drown, and no one will know we had anything to do with it."

"No." I straighten my leg, blocking her path as she tries to crawl across the dock to Nico.

"But I need him to drown, Aidan," she insists, voice rising. "I need him to drown so he can never hurt you or me or anyone else ever again. I can't live the rest of my life wondering if a crazy person is hiding behind a door waiting to kidnap me or cut off the dick of someone I care about."

"He's going to jail for a long, long time, Red," I say gently, very grateful to be alive and someone she cares about. "Give me the gun. As long as he stays put until the police get here, he gets to live. If he tries to run, I'll shoot him, I promise."

Cat shakes her head blearily, holding tighter to the weapon. "No, Aidan. He's crazy. He won't stop until he hurts you."

"I'm more worried about you," I say, wishing my damned arm didn't hurt so much. I would really like to hold her properly right now. "I went crazy when I realized he'd taken you from the cottage. I don't want to lose you, Red, especially not like this."

"I don't want to lose you, either." Her shoulders relax away from her ears, making me think she's starting to come down from her adrenaline high.

"I'm sorry," I repeat for the dozenth time, meaning it more than ever. "I'm sorry I was an idiot who didn't realize he's been in love with you forever until it was almost too late."

Cat sniffs, and her mouth turns down hard at the edges. "You haven't been in love with me forever."

"I have," I insist, tipping the barrel of the gun between us so it points at Nico. The last time I checked, the safety was on, but if there's an accidental discharge, I want to make sure it hits someone worthy of catching a stray bullet. "From the moment you won that first race, the second you jogged across the finish line looking ready to start a fight, I was a goner. I was just too stupid to realize it. But I don't want to be an idiot anymore. "

"You're not an idiot," she says, her expression still wary. "You're one of the smartest people I know. And you don't have to make some big declaration just because you're shot and I was almost kidnapped by my crazy ex-boyfriend."

"I know I don't." The mention of Nico makes me cast another glance his way. But the man is still down for the count, proving, yet again, that my girl doesn't fuck around.

Which means, if I want her to truly be my girl, I can't either.

"I just thought love had to be hard." I scoot closer, inhaling the sweet, Cat smell of her. "My mom and dad made being married look miserably hard, and then Dad and Julie got together and made it look hard in a different way. When they first started dating, they fought constantly."

"That's hard to believe," Cat says with another sniff. "They seem so good together."

"Well, it's true. Ask Julie." I brush her hair over her shoulder, grateful that all that silky smoothness is still attached to her living, breathing body. "And by the time they figured out how to make things work, I was at college watching people even stupider than I was fall in and out of love every few days. I knew way before my friend nearly died of alcohol poisoning after a girl broke his heart that I wanted nothing to do with that kind of love."

She frowns, but tips her head closer to mine. "But you dated. You dated a lot."

"Yeah, a lot. But never seriously. I made sure to date girls who wanted to keep things casual, so there was never a risk of fun becoming anything more." I curl my fingers around her waist, pulling her closer, even though the movement makes my injured thumb throb. "But I made a big mistake."

"What's that?" She tilts her head back, looking up at me, her face pale in the moonlight. Pale, but beautiful.

She's the most beautiful thing I've ever seen, and I want her to let me love her more than I've wanted anything in a long, long time. More than that second location of Ink Addicts, more than freedom from my father's dreams for my life, more than the skills I honed to make my art and do my job.

I have a feeling loving Red will be its own kind of art, one that will never get old or frustrating or make me wish I understood more about perspective. *She* is my perspective. One look in her eyes and I know this is what matters—loving someone enough to put every piece of yourself on the line.

"I forgot to watch out for you," I say softly. "By the time I realized you were way more than a friend, or a bratty little sister stand-in who I enjoyed giving a hard time, I couldn't quit you." Her lips curve, giving me the courage to lighten my tone as I add, "I had to keep writing you notes and texting you and bailing your ass out of trouble because I needed your ass in my life. And not just to stare at to get me through mile five."

I'm hoping for a smartass remark, but instead her smile fades before it can fully form. "But you did quit me, Aidan. Eventually."

"Only because I knew that if I stayed with you that summer I would never have left," I say, bending my lips closer to hers. "And back then I was too stupid to realize that you're way more exciting than studying tattooing in Asia."

"Damn straight," she says flatly, tipping her head to one side, her gaze fixed on my mouth. "Do you hear sirens?"

I listen, catching the high-pitched whine coming from the top of the hill. "I do. Looks like you only have a few minutes left to decide if you want to ride with me in the back of the ambulance."

Her hand comes to my face, her fingers scratching gently at my beard. "Of course I'm coming with you in the ambulance. I love you," she says, sending a wave of relief coursing through my chest.

"I love you, too," I say, my voice rough. "So much."

"I wasn't finished," she says with a smile. "I love you, but I also have to see if you cry when they dig the bullet out of your arm. If you cry, I'm going to make fun of you for years. I had a bullet pulled from my ass when I was twelve and didn't shed a single tear. My dad was so proud he bought me a stuffed boa constrictor."

I shake my head gently as flashlights sweep through the woods near the trailhead. "So is this when you finally tell me what went down in Kathmandu?"

She huffs, her laughter puffing against my chin. "Not a chance in hell. I've given away enough of my secrets for free, handsome. You're going to have to work for the rest of them."

"Gladly." We're so close now that my lips brush hers as I speak. "As long as you'll remind me that you love me every once in a while. I like hearing those particular words from your particular lips."

"I love you," she whispers. "Now kiss me, please."

"Any time, beautiful." My fingers curl around the back of her neck. "Kissing you is my very favorite thing. Ever."

"You're sweet, Mr. Knight," she says, a catch in her voice. "Thanks for coming to my rescue."

"Thanks for coming to mine," I say, meaning every word.

And then I press my lips to hers, saying the rest of the things that need to be said with a kiss.

Chapter Thirty-Eight

Ten months later

From the group text archives of Aidan Knight, Sebastian "Bash" Prince, Penny Pickett, and Shane Willoughby

Penny: I LOVE THESE IDEAS! I LOVE THEM SO HARD I HAVE TO USE ALL THE CAPS! ALL OF THEM!! THEY'RE ALL MINE!! OMG, IT'S GOING TO BE SO AMAZING!!

Aidan: Are you sure?
You and Bash aren't mad at us for stealing your thunder? You were engaged first. So if you want us to wait, we will. It's not a big deal. Nothing is set in stone yet.

Penny: OMG, DON'T BE CRAZY. YOU HAVE

TO GET MARRIED THIS WEEKEND! IF YOU DON'T I'M GOING TO CRY BECAUSE YOU GOT ME ALL EXCITED ABOUT A CHIHUAHUA FLOWER GIRL AND THEN STOLE IT AWAY.
CHIHUAHUA. FLOWER. GIRL!
Seriously, though, all caps aside, Bash and I don't care at all, do we Bash?

Bash: Not even a little bit. And our wedding is still five months away. You're nowhere close to stepping on our toes. I also love your ideas, but what do we do if the dog poops in the courthouse? If I pull strings with Judge Lawrence and then get poop on his carpet he'll tell my mother, and then my mother will rip me a new asshole. I'm sure she's going to dump the judge sooner or later, the way she dumps all her man toys, but for now she's pretty into him.

Shane: I'm on it! I'll bring a cloth runner to lay down, something that will be pretty for Cat to walk down and protect the judge's carpet at the same time. That way, if Fang has an anxiety attack and loses control, we can just wrap it up and take it with us.
But I don't think it will be a problem. She's been housebroken for a while and she's not a nervous dog. She does well in large groups.
I'm more worried about the reception. Are you sure we can fit a hundred people in the new

studio?

Aidan: Totally. It's still just empty space. The floors are done and the window was painted yesterday, but I'm not bringing in the furniture until next week. The rest of the space can be mingle room and dance floor. A friend from the gym is going to D.J.
We can just set up a couple of folding tables for food, Bash will play bartender in one corner, and we'll be good to go.

Penny: He's going to bartend the shit out your reception, buddy.
He's been practicing all week. By Saturday, he'll either be an expert, or signed up for a twelve-step program.

Bash: I will not! I haven't even given myself a hangover yet.
And how am I supposed to know if my drinks are delicious if I don't TASTE THEM, Pickett? You're certainly no help, you lightweight.

Penny: Is it still "tasting" if you taste them all the way to the last drop?

Bash: You're just jealous that I'm so dedicated to my new art. You're afraid I'm going to become a famous mixologist, and you'll have to share me with my hordes of adoring fans.

Penny: Hush. You're ridiculous.

Bash: I am not.

Penny: Please, save it for when we're at home. Aidan is trying to decide serious stuff here, and this is a group text. Keep it classy.

Bash: I am keeping it classy! I haven't used a single farting emoticon.

Shane: Why not? That sounds like fun. I love emoticons!

Aidan: Don't we all? But I'm trying to plan a wedding in less than a week.

Bash: *farting flying squirrel* That's a new one my future sisters-in-law sent me last week. I love how it looks like he's being propelled by fart power.

Aidan: Focus, people. We've covered the ceremony and drinks, now

Bash: *farting Buddha* That might be sacrilegious, but I don't care. The smile on his face as he lets loose a stench cloud is too perfect.

Shane: LOL! Omg, I love it.
He's clearly found enlightenment. I wonder what it smells like…

Bash: Penny, invite Shane over to poker night. I like her. We need more girls who appreciate my sense of humor.

Penny: Done. Now let's get back on task.

Aidan: Speaking of group gatherings, my reception is still not fully planned. What about decorations? Cat offered to—

Bash: One more! *farting celery emoticon*
I'm not sure why someone took the time to code a farting celery, but that's part of what makes it so great. It's really—

Penny: BASH! BEHAVE!

Aidan: DOES THIS REALLY HAVE TO BE LIKE HERDING CATS?!
Seriously, I like you people, but I don't want this to be half-assed at the last minute. This is the only time I'm getting married, and I would like it to be nice for the woman who has so generously consented to marry my ass.
I don't want her to start having second thoughts at the reception, for Christ's sake.

Bash: I'm sorry, friend. Sometimes I forget how squishy your underbelly is these days. And then you say something like that and I remember.
We will not fuck this up. No way, no how.

The wedding and the reception will be amazing. Leave all the food and drink stuff to Penny and me. She was raised by a movie star and is great at this kind of shit, and I am good at doing what she tells me to do. It will be fabulous.

Shane: And I'll handle decorations. One of the benefits of running a charitable trust that throws lots of parties: I have access to TONS of decoration options.
And after a decade of friendship I know what Cat likes. I've got this scattered, smothered, and covered.

Aidan: Thank you. Good. Great.
deep breath
I'm seriously breathing easier.
You don't know what a load off this is. I was so happy that she said yes that I didn't think about how crazy it would be to plan a wedding in a week.

Shane: You're so welcome, Fuzzy. I'm thrilled for you both!

Penny: Me too! IT'S GOING TO BE AMAZING!

Bash: Me three. I'm seriously happy for you, brother. Couldn't happen to a nicer guy.

Aidan: Thanks, people. I couldn't do this without you.

Chapter Thirty-Nine

I should have done this without my friends.

Without my family.

Without anyone to observe just in case Cat comes to her senses at the last minute and decides to make a run for it. We've been running with our new Dasher club almost every weekend, so I know for a fact that she can make some serious tracks. For all I know, she could be halfway to the Bronx by now.

God, what's taking so long?

Bash and I have been in position at the front of the courtroom for a good ten minutes, and from the look on the judge's face, he's starting to regret staying late to sneak in a private ceremony.

"Relax," Bash whispers out of the side of his mouth. "It's going to be fine."

"Where is she?" I mutter, sweat breaking out at the small

of my back beneath my tux.

"Probably just having technical difficulties," he says. "Maybe her dress wouldn't zip or she was allergic to the flowers and they made her mascara run."

I curse softly.

Bash leans close enough to bump my shoulder with his. "Or the dog. It's probably the dog. Fang is probably rolling around on the floor in protest of that flower puppy dress. You know she's too badass for lace."

I swallow hard, trying to come up with an appropriately smartass reply to keep my mind off of my senseless freak out. Cat and I are good, better than good, and deep down I know she would never leave me standing at the judge's desk. But at that moment, the doors at the back of the room open. Seconds later, Fang, dressed in her flower puppy duds, runs down the aisle to jump into Shane's lap with a victorious bark, just like we practiced. The assembled friends and family murmur with laughter, and the judge grunts in approval, but I'm not paying attention to any of them anymore.

My eyes are all for the bombshell at the back of the room.

There she is. Red. My Red, looking stunning in her off-the-shoulder dress, with flowers in her hair and a smile that assures me she's every bit as ready to get married as I am. My heart starts thumping so hard it feels like it's going to rip a hole through my chest. I'm so happy—and simultaneously worried that I'm about to have a heart attack—that I don't notice my father beside her, walking her down the aisle, until they're three steps into the room.

But the moment I see his beaming face, I realize this must be why we're running late.

Jim must have required some convincing to do the

honors. He started acting weird again last week, when I called to announce that Cat and I were doing the courthouse thing instead of a big wedding. If I hadn't been so busy planning everything, to spare Cat the stress, since she's covered up with campaign planning for her city council bid, I would have worried that the old man and I were heading into another rough patch.

But when his gaze meets mine and I smile, letting him see how grateful I am that he loves Cat, too, I know the rough patch has been averted. Cat's made sure of it. She's taken care of me, again, the way she does in a hundred different ways every day. She swears I do the same for her, that she would never have had the guts to run for office without me, and that she's happier than she ever dreamt she could be.

But as she walks down the aisle, dressed in white, ready to say, "I do," for the rest of our lives, I make a silent promise to make her even happier.

"Take care of her, son," Jim says gruffly, as he and Cat stop beside me.

"I will, Dad." I draw him in for a hug. "I promise."

Jim pulls away first, but I can tell he's one happy bastard. So am I. I love that we're in such a better place. But the moment my dad sits down, he vanishes from my awareness. I no longer have room in my thoughts for anything but the woman I'm about to marry.

"Last chance," she whispers as we turn to face the judge. "Dash now or dash never, Curve."

"Never, Panties." I tuck her hand into my arm, folding my fingers over hers. "This Curve is yours for life."

"Lucky me." She grins so hard I know she's thinking naughty things, because she's my perfect match, the kind of girl who has no trouble wearing white while making references to my penis at the altar.

But she still cries during the ceremony. I do, too, a little, but in the car on the way to the reception Cat assures me that no one but her could see. I assure her that I couldn't care less—I'm too in love with her to worry about losing my man card for tearing up at my own wedding—and then we're at the shop, and it's time for the final surprise of the day.

"Close your eyes." I wrap my arm around her waist, turning her to face the street as she steps out of the car.

"Why?" she asks with a laugh. "What have you done?"

"Just a little something, but it has a story to go with it." I tighten my grip on her, refusing to let her turn around. "So close your eyes, woman. Now."

"All right, all right." She closes her eyes and wiggles her ass, rubbing against where I'm getting thicker because that's what two seconds of touching this woman does to me. "Tell me the story."

"Once upon a time there was a man who loved his job," I say, leaning down to murmur the words in her ear. "He loved it so much he named his shop Ink Addicts. And the name fit because he couldn't imagine being addicted to anything else. But he was wrong."

"Was he?" she asks, sounding like she likes the story so far.

"He was," I continue. "Because there was this woman he'd never been able to get out of his head, this amazing, crazy, smart, funny, perfect woman who came back into his life when he least expected it and showed him what he'd been missing."

Her hands fold over mine and squeeze. "And what was that?"

"Everything," I say, my voice catching, because it's true.

She is everything, and I can't believe I ever thought I had a full life without her. "I was missing all the good stuff. But now I'm not. Now I have my favorite person with me all the time, and a place where I'll always belong, no matter where we go or what we do. Because you are my home, Mrs. Catherine Knight, and words can't express how happy I am that you're mine."

"Oh man, I love you," she says, sniffing as I turn us both around to face the shop window. "But don't make me cry. I just got my mascara unsmudged."

I kiss the top of her head. "Okay. I'll stop. I just wanted you to know that I have a new addiction, and therefore, the shop has a new name. Open your eyes and check it out."

She sniffs again, swiping at her cheeks as her eyes open. Almost immediately, she breaks into a delighted laugh. "Oh my God, is that Fifi?"

"It is." I shift so I can see her face. "I was going to make the logo a pin-up style drawing of you, but I decided I didn't want to share you with every asshole who comes in the front door. And Fang looked so kick ass in that leather jacket, it was really a no-brainer."

"The Cat's Fang," she says, nodding slowly. "It's the perfect name. Badass, but adorable, just like you."

"I feel like I should say I'm not adorable, just to maintain street cred. But I already cried at my wedding, so I'm going to let that go without a fight."

"You should." She turns, twining her arms around my neck, beaming up at me. "I love this surprise. And I love you. And I love being your wife. I know it's only been half an hour, but I'm pretty sure it's the best thing ever."

"I'm glad you think so." I hug her closer, setting that now familiar fire to burning in the air between us. "And thanks for the thing with Dad. You made his year, I'm sure. He loves you a lot."

"My pleasure. I love him, too." She wrinkles her nose. "But he *was* asking about kids again today. I get the feeling a Chihuahua grandbaby isn't going to be enough for him for much longer."

"You didn't tell him we were going to start trying, did you?"

She shakes her head, threading her fingers into my hair. "No way. Your penis and my vagina are none of his business."

"Speaking of," I say, my cock thickening. "Think we have time for a quickie in the new bathroom before everyone else arrives?"

"Considering Shane and Fifi are getting out of a cab at the end of the block right now, that's doubtful," she says, laughing. "Don't look so sad, babe. I heard from a little bird that you're getting lucky as soon as we get home tonight. Like, all night long lucky."

I hug her tight. "Yeah? All night long?"

"All night long and into tomorrow," she says, tilting her head back and bringing her lips closer to mine. "Because you look hot as hell in this tux. And since Fifi's staying with Shane until we're back from the honeymoon, we don't have to worry about any spanking confusion."

Spanking confusion—aka when Fang hears me slapping Cat's ass through the door, thinks I'm hurting her mama, and whines like someone's dying outside while Cat and I are trying to come—is a pain in the balls. "Spanking confusion is my least favorite part of being a dog dad. But I like the thought of knocking you up while I'm spanking you and fucking you hard from behind. Is that wrong?"

Her eyes glitter with lust and love and that particular breed of trouble that is hers and hers alone. "If it is, I don't ever want you to be right."

Her lips touch mine, but before we can make the moment into a proper mini-make out session, a firm, wiggling body squirms between our legs. We separate in time to see Fang, wearing the leather jacket I gave Shane to change her into as part of the surprise for Cat, running away down the street, hauling ass toward Washington Square Park. A moment later, Shane streaks after her, moving fast for a woman wearing three-inch heels.

"Fifi, come back here!" she shouts, before waving an arm our way. "Don't worry, I'll get her and bring her back. She'll be fine! I swear! This is a game we play when we go walking in Central Park. She runs away, but she always comes back in a few minutes."

Cat's brow furrows with worry.

Before she can say a word, I assure her, "Of course we're going to help get Fifi back on her leash. We're responsible dog parents, and that's what we do."

Relief, mixed with enough affection to make me sure I'm the luckiest man in the world, floods her expression. "I love you. But don't get any more perfect, okay? Or I'm going to start worrying that I'm dreaming again."

"I'll try," I say, though I have no intention of doing anything of the sort. I'm not perfect, but I'm going to keep being as perfect for her as I can be, from now until the last day I'm lucky enough to hold her in my arms.

As if she knows exactly what I was thinking—which she probably does—she presses a kiss to my cheek with a happy humming noise. "Come on. You call her, and I'll wait behind a stairway and pounce as soon as she gets close."

It takes fifteen minutes, but we get Fifi back on her leash, get Shane calmed down, and get all of us back to the party. And for the next few hours, I celebrate with my friends before going home to make love to my very best friend.

And it lasts all night long, just that way she promised.

EPILOGUE

Two months later

And now something from Ferocious Fang
AKA Fifi, the Chihuahua

The sun is shining, the first hint of autumn is in the air, and it's a beautiful day to be headed for the park! I'm so excited I can't contain a delirious, head to tail, full body wag as I join my Cat by the door. My squirming makes it hard for my adorable human to get my harness on, but I can't help myself.

We're going to the park! The park!

And I'm going to see Lucky, the most wonderful dog in the world! I'm so happy I could bark, and I do, numerous times, until my Cat tells me to shush and picks me up to carry me down the stairs.

Despite good breeding and better training, I tug on my leash all the way down the street to the Hudson River dog run, but Furry doesn't yell at me. He never yells. He's a sweetheart who spoils me rotten and buys me beautiful clothes.

I usually try not to take advantage of his good nature, but with legs as long as his you would think he could move a little faster already!

Unfortunately, Furry is distracted by the tight new jeans my Cat is wearing. He keeps slowing down to check out the view from the rear or finding excuses to run his hand over her bottom. Finally, she smiles and bats his hand away and I dare to hope our progress might speed up a little.

But then my Cat turns to give him human kisses, the really close kind where you can't see what, exactly, they're licking. And they kiss and kiss for what seems like hours, ignoring me until I wrap my leash around their legs and pull hard enough to make myself gag.

Finally, my adorable humans notice that I'm turning blue and stop long enough to detangle themselves and apologize. I cut short my "it's okay" licks to their hands to half my usual duration, but it still takes forever to get to the park. By the time Furry finally closes the gate behind us and unhooks my leash, I'm fit to burst.

I dash madly across the enclosure, leaping over a pair of unfamiliar bulldogs splashing each other in the water feature, and bound straight to Lucky's favorite corner of the park. I scan the area, circle the stone fire hydrants, and sniff the ground near the gate where Lucky sometimes waits, but he's nowhere to be found.

Spirits crashing, I sit down hard on the pavement, fighting the whimper rising in my throat. I'm so upset that my friend Phyllis doesn't even need to sniff my bottom to determine my fragile emotional state.

Hang in there, kid, she says, slapping my paw gently with

her much larger one. *He'll be here. He never misses a Sunday.*

My brow furrows. *But what if his adorable human is sick? Or on a honeymoon? My humans went on a honeymoon and left me with Aunt Shane for ten days. I though they were never coming back!*

Phyllis laughs and shakes her slightly damp red fur, sending droplets of water flying into the air. *There's no honeymoon in* that *human's future, sweetheart. Have you smelled that one? He's had an ear infection for the past three months. Smells like something died in that big melon of his.*

Maybe he doesn't know, I say, feeling compelled to stick up for Lucky's adorable human. *You know our people have terrible noses.*

I don't know about that. But I do know something about you, little miss, Phyllis says with a knowing look at my midsection. *The big question is, do your humans know yet?*

Before I can answer, a joyful, miniature pincher bark echoes through the crisp fall morning. Seconds later, Lucky dashes into view, looking like eleven pounds, seven ounces of heart-stopping, well-groomed, deliciousness, and I can't think about anything but him. I surge into motion, meeting him behind the largest stone fire hydrant, where we kiss and sniff and squirm with delight, proving my adorable humans haven't cornered the market on effusive public displays of affection.

But it's always been like that with Lucky. Since the day we met—moments after I ran away from Aunt Shane the day of my Cat's wedding—it was love at first sight. And in just forty or fifty more days, there will be puppies with his brown eyes and my light fur, and I will be the happiest Chihuahua in Manhattan.

How are you feeling, he asks, when we've finally settled

down enough to keep our tongues off of each other. *I've been worried about you and the puppies.*

We're fine. I wriggle closer to him, dizzied by the delicious smell of him. *I've never felt better.*

But you should have been taken to the vet by now. Lucky nuzzles my neck. *It's been two weeks. I can't believe your humans haven't noticed that you're expecting. What's wrong with them?*

I pull back with a smile, remembering my surprise. *Follow me and smell for yourself.*

I lead the way across the park, swallowing my impatience when Lucky stops to politely sniff a few bottoms and inquire after the state of various friends' humans and puppies. He's a wonderful, loyal friend. It's one of the many things I love about him, even when it makes getting somewhere take twice as long.

Finally, we arrive at the bench where my Cat and Furry are snuggled up, holding hands and gazing out at the Hudson River, talking non-stop, the way they usually do.

They never run out of things to say, do they? Lucky observes with a smile.

I wag my tail proudly. *No, they're wonderful together.*

Like us. Lucky says, but before I can kiss him for being so sweet, he lifts his nose higher into the air, and his ears shiver the way they do when he's solving a scent mystery.

Well, well, he finally says, his tail wagging, too. *Guess we have a lot of things in common. How long until their puppy arrives?*

I don't know, I say honestly. *I only smelled the change in her scent a few days ago. I don't think she even knows yet. But I'm so excited for them!* I stand on my hind legs, bouncing lightly on my toes. *I can't wait for our puppies to be very best friends, just like my Cat and Furry and I are very best friends.*

Lucky licks my face. *You're the sweetest thing I've ever met. Or tasted. Or smelled.*

I laugh, tempted to tease him for being so smitten. But in the end, I decide it's more fun to kiss him and nip his neck and let him chase me around the park again and again until we're both exhausted and ready for a nap in the shade.

When it's finally time to go, I promise him that I'll figure out a way to get my Cat to take me to the vet, swear the puppies will be fine, and kiss him a few dozen more times to give him enough kisses to last him until next Sunday. And as Furry leads me out of the gate and locks it behind him, I hear him tell my Cat that Lucky and I are the cutest little couple he's ever seen.

My heart swells with happiness until I can't help barking out everything I'm feeling. I tell my adorable humans that they are sweet and wonderful and that I'm so thrilled that they found each other and are in love and are having a baby to add to our family. But of course they don't understand a word.

But that's okay.

There are other ways of showing humans how you feel, and as soon as the new baby comes, I will welcome it to our pack with my softest kisses. And we will all live very happily ever after.

I just know it.

The End?

Keep reading for a free sneak peek of Lili's next serial romance, Love and Ruin, coming in September 2016.

Sneak Peek of
Love and Ruin
coming soon!

The Moment I Knew

Ezra

It's late, after midnight, and my room is dark like the inside of a tomb. Dark like a night without stars, like a cave where nothing human has ever set foot, just the way I like it.

But even though I can't see a damned thing and I'm half asleep and my head is pounding, I know the second the door snicks shut—snuffing out the brief flash of light from the hallway—that it's her.

Before I smell her perfume, before she calls my name in a shattered whisper, I know it's Jenny. And I know I'm not going to be able to say no. No matter what she wants, what she needs, tonight I'm going to give it to her.

Tonight I am weak.

"Are you awake?" she asks, her voice thick, sad.

"Yes," I whisper.

"Can we talk?" She sniffs. "Or maybe…not talk? I just don't want to be alone, Ezra. I can't. Not tonight."

I draw back the covers. "Come here. Lie down with me."

In a heartbeat, she's beside me in bed, curling against my side, her hand slipping beneath my tee shirt to rest on my stomach.

That's all it takes, one touch and I'm hard, aching. But I've spent most of the past few weeks hard for her, wanting her, dreaming about all the ways I want to take her even though I know it's wrong. It's so fucking wrong, but as I roll on top of her and capture her lips with mine, nothing has ever felt so right.

We kiss, slow and deep, like we have all the time in the world though we both know we don't. Our lives are crumbling. Everything is going to shit and it's only a matter of time before fate tears us apart, but at this moment, it doesn't matter.

Nothing matters except finally getting as close as we need to be.

I take off her clothes, slowly, deliberately, pressing kisses to each newly exposed plane of skin like a benediction. She is beautiful, sacred. I don't believe in God anymore, but as I slide Jenny's panties down her thighs and kiss her where she's salty and wet—for me, only for me, she whispers again as I fuck her with my tongue—I realize that there are still holy things left in the world.

There is her body unraveling beneath my mouth, her voice calling my name as she comes, her legs wrapping around my waist as I position myself and glide inside her, finding hope, finding home.

And for the first time, it's more than sex, more than fucking. For the first time, I am lost and found, shattered and made whole, destroyed and born again in the circle of her arms.

And that's when I know that I'm ruined.

I never realized that love and ruin had so much in common. But as I fall through the darkness, stripped bare and defenseless, with nothing but the girl I love to keep me from crumbling to pieces, I realize that, for me, love and ruin might as well be the same thing.

I love this girl, but she will destroy me and I will destroy her right back.

Before we began, it was already over.

All over but for the fall.

ACKNOWLEDGEMENTS

Big thanks to the many creative and talented authors whose books inspire me to play and try new things. Things like breaking the fourth wall, writing a chapter from a Chihuahua's point of view, and hiding a little something special here in the Acknowledgements. And even more thanks to the readers who devour every word—even the dedication and acks—this one is for you :)

From the text archives of
Sebastian "Bash" Prince and Shane Willoughby

Bash: Hey gorgeous, just checking in to make sure you'll be at poker night tomorrow. I have a proposition I want to run by you while I'm taking your money…

Shane: Hmm…
Well, you know I love poker night, but that sounds a little ominous…

Bash: Nah, not ominous.
Portentous, maybe.
Or delicious.
Or some other word that ends in "shus" that means fun, sexy things. I think you're going to love what I have in mind!

Shane: Oh God…
You aren't going to ask me to have a ménage with you and Penny are you?

Bash: Fuck no!
Jesus!
No!
I'm a one-woman man. And Penny would cut my dick off if she even thought that I was *thinking about* thinking about something like that.
Which I never would.
EVER.

Shane: Oh, good. So glad to hear that!
I mean, Penny's a hottie, but you're not really my type, pumpkin ;).

Bash: Ha ha.
Christ, you actually made me blush.
I can't remember the last time I blushed.
Penny just asked me why I'm all pink and now she's laughing her ass off. She wanted to be the one to reach out to you about this, but I said I could handle it.
Thanks for proving me wrong, Willoughby.

Shane: My pleasure!
So what are you reaching out about? Now I'm really intrigued…

Bash: You're a mess is what you are.
And that's why you're perfect for this job. I'm in need of a Gorgeous Mess...

Shane: A Gorgeous Mess...

Bash: Yes, a Gorgeous Mess, capable of taking a misunderstood man in desperate need of an image makeover and transforming him into a media darling. All while scaring off the ex-girlfriend determined to ruin his good name and maybe faking a pregnancy if things get really dire. But that's only if stage one doesn't go as planned.

Shane: Faking a pregnancy? What the heck are you...
Oh, no.
No, way.
You're not saying you want me to...

Bash: Work for me? Yes! Yes, I am.
I have a Magnificent Bastard and a Spectacular Rascal, but I don't have a Gorgeous Mess, Shane. In fact, I don't have a single woman on the intervention side of things in the event that a male client approaches me in desperate need of our particular brand of assistance.

Shane: Oh my God. I don't know whether to be flattered or horrified.

Bash: Be intrigued! And excited! You'll be wonderful.

Shane: But I already have a job!

Bash: Not a full time job. You said yourself that your aunt's charity practically runs itself.

Shane: Sometimes, it does, but sometimes I'm very busy raising funds and throwing benefits and changing lives.

Bash: Which is what you'll be doing for me! You'll be changing lives—or at least one man's life. The guy really needs your help.
He's like a big, sad puppy. A big, sad, sexy puppy. (Penny told me to add the sexy part so you would know that spending a few weeks making out with the dude won't be any hardship on your part. And it'll put a cool ten grand in your pocket! You can't beat that.)

Shane: I don't need ten grand, Bash. You know my aunt left me a very *ehem* *comfortable* inheritance.

Bash: So give the ten grand to charity!
It's the work that counts, doll. The good work for a deserving soul who has the right to go about his business without having his good name ruined by a spiteful nightmare of a person who thinks a man

ending a relationship is grounds for her to set a bomb off in the middle of his life.
And who knows, you might even have fun!
Dating an NHL star comes with certain perks. I'm sure he can get you season tickets at the very least. Or maybe a monogrammed hat. Or mittens. You like mittens, right? I mean, who doesn't like mittens? They make you feel like a kid again!

Shane: He's a professional hockey player? You're kidding.

Bash: I'm not.

Shane: But not for the Rangers, though. Some other team?

Bash: No, he's with the Rangers. Why, are you an Islanders fan?

Shane: No, I'm just…
You wouldn't by any stretch of the imagination be talking about Jake "The Dragon" Falcone would you?

Bash: I am. But I swear everything you've been reading about him is a pack of lies. The guy is innocent.

Shane: *snort* Like hell he is.

Bash: No, seriously, Shane.
I mean, yes, he's banged his share of starlets and super models, but I verified his side of this particular story myself. After what happened with Aidan and the mob, I'm taking background checks on the clients very seriously these days.
Jake is being framed. He's a good guy and he really needs our help.
I don't think he has anywhere else to turn…

Shane: You're laying it on pretty thick, Prince.

Bash: The guy is really devastated, Shane. (This is Penny, by the way.)
I just wanted to let you know that I think you would do an amazing job with this intervention and really make a difference in this man's life.
But if you need to say no, I understand. We'll just have to tell him we can't help him and wish him luck finding someone else who specializes in taking down evil ex-girlfriends. I'm sure he'll be able to find someone out there like that.
I mean, I've never heard of anyone who does what we do here at MBC, but…

Shane: Fine! Ugh! I'm helpless against the double guilt trip.
I'll do it. You can fill me in on all the details over cards tomorrow.

Bash: Thank you, Shane! Thank you so much. We really appreciate this. And you're going to have some extra good karma coming your way, Babes.

Shane: Yeah, yeah. Make that a bottle of really nice scotch waiting for me at my poker spot. Scotch goes down easier than karma.

Bash: Done!

Shane: Oh, and Bash. I want my name to be the Miraculous Mess.

Bash: Gorgeous wasn't alliterative enough for you?

Shane: No.
Because if I'm going to get "The Dragon" Falcone out of the public relations shit pit he's in, I'm going to have to be a fucking miracle worker.

Miraculous Mess is coming your way Fall 2016!

Tell Lili your favorite part!

I love reading your thoughts about the books and your review matters. Reviews help readers find new-to-them authors to enjoy. So if you could take a moment to leave a review letting me know your favorite part of the story—nothing fancy required, even a sentence or two would be wonderful—I would be deeply grateful.

ABOUT THE AUTHOR

Lili Valente has slept under the stars in Greece, eaten dinner at midnight with French men who couldn't be trusted to keep their mouths on their food, and walked alone through Munich's red light district after dark and lived to tell the tale.

These days you can find her writing in a tent beside the sea, drinking coconut water and thinking delightfully dirty thoughts.

Lili loves to hear from her readers. You can reach her via email at lili.valente.romance@gmail.com or like her page on Facebook www.facebook.com/AuthorLiliValente?ref=hl

You can also visit her website: www.lilivalente.com

The complete Under His Command Series is Available Now:

Controlling Her Pleasure

Commanding Her Trust

Claiming Her Heart

The complete Bought by the Billionaire Series is Available Now:

Dark Domination

Deep Domination

Desperate Domination

Divine Domination

The complete Dirty Twisted Love Series is Available Now:

Dirty Twisted Love

Filthy Wicked Love

Crazy Beautiful Love

One More Shameless Night

The complete Bedding the Bad Boy Series is Available Now:

The Bad Boy's Temptation

The Bad Boy's Seduction

The Bad Boy's Redemption

Printed in Great Britain
by Amazon